Fate Undenied

Book 1

FATE UNDENIED

BOOK 1

Ana Bice

THE REGENCY PUBLISHERS

Copyright © 2022 by Ana Bice.

All rights reserved. No part of this book may be reproduced in any form or by any electronic or mechanical means, including information storage and retrieval systems, without permission in writing from the author and publisher, except by reviewers, who may quote brief passages in a review.

ISBN: 978-1-959434-22-1 (Paperback Edition)
ISBN: 978-1-959434-23-8 (Hardcover Edition)
ISBN: 978-1-959434-21-4 (E-book Edition)

Some characters and events in this book are fictitious. Any similarity to the real persons, living or dead, is coincidental and not intended by the author.

Book Ordering Information

The Regency Publishers, US
521 5th Ave 17th floor NY, NY10175
Phone Number: (315)537-3088 ext 1007
Email: info@theregencypublishers.com
www.theregencypublishers.com

Printed in the United States of America

Contents

Dedication

THIS IS DEDICATED TO THE GREAT ' I AM',
MY MUSE AND INSPIRATION

CHAPTER 1

EVE ANNE'S LOVE

The sun was setting over the Pacific Ocean on that late autumn afternoon. From her tenth-floor office in the city of Santa Monica, Eve Anne had an unobstructed view facing west, less than half a mile from the beach. In the distance, she could see the surfers carrying their boards, rushing into the water and swimming out to catch some waves while there was still some daylight left.

On any other day she would muse about their perceived free spirit and wished she was alongside them. But on that afternoon she was too busy putting the finishing touches on her latest assignment with the magazine. She was also getting ready to go on vacation the next day to spend the holidays with her parents and do some hiking if the weather allowed. Not too long after that she was going to Europe, where she was scheduled to start work on her first two reporting assignments for the following year. At the moment however, she was just happy to be done with the latest project so she could go home and nurse her migraine headache. The pain pills she had taken earlier were beginning to wear off and she wanted to get out of there as soon as possible. Fortunately for her, these episodes never lasted more than a few hours and the pain was significantly reduced with medication.

She wanted to leave the office in time to get her packing done and start her trip early the next morning. That wouldn't be a problem, since she had plenty of practice traveling because of her work. There was a gentle knock on the door and she looked up from her computer screen.

"Come in, Matt," she said.

"Are you ready for your vacation?" Matthew asked.

"Yes, pretty much. But right now I'd just be happy to go home," she said, massaging her forehead.

"Having one of your reincarnation headaches?" he asked jokingly.

"If that's what you call them," she said, squinting from the pain.

"I'm sorry," he said, immediately regretting making fun of her. "I didn't mean to make light of your pain; it just came out without thinking."

"Don't worry about it. It's not a big deal," she said. "And to answer to your question, yes, my head is killing me and I'm just about ready to get out of here. What about you? Any plans for the weekend?"

"I'm going to Mammoth to visit a college friend and go snowboarding," he said.

"That sounds like fun. Do they already have enough snow for skiing?" she asked.

"They had their second big storm in a week yesterday, which dropped eighteen inches on top the sixteen they got a week ago," Matt said.

"Very good then, have a wonderful time."

"Thanks, I will. You have a great time with your folks, and I'm sorry about the reincarnation joke."

"Don't worry about it; you know I don't believe in reincarnation. I think that human beings are more than just recycling matter," she said.

"I agree with you, but the witch doctor in that tribe didn't share our views; in fact, he was completely sure of what he thought he saw in your 'spirit aura.' Is that what he called it?"

"Something like that," Eve Anne said.

"I'm curious," Matt said. "Why didn't you let him lay hands on you like he wanted and tell you what he believed was the reason for your headaches? It wouldn't have hurt."

"Because it was a complete waste of time. An African witch doctor telling me that my headaches were remnants from my previous or future lives made absolute no sense to me, especially while I was in the middle of a migraine. At that time I just needed to take my medication, lie down, and go to sleep," she said.

"What happened to the follow up article on the Chainica tribe?" Matt asked.

"They want the Romanian orphanages article as a first priority, and I totally agree. These children are in dire need of help. Every day that passes without getting the proper care could mean death for some of them," she said.

"The first article two years ago generated a lot of attention," Matt noted.

"Yes it did, and for a while after that they were receiving a lot of financial help as a result. Unfortunately, the contributions have slowed down considerably since then because the information isn't fresh anymore. I hope that this article will help bring back the exposure they need. The aim is to raise more awareness of the difficulties these children and many like them face every day."

"If we can do that, we'll accomplish our objective," Matthew said.

"God willing," Eve Anne said.

Matthew looked at his watch and realized it was close to five o'clock in the afternoon.

"I'm sorry for holding you up; I just came in to say goodbye, happy holidays, and I'll see you in Belgrade," he said.

"Thank you. I hope your holidays are great too," she said, getting up from her chair and giving him a hug. "It'll be nice working together again."

"I assure you, it's my pleasure."

"Ah Matt, full of compliments as usual; thank you. Just remember the rules," she warned him.

"Yes, I remember them well. No mixing personal life with business," he said.

"You're a great friend," she said smiling.

"Okay. Go home now," he said walking towards the door.

"I'm on my way out right now. I still have some packing to do."

"Have a fun and safe trip," he said.

"I will," she said. "You do the same."

As Matt walked out of the office, she reached into her purse for a pain reliever, which she took with some water. After making sure everything was in order with her completed assignment, she e- mailed it to her editor and shut off the computer.

Looking around one last time, she grabbed her purse and turned the lights off before going out the door. Just as the sunset was setting over the Pacific Ocean, she was pulling out of the office parking structure and on her way home to get ready for the next day. She hoped to feel better by morning because she hated to disappoint her parents who were expecting her to join the rest of her family for Thanksgiving, two days away. When she got home her headache had subsided giving her an energy spurt when the medication took effect.

Her packing skills were down to a science, thanks to the extensive traveling involved with her job. A short time later, she was ready for her trip. She went to bed early enough to get eight hours of sleep.

The next morning, she was ready and in her car before six o'clock. Once again she was eager to experience the beauty of the drive that waited a few hours into her trip. As she merged into the highway morning traffic, she couldn't miss the beautiful sunrise behind her, reflecting in her rearview mirror as if joining in her journey that day.

Less than six hours later, she got off the main highway and stopped to grab a bite to eat. After having lunch in St. George, she got on the scenic Route 9, a path that would take her through Zion National Park, then to Highway 89, a spectacular drive leading to Bryce Canyon. The beginning of the detour was carved through canyons and towering rocks, soaring thousands of feet up, and then opened into a breathtaking, sweeping view that seemed to stretch forever. It was the beginning of a drive that Eve Anne Vinson had made countless of times. Still, the natural beauty displayed before her had a magnetic calling that she had felt and heard forever—as far back as she could remember.

Visiting Grandma and Grandpa Conley in Colorado was the highlight of her summers for that reason. She especially enjoyed summer camp at the Bryce Canyon! There was something about the Utah and Colorado canyon parks she loved—the rocks and the magnificently tall columns and rock patterns reaching to the heavens, defying human description. The Walls of Windows in the Peekaboo Trail at Bryce Canyon, resembling ethereal and mystical buildings, seemed to her like a place where happy beings dwelled. In such an imaginary place sadness didn't exist, only joy, and from its highest point you could see all that your heart desired in any realm of existence.

Her fertile imagination as a writer gave the canyons a life of their own when she visited. They became more alive to her each time, as if rewarding her lifelong obsession and love affair with that part of nature.

The chill in the air that afternoon was exhilarating as she stepped out of her car to stretch out her legs and enjoy the beauty of Zion National Park. She stopped along the way often when she made the trip, rewarding herself with the scenic views of the incredibly beautiful landscape. Rising out of the earth and morphing into unbelievable shapes, it gave testimony of the ongoing process that started millions of years ago, and would likely go on long after mankind's existence came to an end. For Eve Anne, the trip was never just about reaching her destination; she enjoyed the spiritual communion she experienced with everything around her, especially when she made the trip alone. The journey in itself was her reward.

By late afternoon, she was driving through the park entrance at Bryce Canyon and heading to the nearest scenic stop. She parked her car and decided to walk the Navajo Loop Trail, a mile and a half round trip hike from the parking lot.

"There is no peace like this," she whispered as she took a deep breath and slowly turned 360 degrees to take it all in. The sunset cast shadows on the sandstone formations continuously changing the look and colors, giving them a feeling of evolution. She sat on a bench to enjoy the aptly named Sunset Point and before she realized it, the sun had set completely and daylight had given way to early-evening.

She walked back to her car and drove to the Bryce Canyon Lodge where she got a room for the night. The twinkling light of stars was beginning to appear in the early evening sky when she walked to the restaurant for dinner.

The next day she got up early to begin the second half of her trip. Having done the most time-consuming part of her drive the day before, the remaining distance would normally take five hours, getting her to her parents' home in the later part of the day.

Spending the holidays surrounded by family would inevitably remind Eve Anne of her beloved grandparents. She felt especially close to them around this time, and sensed their comforting presence. They were a big part of her life, nurturing her innate love of nature, which she was sure to have inherited from them.

When Barbara and John Conley, her maternal grandparents, grew older and needed care in their later years, her parents moved the family from California to look after them until they passed away.

Eve Anne and Hannah moved back to California after graduating from college and lived within two hours of each other. Ideally, the two sisters would have wanted to have their parents closer to them, especially now that Hannah was expecting her first child, but convincing them was difficult. Eve Anne lived in Marina Del Rey, a Los Angeles beach town not far from her office in the city of Santa Monica, and Hannah was a pediatrician specializing in cancer research in San Diego. Andrew, the younger brother, was away at college.

A photo journalist and reporter, Eve Anne worked freelancing for a number of magazines and a network broadcasting company. She was fluent in four languages: English, Italian, Spanish, and Chinese. She had been studying Arabic and was planning to spend a year abroad in a language immersion program. Her family, however, was opposed to the idea of her travels to the Middle East or anywhere they perceived dangerous. For now she was making them happy by not considering assignments offered to her in that area of the world.

As she drove up and into the driveway of the Vinsons' neatly manicured home, she noticed Ethan's car parked up front and let out a sigh. Although she had dated a few times since they broke up, he was the only serious boyfriend she ever had.

"How cliché! And how young!" she thought. Now she only wanted him to truly fall in love, because it was clear that they weren't right for each other, at least not on a romantic way. Still, she hated the thought of losing him as a friend, as well as her hiking and rock-climbing partner. Up to now, she could always count on him to join her on short notice for an outing, but having a girlfriend would change all that.

No one understood her passion for rocks better than Ethan; even so, she felt that her innate attraction to the canyons was more than he could handle at times. He would often tell her that the true love of her life was out there, in those breathtaking panoramic scenes that she was obsessed with. He always felt as if he came in second place to her love of nature. He let her know his feelings but never tried to change her, and although she made an effort for him, the changes were always short lived, and her tendencies regressed.

The sound of her car had alerted the family of her arrival, and a group of them were coming out, bringing her back to reality. As she got out of the car, her mother and father were coming toward her with open arms, followed by her brother Andrew and Sister Hannah with her husband Steven.

Living alone made her appreciate being with her family, making the times together more meaningful. She would never outgrow the feeling of peace and nurturing she got from visiting her parents and being surrounded by family. After losing her grandparents a few years before, she never took her family for granted again. Hannah was beaming. There was a glow about her that radiated and Steven was grinning from ear to ear. It was the same big grin Eve Anne had seen two weeks earlier when they told her they were having a baby. After happily hugging her parents and sister, she turned to her brother.

"What's up, punk?" she asked, giving him a hug and a kiss on the cheek.

"You know Sis," he said, grinning, obviously happy to see her, "I'm just doing the family duty, the self-sacrificing guy that I am, by giving up my parties just to be here with all of you."

"Yeah right, my heart bleeds for you, sweetie," Eve said, hugging him again and patting him on the back.

As she looked beyond Andrew, Ethan was smiling at her from the front door of the house. She walked over and hugged him.

"Long time no see," she said to him.

"Yeah," he said. "It's been a while, and you look great."

"Thanks, so do you. How've you been?" she asked.

"I'm doing well. Nothing's changed since I last talked to you. How have you been?" he asked, genuinely interested.

"I've been good. Glad to be home."

"It's good to have you around for the holidays. Maybe we can do some skiing while you're here; Breckenridge has great snow conditions," he said.

"That sounds wonderful. I definitely want to go skiing before I leave. It's great to have enough snow this early, otherwise I'd miss the whole season," she said.

"I guess the weather is cooperating with you."

"I'm glad. By the way, whatever came of the resumes you submitted to the agency looking for a design architect?" Eve Anne asked.

"I've narrowed it down to two companies—one in New York and the other in Texas. But I'm not in a hurry to change what I'm doing right now; it has to be an incredible offer to make me leave the firm," Ethan said.

"It's a good company to work for, and you can't put a price on being happy with your job. But something must be missing if you're looking around," she said.

"I just don't want to look back on wasted opportunities later in my life. I would at least like to know how much in demand my skills are and what I'm worth."

"It's good to know what opportunities are out there. You are the one deciding who you'll work for, instead of the other way around, and that's a pretty good feeling," she said.

"Yes, it is," he agreed.

"Okay, you two! No shop talk for now! You can get caught up on all that work stuff later. Right now it's dinner time. Let's get to the table," Emma Vinson said to her daughter and Ethan.

They smiled at each other as they made their way to the dining room of the festively decorated home, where the table was set for seven.

In his characteristic gentlemanly manner, Ethan pulled out Eve Anne's chair for her to sit.

"It's so good to have you home, honey, but we were beginning to wonder if you'd be too late for dinner. We thought you'd be here earlier," her father Daniel said.

She walked over and gave him a hug.

"You know how much I enjoy the drive. Sometimes I lose track of time, but it's great to be here with you, Dad," she said.

"Did you say sometimes you lose track of time? It's more like always when you make that trip," her mother said. "Speaking of enjoying the drive was your cell phone turned off?" she asked.

"Yes, but this time it wasn't on purpose. I just forgot to turn it on this morning. Did you try calling me?"

"Yes, but I don't even know why I try. I should know by now that when you make that trip, nothing else matters," Emma said.

"I'll work on that Mom." she said, smiling sweetly at her. "I should have called you last night but I was exhausted."

"Yes you should have," her mother said. "I worry when you are on the road alone. A lot of things can happen."

"I'm sorry Mom," she said.

"All right, then! Let's say grace because I am starving!" Andrew said.

"Great idea, Andrew, and since you're in such a hurry, you can do the honors in saying grace tonight." Daniel Vinson said to his son.

"Fine!" Andrew said, unhappy to be put on the spot. "Good food, good meat, good God, let's eat," he said, trying to hurry into dinner.

"Now, Andrew! That's not going to work. You have to say grace from the heart," his mother said.

"Okay," Andrew said grudgingly, and proceeded to give heartfelt thanks.

Everyone enjoyed the hearty meal of ribs and vegetables, one of the family's favorite recipes, followed by dessert. Eve Anne smiled as she sat back, listened, and watched; she found people a fascinating breed and her family was no exception. Someday she wanted to have one of her own, but she didn't feel the rush to settle down, much to her mother's disappointment.

"You want to have your children while you're still young enough to keep up with them," her mother had said the last time the subject of a family came up between them.

"I thought age was a state of mind," Eve Anne retorted, smarting off.

"Say what you like, the older you are the harder it is for your body to deal with the stress of pregnancy."

"Okay, Mom! It's not like I'm that old. I've still got a few years before my biological clock starts ticking."

"I won't say anything anymore," Emma said.

That conversation had taken place two years before and her mother had kept her word. "No one better than Mom to get you thinking of life in the big scheme of things," she thought, "especially when you get the feeling that she's giving you the silent treatment about the subject."

Of course, she would often wonder why she and Ethan weren't destined to be with each other; after all, everything seemed right in so many ways. He was caring, smart, and shared her spiritual values. Their families knew each other for many years and he was very handsome, with dirty blond hair, hazel eyes, and a six-foot-tall frame that any woman would love, but not Eve—not in a romantic way.

CHAPTER 2

JONATHAN'S CELEBRATION

Earlier that same day, on the East Coast in Long Island, New York, William Fitzgerald, owner and president of Fitzgerald International, had set up a meeting in the small auditorium on the top floor of the Fitzgerald building. On this day before Thanksgiving, he wanted to make his announcement of the upcoming management changes to the staff, which he considered like his family. He was sure they would all share his enthusiasm for the appointment of their new boss.

After all the employees took their seats, William greeted them and started by giving account of Fitzgerald International's fiscal reports for the year. He followed with future projections of the company profit earnings and stock value.

"I would like to thank every one for your contributions to Fitzgerald International and for the part that each one of you plays in our success. You are all an important building block of this company's accomplishments. Our production and profit margin this year far exceeded our expectations, and Jonathan is a big part of our success. As you all know, my wife Sophia and I have been talking about retirement for some time. Although, I am not ready to stop working altogether, I feel it's time to start enjoying the fruits of our labor; it's time to give Jonathan the title for the job he has been doing for a while now. He has proven himself the last three years, working harder than anybody to obtain international contracts, permits, and financing in Central and South America. He has remarkable insight, recognizing the ideal strategy to market our homes. Ladies and gentlemen, I give you the new President and Chief Executive Officer of Fitzgerald International, my son, Jonathan Fitzgerald."

The room erupted into applause in a clear expression of

approval. Jonathan was William Fitzgerald's only son and heir. Jon, as he was affectionately called, was an unassuming young man, unspoiled by the comforts that surrounded him growing up. He wanted to earn his way by working harder than anybody else. Becoming the leader of the company, a position that he was born into, was not something he took for granted. Instead, he sought to earn it with his hard work and down-to-earth style of management. It was easy to see why he inspired loyalty with this kind attitude, and his employees admired and respected him.

As he made his way to the microphone, all eyes were on him, especially the women's, whose admiration was for more than just his performance on the job. They loved the eye candy as well.

"Thank you Dad, for your kind words," he said as he slightly bowed his head and began addressing the small crowd. "I will certainly do my best for the good of the company and its employees. All of you know me. A title won't change my accessibility, and I will need your expertise as much as I always have. I couldn't do my job without you doing yours well too, and I thank you for that. This year we did very well as a team. The company exceeded our forecast and Fitzgerald International would like to show you our appreciation for playing an important part. Your bonus checks will be issued to you by the end of December as a small thank you.

The applause of grateful employees filled the room but Jonathan motioned them to stop.

"Thank you very much. I think that we've covered everything and I'm sure we're all anxious to start our nice long weekend. All that's left is to wish you a Happy Thanksgiving to you and your loved ones," he said waving as he walked away.

Within a few minutes, all the thankful employees cleared the conference room and soon were on their way to begin their long holiday weekend.

***

William Fitzgerald started Fitzgerald International with a visionary dream: to make home ownership attainable for retiring citizens on fixed incomes. Thinking globally, he started to invest in third world countries where he could find reasonably priced land to build affordable housing. His idea was that as the baby-boomer generation aged, more retirees living on a small income would find owning a home in these places desirable and within reach. To many of them, going back to their birth places and living their twilight years able to afford a better standard of living, was a dream come true. In addition, the company created jobs locally that were badly needed, giving it a very favorable reputation.

Originally, William started his business venture with his longtime friend, Oliver Spellman, as a partner. But due to their differences in philosophies when it came to the direction the business was taking, they ended their business partnership amicably. After William bought Oliver's share in the company, Oliver pursued his idea of building luxury homes, where the profit margin would be larger. In comparison, the housing tracts William was interested in building were modest and affordable.

Not long after parting ways, William's father passed away and with the inheritance left to him was able to start his first major project in Ecuador. Within a few months of its release, all one hundred units were sold and William was on his way to building a solid reputation for being an honorable businessman with a strong sense of community giving.

The mortgage company created later on was an evolution spurred by the needs of buyers and sound advice from William's business associates. Offering financing of homes built by Fitzgerald International turned out to be a lucrative venture, because soon they had more business than they had planned for and had to farm out loans.

William felt like a very lucky man to see his son shared his philosophy that responsibility came along with privileges. Company profits always came second when it came to making a difference in people's lives, and his son had learned this early in life. Along with the compassionate heart and good looks inherited from his mother, he was a young man any father would have been proud to have. "Indeed," he thought to himself, "I have so much to be thankful for."

After officially relinquishing his position in the company to his son, he had no doubt it was the right thing to do; a sense of liberation validated it further. He had dreamed of the day when he would hand the reins of the company to Jonathan, and now that it had happened, he couldn't have been more content. This year he looked especially forward to their traditional Thanksgiving party and beyond that, to the beginning his life of semi-retirement.

Every year, Sophia and William Fitzgerald had a Thanksgiving dinner party. With everyone in the family busy and going all different directions, they liked setting aside the whole weekend for a little catching up with events in the lives of their loved ones. Friends and family were very important to the two them. When they started their married life together many years before, they hoped for a large family, but were blessed with only one son. Jon was their pride and joy and when he decided to major in Architecture and International Business Law to join the company, his parents couldn't have been happier. William wished nothing more than to have Jonathan take over the business when he was ready to step down completely. At sixty-five, he still felt he had a lot of life ahead of him to enjoy. He especially looked forward to the time when the grandchildren would come.

As the early evening started to cast its shadows over beautiful Alexandria Bay, a small army of workers was moving about the mansion, checking over the last details before the first guests arrived. Flowers adorned every area of the estate, and guest rooms were provided with every amenity for the weekend. The kitchen was abuzz with all the food preparation, which was closely overseen by Sophia. She often enjoyed cooking alongside her help, but more so during Thanksgiving because she liked putting her personal touch on every part of the evening celebration.

Shortly before six o'clock, the guests started to arrive; some to stay for the weekend and still others were only there for the evening festivities. Maxwell Adams, Jonathan's best friend, was the first to arrive. The two men had met at a summer camp in Colorado when they were nine years old and became inseparable from the beginning. Max was like the brother Jon never had, and they remained close through the years. They went to the same schools and graduated from the same university, with Max majoring in Business Administration. Soon after, Max came to work for Jon at Fitzgerald International and became the controller and his right-hand man. The trio of friends was rounded off by Bradley Spellman, son of William Fitzgerald's friend and one time business partner, Oliver Spellman.

One of the last guests to arrive that evening was Madison Shelton, Jonathan's girlfriend of over two years. She looked stunning as she made her way toward him, dressed in a white mink coat below the knee. Underneath it, her sparking pale yellow dress accentuated her beautiful curves, which she was only too happy to flaunt. She loved making a grand entrance and having all eyes on her.

"Hi, honey. I didn't miss anything, did I?" she asked with a deceitful sweetness.

"No party is complete until you get there," he said.

"Now you see why I think you are an absolute keeper," she cooed.

"And you look beautiful tonight," he said gallantly.

She gave him a seductive look.

"Tonight?" she asked, batting her eyes at him.

"Always," he told her, correcting himself.

She smiled, touched his cheek, and handed him her coat before walking away.

"I have to say hello to everybody," she said waving and giving him a flirtatious look.

Max, who had been observing the scene from nearby, walked up to Jon.

"Are you sure you want to do this?" he asked in a low voice.

"I have to do something. It's not fair to Madison; I have to make up my mind, and just can't see myself walking away. Look at her, she's beautiful."

"I can't argue that. I know she is beautiful. That's obvious. You think you're in love, but what makes her the One? You have to agree, the two of you are very different people."

"I think that Madison and I are past the 'in love' stage of our relationship after more than two years together. We love and respect each other; besides, at thirty-three years old, it's time for me to settle down."

"I'm all for you being happy. I just don't want to see you do it for the wrong reasons and being thirty-three is not a good one."

"Don't worry Max. Everything will be alright," Jon reassured his friend.

Just then, Bradley walked into the room and joined them.

"I see Miss Shelton is in the area," he said, looking around and then at the coat Jon was holding. "I'll take it and put it up for you," he volunteered.

By now, everybody had started making their way to the large, beautifully decorated dining room, bursting with festive autumn colors. They were all eagerly anticipating the legendary Fitzgerald delectable Thanksgiving meal to come. Soon, everybody was seated in the spacious formal dining room, built especially for this occasion. William stood up and, raising his wine glass, gave his always moving and eloquent message of thanksgiving.

The melodic sounds of crystal filled the room as everyone raised their goblets to toast; soon those sounds were followed by silverware against fine china as everyone started to enjoy their feast. There was a brief silence, followed with well-deserved compliments to the hosts on another memorable dinner experience. After thoroughly enjoying the traditional turkey dinner with all the trimmings and delicious desserts, they moved leisurely to the living room to enjoy coffee and after-dinner drinks.

In the next room, the small band hired to entertain the younger guests was beginning to test their equipment and warm up. Before the crowd started to disperse to different rooms, Jonathan walked over to his parents holding hands with Madison, and standing in the middle of the room addressed the guests and family.

"Everyone, I have an announcement to make," he began. "As most of you know by now, my father officially appointed me the head of Fitzgerald International yesterday. I'm honored that he has enough confidence to trust me with such responsibilities, and hope that I can live up to his expectations. In light of this, my friends and family, I think it's time for me to take the next logical step in my life, and after almost three years, I have something to ask Madison." He held her hand and got on one knee. "Madison, will you be my wife?" he asked.

Her eyes opened bigger than saucers when he pulled out an exquisitely expensive jewelry box and opened it, exposing a sparkling white, three-karat pear solitaire diamond ring.

"Oh Jon, I had no idea! Yes, yes I will," she purred as Jon slipped the stunningly beautiful engagement ring on her finger. Then they kissed in front of surprised guests.

Everyone gathered around the couple, offering their congratulations and best wishes. Jonathan's parents seemed to be a bit stunned at his announcement but avoided showing their feelings. It wasn't like their son to make major decisions without at least letting them know ahead of time. Sure, Madison was a beautiful woman. Her green eyes, blond hair, and model figure was the reason they believed their son was first smitten with her, but they wanted more than that for Jon. They wanted nothing less than true love for him and they weren't sure Madison was the right one for Jon. Maxwell had his doubts all along, and Bradley seemed ambivalent about the whole scene.

"Darling, this is the best news! I am calling my parents right now," Madison said, ecstatic.

When she walked to the phone in the garden room, Jonathan motioned Max over to the adjacent study.

"Well, I did it," Jon said, as if he had just cleared a hurdle.

"That, you did," Max said, giving him a hug. "Congratulations, my man. I hope she makes you happy."

"Thanks Max, it means a lot coming from you. By the way, I called you here because I'm going to the office tomorrow morning.

I left some papers with information I need to complete a transaction to my Swiss bank account. Are you up for golf afterwards?"

"Come on Jon, when was the last time I turned down golf? But what is so important that can't wait until Monday?" Max asked.

"My dad insisted on giving me a signing bonus for my promotion, as you know, and wouldn't take no for an answer. So I am going to use it to build the chalet Madison has said many times she dreamed of having in Switzerland. It's going to be my wedding present to her and I want it to be a total surprise."

"Knowing her taste, it will cost you plenty," Max snickered.

"It won't be more than five million dollars which is what my dad gave me as a bonus. Whatever it buys will have to be enough because I'm not willing to spend any more than that," Jon replied.

"Five million signing bonus? You are worth more than that. Your father knows it."

"I told him that I didn't need a bonus to go with my promotion. After all, it's our family business, but he insisted on it. He said that it would cost him a lot more if he had to find his replacement outside the company."

"He is right about that too," Max said.

"I know. But this is not about business; it's about family," Jon said.

"You're just going to have to humor him and let him dote on his only son."

"You're right, and that's what I thought, too. Who am I to argue with my dad? I'll just let him have his way this time," he said with an impish smile.

"It makes him happy to do that," Max said.

"Yes, my dad's a good man. By the way, I'd also like you to come to the office with me tomorrow because I'm putting you down as my secondary signature on the Swiss account."

"What's wrong with putting your dad's signature instead?" Max asked.

"He would probably think that spending that much for a place you would only use a few months a year is a waste and that there are better things I could do with the money."

"I'd say he has a point," Max said.

"Yes, I know," Jon said.

"Okay. I'll go with you; in fact, I want to check last quarter's report for mortgage loan figures. I think I saw a discrepancy in the totals for the last quarter, and I can do a quick check on it when you do your bank transaction—while it's fresh in my mind. Some figures don't match, and you know my philosophy: Numbers don't lie," Max said.

A gentle knock on the door alerted them to Madison's presence.

"Are you guys talking business? My mom just can't wait to see my ring! If you don't mind, honey, Bradley can drop me off at my parents' that is, if you are too busy."

"Madison, of course I am not too busy for you," Jon said.

Bradley peeked from behind Madison.

"Does the lady need my services?" he asked, as if he'd overheard.

"No, she doesn't, but thanks anyway, Brad," Jon said, putting his arms around her waist. "By the way, are you up for golf tomorrow?"

"I wish I could, but I have family stuff to do. In fact, I've got to get going now because I still need to stop by my parents' house, and on top of that, I got a busy day tomorrow. I'm really sorry to miss it."

"There will be other times," Jon said.

"There's no doubt about that. For now, I bid you goodnight and congratulations, to the both of you," he said, giving Madison and Jon a hug and walking to the door.

"Well then, let's go sweetie. You can just take me to my parents' because I'm spending the night there," Madison said to Jonathan.

"I'm ready when you are," he said to her after checking his watch.

"Let's go!" she said, giddily staring at her ring as they walked out the door toward Jon's car.

"I'm glad you like it," Jon said to her, noticing her happiness.

"I love it! I can't wait to show it off to my whole family. I just hope everyone is still there."

"Didn't you call them from the house to give them the news?" he asked her.

"Yes, but all I said was that I had surprise for them," she said.

"Call them from your cell and tell them to wait until you get there."

"I left my cell phone at home."

"You can use mine," he said, handing her the phone, as he made his way around the circular driveway and drove away.

Twenty minutes later, the two of them were at her parents' home, basking in the congratulations and best wishes from friends and family at the Shelton's home. Shortly after midnight, Jon kissed his future bride and went home, blissfully unaware that not everything around him was as it seemed.

***

The morning daylight, filtering through the slightly open drapes, slowly shed light in the bachelor bedroom with windows that faced a view of Alexandria Bay. It was the morning after her engagement to Jon and Madison opened her eyes and stretched out her hand to look at her lavish engagement ring in the light. She reached over to her bed companion and ran her fingers down his chest, as she pressed her naked body against his back.

"Come on, handsome, wake up," she whispered lustfully in his ear.

He slowly turned around and stared at her with a seemingly impassive look.

"You're just a little whore, aren't you?" he said, clenching his fists.

"That's right," she said in a low sultry voice. "I'm your little whore, lover."

He turned his face away and was silent.

"Bradley, are you upset about the engagement?" she asked surprised.

"It does not fit very well in the present situation," he told her, grinding his teeth in anger.

"Look, baby, things won't change that much for you and me. Jonathan will go on trips just like he always has and I need you to satisfy my needs. You're so good at that."

"What about Jon?"

"He is a good man and he'll make a great husband and father of our children, but sexually speaking he is too conservative. I need the cutting-edge sex you and I have."

"You have no shame," he said.

"Shut up and do me right now," she shamelessly demanded.

She was so infuriatingly beautiful and knew how to make him angry and want her at the same time. He got on top of her and pinned her arms down with force, wanting to hurt her.

"Oh lover, I like it when you're bossy," she said, pleased to see him lose control of his emotions

"Shut up!" he said as he kissed her furiously.

She started to moan and he put his hand over her mouth. "That's the sound I want to hear," he said to her.

Madison and Bradley had been carrying on their deceitful affair for more than two years. It was instant sexual chemistry when they were introduced shortly after she started dating Jonathan. Being his friend and girlfriend respectively didn't prevent them from jumping into an affair not long after they met. Jon was a nice guy who thought he fell in love with her, but she had a wild sexual side that Brad not only satisfied but encouraged. They were surprisingly candid with each other from the start about what they wanted out of their relationship. She wanted to satisfy her taste for sexual adventures and he was deeply resentful and envious of Jonathan all of his life. In Brad's twisted mind, half of Fitzgerald International should belong to the Spellmans. It's the way it would have been if William had remained partners with his father years ago. Bedding Madison made him feel superior, as if he was taking her away from Jon and relished the thought of getting away with it.

Their convenient arrangement worked well for them because it was based on their shared greed for material possessions. She wanted to marry into a lot of money, and Jonathan fit the bill. Bradley, on the other hand, wanted a piece of Fitzgerald International. In his twisted mind, fate had cheated him, but he decided long time ago to take matters into his own hands, and his first step was going to work for Jon. Naturally, their uncharacteristic honesty with each other was a mutual benefit of their unholy alliance. Being privy to their mutual dirty secrets was their insurance against each other. It was a calculated move by both of them; after all, they knew that they were too much alike to be trusted.

Growing up, Bradley became bitter and resentful of the success of Fitzgerald International. Over time, his concealed anger grew more with the success of the company. Ever since he was a boy, he knew of the partnership of his father with William. In fact, the two men had remained friends through the years. His father's business was successful enough to support the family comfortably and to give them the best money could buy. But it was not nearly the booming success that Fitzgerald International came to be, and that caused Bradley's anger to simmer. When Oliver, his father, had retired a few years before and put him in charge of the business, Bradley convinced him to sell, and went to work for the Fitzgeralds as soon as he found a suitable buyer. Using his friendship with Jon and his parents, he lobbied for a high-profile job, which he got without much effort. Eventually he became head of Finance at Fitzgerald International, working under Max, where he was just waiting until he refined his plans to get back what he thought was rightfully his.

***

Two weeks later it was a clear December morning, but the sun belied the cold temperatures at the home of the Fitzgeralds in Alexandra Bay. Jonathan parked his car by the gate and walked the circular driveway bordered with plants and flowers, leading to the breathtaking garden in the back of the house. Bundled up in a hooded sweater and gardening gloves, his mother was checking over the plants and making sure all the right bulbs had been put in the ground. It was another one of those things that, with the help of her gardener, she enjoyed doing often.

There were always flowers everywhere in the Fitzgerald house, or at least ever since Jon could remember. His mother inherited the love of plants from Jon's grandmother, Angela Millett. She was the most enthusiastic nature lover Jon had ever met and could make anything grow. There was something timeless, youthful, and happy about her that he missed.

"What brings you here at this hour of the day?" his mother asked him, bringing him back to reality. She walked up to hug him and kissed his cheek.

"Max and I are flying to Portland this afternoon. I just came by to tell you that I'll be back soon," he said to his mother.

"You do that," she said. "Be safe and come back to us."

"I'll be back," he said. It was always the way he said goodbye to his mother. She didn't like saying the word goodbye to him. It seemed too permanent.

"I would ask if you want to have coffee or tea with me, but the earlier you leave the better. Don't get caught flying in the evening and chance bad weather."

"Yes, Mom," he said. "By the way, Madison will be calling in you the next few days to go through the wedding locations she has narrowed down in her list of possibilities."

"That'll be lovely, dear," she said, smiling sweetly for the benefit of her son, while deep inside she pleaded silently, "Give me strength!"

"Thanks Mom, you're great," he said.

"Thank you dear," she said, giving him a hug and a kiss as Jon got into his car. "You take care of yourself." Sophia leaned over the driver window and kissed her son's cheek one last time.

"I will be careful," he said to her.

"I love you, son. Please be safe," she said lovingly.

"Don't worry. I'll be fine. I love you too, Mom."

And with that, he was gone, watching his mother waving at him in the rearview mirror.

Half an hour later when he got to the airport Max was already waiting.

"Good old Max," he thought, "Always on time and always a friend."

"How do you always get to the airport before me?" he asked Max.

"I'm always packed," Max replied. "My carry-on suitcase always has the basic traveling necessities: passport, some cash, and clothing essentials. There isn't much packing left for me to do on short notice."

"You're such a boy scout," Jon said, patting him on the back.

The two men walked toward the Cessna Citation XLS eight-seat plane owned by Fitzgerald International. Flying had been a passion of Jon's since he started taking lessons at thirteen, and became licensed as soon as he was old enough. For him, there was nothing like the feeling of flying, and he took advantage of every opportunity to do it. As two ground crewmen finished getting the plane ready, the friends boarded and threw their carry-on suitcases on the seats in the back. Within minutes, their plane started to taxi and prepared to take off.

At 2:30 in the afternoon, Jonathan Fitzgerald and Maxwell Adams started their fateful journey the same way as many trips they made before. More than two hours into it, while flying at 20,000 feet altitude, Jon activated the automatic pilot, stood up to stretch, and sat back down. He enjoyed the view from the sky as much as he loved flying. Over the horizon, the sun was approaching a spectacular sunset with a few scattered, puffy clouds; to the right side of them was the majestic sight of the Grand Canyon in its incredible splendor. The two men pensively enjoyed the view for a few minutes and then Jonathan turned to Max. They looked so much alike they could have passed for brothers, and in fact they did so many times while growing up, often as a prank. They had the same build, with light brown hair and blue eyes. But while Jonathan's future looked full of success and promise, there was a cast of deep melancholic sadness in Max's eyes that had been there for a long time.

"You've been awfully quiet," Jon said to his friend.

"Well, I was trying to figure out how to talk to you about marrying Madison, and my mind wondered to Elise. I miss her so much; I'll never stop missing her," Max said with deep sadness in his voice.

Jon reached over and patted his friend on the shoulder.

"Yes buddy, I know. She was a beautiful soul inside and out. Even I miss her sometimes and she was just my friend, not my wife. After all this time, I still am so very sorry that you lost them both so soon."

Max nodded, trying to contain his emotions that always surfaced when he talked about her.

Elise was Max's wife and the love of his life. They were college sweethearts and soon after graduating they got married. After three years of trying to conceive, Elise finally got pregnant and they could hardly contain their joy when they told "Uncle Jon." Elise looked absolutely radiant and Max was on top of the world.

Four months into the pregnancy, on her way home from work, there was a loud rattling noise in the rear of her sports utility vehicle and she stopped on the highway emergency lane. When she got out to check the problem, a drunk driver being pursued by the police hit her, the impact throwing her up in the air and into the hood of an oncoming car's windshield. Elise died instantly along with their unborn child, and Max's world was shattered forever. It had been more than five years since then and the pain of losing her never went away.

"My love for her is the reason why I feel compelled to tell you frankly what I think," Max started. "I've heard your reasons for getting married and I don't buy them. I'm more inclined to think that, after almost three years with Madison, you are in a commit-or-get-out situation. You're a nice guy who talked himself into thinking that you have enough in common to build a life together. But what would happen if the love of your life, your soul mate, comes along when you're married to the wrong person? Pragmatically speaking, it would cost you a lot, and I'm not just talking about money."

"I hadn't looked at it that way," Jon said.

"Please think about it carefully," Max continued. "Talk to your parents or someone who can give you a wise perspective. You may feel in a bind right now, but be careful not to create potential for worse later," he said with a feeling of relief. "There, I said it. I wanted to get that off my chest for a while."

"I'd be lying if I said that Madison and I have what you and Elise did. But I think that few people ever find that. You were the lucky ones. Me? Well, I'm not so sure."

"And how do you know that?" Max asked.

"I'm basing my opinion on what I see around me," Jon said.

"I'm surprised that you'd have such a cynical attitude about marriage. You have a wonderful example in your parents! Don't cheat yourself and settle because you think it's time to get married. Ultimately, however, it's your call. Only you can decide if Madison and you can last forever."

"You make a solid argument, and since you feel so strongly, I'll think about it; and thanks, Max. I know you want nothing but the best for me."

"You're my brother," Max said, shrugging his shoulders and lightening up the mood, "I had to do it."

"I promise you that I'll seriously think about what you said."

"That's all I'm asking," Max said, patting Jon in the back.

"Hey! Let's fly over summer camp!" Jon said on a whim, after a brief silence. Max gave him a broad smile.

"That's a great idea!" he said enthusiastically. "It's been a long time since we've done that."

"Let me file the changes of my flight plan," Jon said as he proceeded to communicate the changes to his original course.

Summertime at the camp was always a blast for the two of them, and it had a special meaning because they had met there as boys and instantly became best friends.

Jon set the plane's the course in the direction of the Colorado Rocky Mountains as he reflected on Max's advice. His points were worth considering. He had to be sure that he was getting married for the right reasons and needed to talk to his parents about it and seek their advice. In hindsight, he thought his parents' input should have been considered before asking Madison to marry him.

Max leaned back in his seat and closed his eyes, hoping to catch a power nap; Jon just closed his eyes and reflected on what was just said. Immersed in their thoughts while darkness was falling, neither one noticed the size of the dark clouds ahead until they were going through them. Suddenly a gust of wind shook the plane, making it drop down all of a sudden, getting both of the men's attention. They had unwittingly got caught in a massive snowstorm as the plane started shaking violently. Jon struggled to get it under control as the instrument panel started vibrating and every indicator went wild. All of a sudden, he couldn't see anything in front of him—only darkness and snow flurries swirling around, illuminated by the light from the plane.

Realizing he was not getting the situation under control, Jon tried to glide with the current of the storm, trying to keep the plane from breaking into pieces. But there was another big gust of wind immediately, followed by a major drop in altitude, as the violent windy conditions tossed the aircraft around. A few minutes later, the rear of the plane clipped a tree on the side of a mountain. The impact broke the plane in two, ripping Max's seat off and pushing him all the way to the tail end. The rear section plummeted down a steep mountain and into a dark abyss of snow, completely disappearing along with Max. Jon tried to save what was left of the craft until the last second, but his heroics came to an end when the remainder of the plane crashed against a towering rock and finally came to rest at the edge of a mountain cliff, killing him instantly.

Suddenly the two friends felt as if they were ejected from their bodies and found themselves hovering over the crash site. Time seemed to stop as they looked at each other and could hear one another's thoughts without uttering a word. They didn't feel physically hurt or sad—not even cold—but the moment of confusion soon faded when they realized that they were no longer physical beings. Having shed their bodies, the feeling was that of unbelievable lightness and freedom.

They looked at Jon's mangled, lifeless body in the wreckage of the plane, slumped over and still strapped to his seat. Then they looked at the spot where Max went down. His lifeless body was buried beneath the snow below them; even the tail of the plane had completely disappeared. And yet they could see it all clearly through the falling snow, in what they knew to be night just a few minutes before. At that moment, a wind tunnel came from underneath them, moving upward and sucking them through total darkness, whirling them toward a light in the distance. As they got closer, the light completely overtook the darkness and exposed a vision of the most incredible world. Mortal words would completely fail to relate its reality, and new souls such as Jon and Max could only stand in awe of it.

The beauty everywhere was astonishing and beyond belief. It was all not merely there to be admired, but to experience and become one with, if so desired. It was a world made of the purest crystal imaginable, with an immense dome and a roof made of crystallized colors, emanating heavenly melodious notes. An elliptical passage way connected as a bridge portal to a never-ending mansion carved in shapes that reminded Jon of canyons and rock formations. From there they could see reflections of an array of colors beyond belief. As they paused on the bridge, they could see what seemed like the whole universe displayed before them. A benevolent, loving spirit appeared at that moment.

"Welcome," he communicated silently. "I am Apollo, the gatekeeper. I will be your guide until you find your home."

"Our home? Isn't heaven our home now?" Max asked.

"You are not in heaven yet," Apollo said, "this is just a glimpse of what's yet to come. However, I perceive one of you is ready for it but not the other," he said turning to Jon.

"What do you mean?" he asked surprised.

"I mean that heaven was a choice offered but you never decided. It's very simple, really. Just like a contract, you have to accept the offer and its conditions."

"I don't remember the offer ever being made to me, much less conditions of acceptance, which by the way, what are they?"

"You knew that some day you would die. It's an inescapable fact for humanity. Didn't you stop to think about your existence beyond that life?" Apollo asked.

"I guess I was too busy to think about that stuff. I'm embarrassed to say it, but I always thought I'd have more time."

"Most humans do. They think of death as something that's going to happen last in their lives, which is true, but sometimes it happens sooner than they think."

What happens to me now?" he asked anxiously.

"Fortunately for you, you've been given a second chance. Soon you'll be able to make your choice and live in your paradise forever."

"What do you mean when you say live in my paradise?" Jon asked.

"It's different for everybody. All human beings have an instant when their joy is so complete, they experience a moment of complete rapture when time stands still, almost filling the gap between the spiritual and the physical realm," Apollo said. "It's the closest description I can give you."

"Does every human being go through that experience? I don't recall anything like that."

"The only exceptions happen when a soul arrives here before it's time, such as your case."

Jon looked confused.

"I don't follow you," he said.

"You are slightly ahead of your time and need to adapt to your new existence. I will be around when you need me," he told Jon, then turned to Max. "Welcome to heaven's realm." With that said, Apollo disappeared.

Max smiled. He knew what his paradise in heaven was, but was it possible not only to be with Elise but also with his child? He looked ahead and there they were! Just like in his dreams, when he fantasized that his child was a daughter as beautiful as his Elise. His soul felt finally set free as his spirit raced toward them.

"I've missed you two so much!" he exclaimed through tears. "I can't believe that I'm finally home," he sighed.

Elise and his daughter smiled and Max felt himself enveloped in total love and irresistible joy. His grandparents, as well as other loved ones who had passed on before him surrounded and greeted him, communicating their happiness to have him there. He understood at that time why no human being could ever be capable of surviving the experience of complete and absolute love. The only way to experience its total power was in the spirit, and his soul overflowed with happiness, knowing that at last he would never part with Elise.

"Many things will become clearer now that you are no longer a physical being. Knowing the secrets of the universe is not something left to mortals," said Max's grandfather, interrupting his thoughts.

Jonathan observed from a distance and wondered to himself what his paradise would be like, as he watched Max disappear with his family into their heavenly home. Looking through its crystal clarity, he could see into the garden decorated with twinkling wind chimes that made the most melodious music he'd ever heard. Max was a music lover and Elise loved wind chimes; in fact, the first gift Max gave Elise was a string of hearts made of thin white rock, which she hung over her dorm window.

Jon was overjoyed for Max but uneasy about himself.

"It will all come to you," he heard his grandmother's voice say.

Instantly he found himself in the most beautiful garden he'd ever seen. There were flowers everywhere—of every kind, every color, and every shape imaginable. There were colors he'd never seen before, trees that sang beautiful songs and gave him constant shade as he moved about. The gentle mist through the branches mixed with the filtering light cast the perfect rainbow colors over his grandmother's garden.

The waterfalls were surrounded by never-seen plant life in countless forms and color shades. "Grandma!" he whispered, "I feel the awe of your paradise."

His Grandmother smiled. She looked just the way Jon remembered her in his childhood: young and beautiful. The warm feeling of joy and unconditional love emanating from her permeated him. He felt what being love itself was like—what it felt to be joy—because it was all around him, and in everything his spirit had experienced in this new realm. As he looked into the petals of a gardenia, his favorite flower, he could feel its beauty and scent, and a softly fragrant breeze surrounded him. He turned and walked toward a rose plant in the distance, bursting with blooms of innumerable colors and sizes. As he got closer to take a better look, he could hear and feel the cheerful chatter among them, but when he got near they became silent. Everything was alive and communicating in a seemingly universal language that he understood as if it was second nature.

"It's so beautiful it's almost overwhelming," he said to his grandmother.

"If you were human, it would be unbearable" she said.

"I keep forgetting I'm no longer a human being," he said to her.

"Hmm," she mused.

"Is something wrong?" he asked.

"I don't know. I never heard that phrase here before. I thought it was impossible to forget our spiritual state," his grandmother said.

"Did I disappoint you?"

She laughed. "Of course not!" she said emphatically. "You know better than anyone how much I love you."

"Thanks, Grammy, I love you too," he said, as she smiled at him.

He looked beyond the garden and his spirit floated along with his thoughts rising high above. From there he could see his loved ones' as well as countless of other souls' paradises, each one blending seamlessly to create a quilted vision that could only be described as heavenly.   The beautiful tapestry below was visible in glorious splendor. Even so, as he contemplated its beauty, the magnificence of his grandmother's garden stood out in his eyes.

He felt himself soaring like an eagle, jubilant that he was able to do what he could only dream when he was alive. He was like a child at a free candy store who couldn't have enough—doing loops and pirouettes, acting as if he had wings, maneuvering any way he pleased.

As he was making one of his many make-believe landings, he saw his grandfather floating toward him, looking younger than he was the last time Jon had seen him. Instantly the two were transported to a sandy white beach with water so clear he could see every oceanic living thing. Anchored not far away was My Fair Lady, the last yacht his grandfather owned. They soon found themselves on the deck, guided by their thoughts. Jon's grandfather sat on a stool in front of a white crystal canvas screen, surrounded by the ocean and the most incredible sunset Jon had ever seen. With a small motion of his brush, the colors began to flow, and as he painted on, the sunset in the canvas came alive with orange hues blazing trails of indescribable colors and lights.

Off in the distance, Jonathan could see a school of white dolphins frolicking in the water, coming toward them, as if knowing his wish to see them up close. A big wave came behind them at that instant and lifted them up. They applauded and happily played with each other talking amongst themselves, all of which Jon could understand. As they rode the wave, he could see their soft silhouettes reflected through the curtain of water and the luminous sunset behind them, making it a spectacular sight. Trailing the dolphins was a manatee tribe of three, gliding and moving as if dancing to the most beautiful classical music piece he had ever heard.

"Welcome home, Jon. I am overjoyed that you are here," his grandfather's spirit said, silently conveying his joy at being reunited, enveloping him in his love.

"I couldn't be happier to be with you, Grandfather. It has been a long time," he said feeling like a little boy reunited with his grandfather at last.

"A long time for you, for us time isn't relevant."

"What do you mean?" Jon wanted to know.

"I mean that you don't feel the passing of time. The physical experience of it is no longer part of our existence, but we still are witnesses of everything that happens on earth."

"Alright, I think I get it. Time is a physical concept which doesn't apply in the spiritual world."

"Something like that," his grandfather said.

It was his grandparents' lifelong dream to sail along the Americas and go island hopping in the Caribbean Sea. His grandfather was an avid seaman when he was alive and together with his Aunt Ingrid, who was recuperating from a bout with breast cancer, they had set out to make their dreams a reality. Not wanting to take chances, they had hired an experienced captain who knew the itinerary they intended to take very well. The first half of their trip had been every bit as good as they had hoped, with perfect weather cooperating and winds often favoring their direction.

Unfortunately, what should have been a happy time for them as they were making their way back turned out to be their farewell. The night before leaving the Bahamas, where they had stopped for two days, while they slept, there was a gas leak in the line to the kitchen adjacent to their sleeping quarters. His grandparents and Aunt Ingrid died in their sleep. The captain and two other crew members, who slept on the other side of the yacht, survived after a stay in the hospital. Jonathan was devastated. He was very close to his grandparents, and being an only child, they doted on him. In fact, he was named after Jonathan Holmes, his maternal grandfather. And his Aunt Ingrid—she was gone in the prime of her life! He could imagine her on a golf course getting ready to hit a spectacular shot.

"Around here all rounds are under par," he heard her voice say as he was about to ask his grandfather about her.

"Of course!" he thought to himself. "You could always find her at the golf course on her days off."

In fact, she gave him his first set of children's golf clubs and took him to his first lessons. It was obvious to him that his aunt's paradise would have golf written all over it and, of course, she would have her own golf course.

"A golf course?" she asked with a laugh. "Nephew, this is paradise and you can play any golf course you could imagine and even some you can't even envision. You can play forever, anywhere and everywhere in the universe."

"The universe?" he marveled.

"In all of creation, and it's always your tee time. All your shots go exactly as you want them, as far as you wish. You can hit the perfect shot every time," she said smiling.

"Well, that is golf heaven," he said.

"When you get to paradise, there are no limitations," she said to him.

He wondered what exactly she meant by that. He had no personal concept of heaven or paradise. Although as a spirit his soul felt incredibly comforted and free, something was still missing. Being there with long-gone family members and loved ones, alive and free of all mortal pain and sadness, was a beautiful dream becoming reality. He had missed them so much when they passed away that seeing them again was spiritually satisfying beyond what he imagined. Still, he had no idea where to begin his journey into this paradise. It wasn't something he had given much thought to when he was alive.

"You were too busy to pay attention to the reality of afterlife," Ingrid said to him, reading his thoughts, and then she laughed. "Isn't it funny? You put so much time and effort towards insuring your material future for retirement, yet you rarely considered eternity. Silly, isn't it? We worry and plan our physical life, which lasts, at the most a little over a hundred years."

"Maybe because we can only relate to our physical existence," he said.

"Perhaps, but in retrospect, would you agree that it pays off planning for eternal existence? If souls will go somewhere after dying, as you can see now, you must choose your destination because there's more than one place to go," his grandfather said.

"Sure, I agree now. But hindsight is always 20/20."

"Of course, but nobody has a lease on life, we all know that."

"That's true. Eternity was a far-away concept to me. I never gave it much thought, figuring that I would have plenty of time later for things like that. It's like dying; we know it's going to happen to all of us, but still, deep inside, we think of it as something that happens to somebody else," Jon said.

"It's true. When you think about it, it makes sense to plan for your soul's future. People plan a long time for retirement, and that's not nearly as long as eternity." Ingrid said.

"Humans are busy living. The afterlife is not reality for them," Grandfather Holmes said.

"Sooner or later, we all have to face it. We don't live in the physical realm forever," Aunt Ingrid said.

"You're right about that," Jon said to her pensively. "Indeed if this is not a dream, heaven must be beautiful beyond description."

"It's unlike anything a human mind could grasp. Words couldn't begin to do it justice. You'll see what I mean soon. I'm sure Apollo will clear things out for you," she said.

Jon smiled at her. "You've given me a lot to think about."

"It's really not that complicated."

"Easy for you to say!" he said.

"Don't worry. It's all good," she said smiling, and with that she was gone.

Finding himself alone for the first time since his arrival to his new world, Jon decided to wander around and explore his newfound existence and its seemingly endless surroundings.

CHAPTER 3

DREAM SO REAL!

Back in Colorado, at the exact time of Jonathan's plane crash, Eve Anne was having a vivid dream. Struck with the flu the week after Thanksgiving, she had gone to bed early after taking some medication. She immediately fell asleep and found herself back in summer camp when she was young—very young. It was early morning and Mr. Kessler, one of the camp guides and counselors, was leading a group of youngsters headed for a hike and climbing trip. Eve Anne had discovered her love for rock climbing the year before and took every opportunity to do it. In fact, despite her young age, she was getting very good at it. The group of three boys and two girls hiked two miles from camp in the Zion National Park. The canyons and majestically immense rocks pointed to the heavens, offering only a glimpse of the awesome beauty that waited to be discovered by nature lovers.

As the group climbed their way up, Eve quickly got ahead, leaving the rest of the group behind. The boys, feeling their egos challenged hurried up, almost catching up with her, with Mr. Kessler who was close behind acting as the belayer, and urging them to slow down. At eight and ten years old, they were at the age when teasing or picking on someone was the way to handle their crush on them. Eve had nothing to say to them. Her exasperated look said it all as she briefly glanced at the two boys following behind her, who were asking if she was Super Girl, laughing at her and carrying on. As she looked away, she heard the sound of a snap. When she looked down, she saw one the boys who had just been teasing her falling off the cliff, gear and all, trying hopelessly to grab onto something that wasn't there, with a panicked look. Her own screaming woke her up, jolting from her sleep, covered in sweat.

"That was too real!" she exclaimed, glad that it was just a bad nightmare.

She drank some water and went back to bed. The dream was vividly unsettling and she couldn't go back to sleep right away, but after a while she convinced herself that the medication, combined with her fever was to blame for its intensity.

***

In Alexandria Bay, the search started the day after the crash. Aware that Jonathan and Max never made it to Portland the evening before, their parents were worried that something horrible could have happened. Jon was always diligent about calling them when he got to his destinations because he knew they would worry otherwise. Before too long, it was established that the friends never made it to Portland and there had been no contact with their plane since early evening the day before.

The Federal Transportation Agency began their investigation as soon as they were reported missing and the change of course was discovered. The anguished parents wasted no time making arrangements on their own.

The search team assembled by the Fitzgeralds and the Adams took off and traced the course of the flight last reported. They knew the final contact with the plane was while they were flying somewhere over Arizona, which eliminated a lot of territory to cover, but there was still a lot to search. Over the next two days they traced what should have been Jonathan's amended flight plan, but came up empty.

The Fitzgeralds spared no expense or manpower of their own in their search, but as time went on, hope of finding them was wearing thin. They had to look at the possibility that somehow the plane didn't follow the exact route. In which case, what direction did they change it to? Desperate for clues, Kemper Shrout, the head of the Fitzgerald's searching party, requested a more detailed weather report of the surrounding areas at the time the plane vanished.

What he saw gave him a chill. Severe winds and snowstorms were recorded northeast from the last point of contact with Jon the evening the plane disappeared. He seriously hoped that his gut feeling was wrong and that the weather would cooperate in his search.

At the home of Sophia and William, friends and family offered their words of encouragement and hope that Jon and Max were somewhere alive, but unable to get in touch. As much as the Fitzgeralds appreciated their kindness, the focus for them was only on finding their son and Max. All the people's support did little to appease the feeling that the longer it took to find them, the worst the prospects looked. Two days didn't seem like a long time, but for them it felt like an eternity.

Two people however, were not affected by the events the same way as everyone else. After putting on the act of sorrow and despair for the parents, Bradley and Madison found something positive about the whole situation. After leaving William and Sophia's home that day, they couldn't contain their gladness.

"How lucky am I?" Brad said, as they were both getting in his car. "If Jon and Max don't come back alive, the logical person to succeed Jon would be me. All the time I spent planning and plotting, now it may all fall into my lap without having to lift a finger," he said with a smug look.

"Now we will be able to be together without hiding our love," Madison said. "Of course, I have to mourn Jon for the customary period. In the meantime, you will be my comfort, and conveniently we will fall for each other. No one will be the wiser."

"Oh Yeah! I like the way your mind works."

"Now all we can do is wait and see," she said.

"For my part, I will have to show William that I am more than the Controller. With Max gone, I am in for vice president of the company guaranteed, and then it's just a matter of time before I take Jon's place, there's no one else but me. I will make old William see that I am the logical choice to head the company in his absence. It won't be hard. The old man has a soft spot for me," he said confidently. "Someday Fitzgerald International will be mine."

"I love it when good things happen to wicked people," Madison said, laughing.

As far as she was concerned, if Jon didn't come back, it wouldn't be the end of her world. In her mind she felt it would be a win-win situation, even if Jon made it back. She could ride her way to the money train with Jon or Bradley, it didn't matter to her as long as the end result was the same.

On the third day, the search party got underway again, but this time they started in the area where the last contact with the plane was recorded. From there, they searched north east, where the bad weather had been reported that night. Four small private planes along with the Department of Transportation set out to search. When they got to the starting point, the sky was clear, without a cloud or trace of wind, but after following the probable direction for over fifteen minutes, far in the distance they could see a great deal of snow on the mountain tops. They divided the area into five sections, with each plane to comb over as much of the territory as possible. Hope springs eternal and they all prayed that against all odds, in the snow-covered terrain, the missing men had hopefully found refuge somewhere in a canyon.

They toiled without success all morning and into the afternoon. It was like looking for a needle in a haystack of snow. Toward the end of the day, not willing to give up yet, Kemper decided to go over the area one last time, and as flew east he saw a light that looked like a mirror's reflection in the distance. His heart skipped a beat. "Is that Morse code?" he wondered. He got on the radio and summoned the rest of the search party that was ready to leave for the day.

"This is unit one," he said, "I think there is something over here we need to check out. I just saw a light or some type of signal."

As they surrounded the area for a closer look around the mountain they could see a reflection, but they could not get close enough to identify what it was. They quickly summoned a helicopter. By the time it got to the site, the sun had set over the west and they could no longer see the light they were looking for.

But after narrowing down the area, they came upon their find with the use of telescopes.

The light Kemper had spotted was a reflection of the windshield of Jon's plane. A crew member was lowered with a rope ladder to take a closer look and it was confirmed: this was the front half section of the plane with Jonathan's lifeless body slumped over the pilot seat. But there were no signs of the rest of the plane or other remains, and because darkness was setting in, the recovery had to be postponed until the next day.

The subsequent aerial search for Max's body was intense, but fruitless. The snow that had fallen the night of the crash made it impossible to put any men on the ground. The only choice they were left with was to monitor the area until the snow melted enough for a ground search. Unfortunately, it was going to take some time before the conditions would allow that.

The news, although not unexpected, were devastating to the Fitzgerald and Adams families. The worst part for the Adams was the almost certainty that Max was dead, but without recovering his body there couldn't be closure. They were sure that the remains of their son lay somewhere in the area of the mountain where Jonathan was found. Until then, they wanted to keep the hope that, against all odds, he might return.

For their part, after hearing the news, Madison and Bradley each geared up to put their next plan into action. With the confirmation of Jonathan's death, she focused on Bradley. Now that the door was open for him to ascend the ladder of Fitzgerald International leadership, he had become the next best thing to Jonathan, and subsequently, her next best catch. After all, they complemented each other so well. For his part, Bradley was thrilled, as he realized the opportunity he had ahead of him was better than he could have ever imagined; more importantly, there would be no one scrutinizing every decision he made. His personal fortune would be multiplying sooner than he thought. His plans could be accelerated and no one would suspect a thing.

Jonathan's parents on the other hand, were too immersed in their grief and busy making arrangements for Jon's funeral to pay much attention to other things around them. They wanted the memorial service to be a celebration of their son's life.

Two days later they were joined by family and friends to pay their respects, many who gave eulogies and shared personal stories that had the same thing in common: his passion for life and nature was only second to the love he had for his family and friends. He shared his love and himself, unselfishly touching and leaving his mark on their lives forever. Those who were fortunate to know him related how he loved with his actions—always helping, always caring.

His father reminisced about the time when the summer camp counselor called to tell him that Jon and Max had gotten in trouble. The two boys wandered away from the group while on a hiking trip.

"They decided to go on their own hike, leaving the camp guide worried sick when he noticed them missing. The group immediately turned around and went back to camp to notify of the missing boys, only to find them sitting on a tree stump by the entry gate of the camp." William stopped for a moment to compose himself before continuing.

"Then there was the time when he could have gotten seriously hurt," he continued. "Once again, after not paying attention to his guide's instructions on securing his rope line to the rocks, he started to climb. He failed to properly fasten the last stop and fell fifty feet down dangling in midair. But Jonathan seemed to be prepared for such an eventuality. Before the hike, he had apparently wrapped layers of bubble wrap around his body, which triggered a chorus of firecracker sounds when his body hit the side of the rock wall repeatedly as he swayed back and forth. At first, everyone panicked at the popping sounds, but after the confusion cleared they realized that Jon was fine. They all roared with laughter as the sounds slowly waned when he stabilized himself, climbing to his last tightly secured stop. That was Jon," his father said, "fearless but safety conscious, most of the time," he paused to clear his throat and contain his tears.

"The next year he discovered parachute jumping," he continued, "and from there he made his way to freefalling, jumping from mountain rocks into canyons and sometimes into snow-covered grounds.

***

Back in the spiritual realm, Jonathan's soul was reflective and searching within. He thought of his parents, who were no doubt overcome with the grief of losing him, and wished he could reach out and tell them that his spirit was alive and well. He knew if they could somehow sense his presence in a tangible way, they would understand his message and be more at peace. But how could he let them know?

In that instant Apollo appeared. "Our world communicates with the physical world constantly. We obviously cannot physically connect with those left behind because we are no longer physical beings, but if our love and spiritual connection is strong, it will transcend the change of existence."

"You mean it's true that love truly never dies?"

"You are proof of it right now. If it were not for love, you would not feel the need to protect them from their pain."

"So I can communicate with them!"

"Yes, but it's not entirely up to you," Apollo continued. "The more spiritually aware of their surroundings they are, the more openness there will be for them to feel your presence."

John felt a sense of peace come over him just knowing he could see and communicate his parents even as a spirit. He also thought of Madison.

"Remember," Apollo interrupted him, "some people you can't reach. Without a spiritual radar, they are unable to receive or send communication to us."

"Hmm... how interesting!" Jon said.

"Of course, the more spiritual the person, the better the

possibility of communication. They are better able to sense your presence, and of course, it's even easier for us to receive their messages."

"How?"

"As easy as it is to listen. Think of a place where you envision your parents."

Jon did as Apollo said and instantly felt his spirit soaring over his own funeral, weaving through the crowd of mourners. His parents were sitting on the first row, holding hands now after William's eulogy. That's the way Jon always remembered them: loving and finding strength together. Next to them were Max's parents, Sarah and Patrick Adams, trying hard to contain their immensurable grief as well. They were two sets of grieving parents bound together by love and tragedy.

Behind them sat Madison with Bradley. Jon was glad that his friend would help Madison through this difficult time. "Poor Madison! I almost forgot about her. She must be devastated," he thought.

Apollo, reading his mind, said to him, "Remember that not everything is what it seems."

"What do you mean?" Jon asked.

"You will soon find out. Right now, sit between your parents and comfort them."

When Jon did as Apollo said, William and Sophia looked at each other through veiled tears and lovingly caressed each other's cheeks, reaching to each other and holding his spirit in their embrace.

"We were blessed to have had him for as long as we did," William whispered, wiping away her tears.

"Yes," Sophia said, "and I know he'll always be with us. I feel as if he is with us right now and I don't ever want to lose this feeling."

"Sophia, my love, Jonathan is as big a part of our life as we were of his. We can't feel whole without him because that part of us is missing. In the same way I hope that somehow that part of us that we gave him will seek to be with us, regardless of the circumstances," William said.

Sophia reached her arm around William's shoulder and he did the same, unknowingly encircling Jon's spirit, looking into each other eyes, silently holding each other up. They took a big breath and smiled at each other, dried their tears, and sat up straight as if they had just been given a boost of strength. How Jon wished he could wipe away their tears and audibly express his love! For all the freedom the spirit world afforded him when he passed on, he felt very restricted relating to the physical realm.

Apollo watched from a distance, aware of everything that was happening. It was not unusual to have newly arrived beings feel drawn to their loves and relationships in their past lives, especially when they passed on so unexpectedly like Jon. But he was slightly concerned about what he perceived as too strong an emotional pull from the physical world. Jon was going to need help in the transition to his new existence, but for now it was good for him to search and find closure to his seemingly too human emotions. Apollo noticed that when Jon moved through the crowd and brushed against Madison, she was totally unaffected by his presence, unlike his parents. She didn't seem like a grieving fiancé but acted rather content sitting next to Bradley, which puzzled Jon; yet he felt no emotional attachment to either of them.

"I guess that means there was never a true connection between us," he said to Apollo.

"You guessed right."

"Max was right, then."

"Max, your parents—"

"Yes, I know how my parents felt. That's why I didn't consult them before proposing; I didn't want them to tell me something I didn't want to hear."

"Things always look clearer after the fact," Apollo said.

"Indeed," Jon said as he stepped back and observed.

It was the end of the memorial service and many went up to the Fitzgeralds' and Adams' to offer their condolences as the crowd started to disperse and go to their cars. When only their small group was left, William and Sophia walked over to the mahogany casket and each of them kissed it before laying a long-stemmed white rose on it. Deeply grieving, they walked away to their car, unable to contain their weeping.

Friends and relatives gathered together afterward in remembrance of Jon at his parents' home. It seemed surreal for him to attend his funeral, and now even though he was with his loved ones, he nevertheless felt like the missing part of the reunion— alive and aware of everything, but silent and invisible to all.

"Silent and invisible, yes, but not at all undetectable," Apollo said, reading his mind.

"What do you mean?" Jon wanted to know.

Immediately he found himself in his mother's favorite room. It was large and decorated in warm floral patterns. Two large rocking chairs, one on each side of the bay window facing west, looked out into his mother's favorite part of the backyard, the garden. Between two other plush chairs across the room was a beautiful mahogany side table with a tiffany lamp in a pink rose's motif. A matching coffee table was set in the middle of the room with furniture pieces arranged around it. Two of the walls were covered with photographs of the whole family, many spanning a few generations. However, the overriding theme was Jonathan's life, chronicled in the images across the rest of the walls and, indeed, the whole room. Framed photographs of him were on the coffee and corner tables. Photo albums were stacked up on the bookshelves that covered half of the third wall.

"Now, wish for your mother to come into this room," Apollo instructed Jon.

Jonathan did as he was told. At that moment, his mother walked into the room and stood looking around at his pictures hanging on the walls. She ran her fingers across the top of the frame of one of Jon's photographs on the table below.

"Now," said Apollo, "with your mind, force one of those photos to fall to the floor."

"Any of them?" Jon asked.

"Choose one which will be of significance to your mother, one which will convey that you're trying to communicate with her."

Jon concentrated his focus on a frame with one of his camping photographs on the table next to his mother. The photograph fell to the floor and the frame came apart, revealing a note that was tucked behind it. It was a short letter Jon had sent to his parents during his second year at summer camp. It read: "Dear mommy and daddy: It's pretty cool at camp. I got a new friend and his name is Max, but I still miss you a little. I love you to the last number, see you soon. Love, your son Jonathan."

Sophia bent down and slowly picked it up. With tears rolling down her face she the nodded looking up, acknowledging his presence.

"Yes, son. Someday we will all be together. I miss you and love you so much," she whispered, bittersweet tears rolling down her face.

Jon realized that his mother did understand and acknowledge his being there as she clutched the photo and letter close to her heart. He couldn't help the loving urge to embrace her and reassure her spiritually, which she instinctively felt and understood. There was peace and acceptance in her heart and Jon felt good knowing that somehow they would always be connected. Looking back, he wished he had told his parents how much he loved them more often, even if they knew how he felt. How right they were when they used to say "love never dies."

As his thoughts turned to his father, he found himself and Apollo in the family room where William and his younger brother, Vincent, were discussing the impact that his and Max's passing was having on Fitzgerald International.

"Right now it's hard for me to think clearly about anything," William started, "but we have a responsibility to the people that work for us. I know you have always been your own man, forging your life independently, but now I need your help. You are the only one I can trust completely to take over Jon's office until things settle and I can make choices with a better frame of mind."

"Of course I am here for you Will. You can count on me for anything you want— anything," Vince said.

"Thanks, Vince," William said. "I know we can always count on each other, but hearing you say that is a tremendous relief."

"Come on, brother, I'd do anything for you, you know that. It's just that, up until now, you didn't need me."

After getting his college degree in Economics, Vincent Fitzgerald declared his independence by traveling around the world and then backpacking through Europe. A tall man with medium build, he exuded warmth with an open smile and unassuming ways. He was not one to be inclined to climb the ladder of material success, but devoted himself instead to his wife and children, two girls and a boy. His management position in an electronics development company had afforded him with a comfortable life for his family, without sacrificing his priorities. Although he had never needed his brother's help, he knew it was always there. In fact, William had made him plenty of job offers through the years. But this time it was different because his brother truly needed him and Vincent was fiercely loyal to his family.

"Besides, Vince, you might as well get involved in the business. Without Jon, you are our closest family, our heir, Sophia's and mine," William said, taking Vince away from his thoughts.

"You know that having a lot of money was never important to me," Vincent said.

"Yes, I know. The message was clear to me when you wouldn't take the inheritance our parents left you. But the reality is that you have been a large stock holder in Fitzgerald International for some time now. After you repeatedly rejected my offers for help, I started putting a quarter percent of our company profits into a financial portfolio for you, with the majority of it going to our stock. As the company grew, so did your fortune."

"You mean—" Vince asked, trying to fully understand what William was saying.

"I mean that you're a major stockholder in the company. I hope you don't mind that I've been voting for you all these years."

"You didn't have to do that!"

"No, I didn't. But it's the right thing and I wanted to do it. Is that all right with you? This is why you didn't have a choice in the matter until now," William said.

"William, that's way too generous, you really shouldn't have," Vince said.

"Don't fight it. You don't have a choice. And remember that it's not all about you. Laura and the kids should have their say too."

Vince realized he was defeated and out of arguments. "Oh Wills, thank you. I'm so overwhelmed by all of it."

"If things were reversed, you'd give me more," William said.

"When you put it that way, I don't know what to say."

"Don't say anything," William said, hugging his brother.

"I guess I have a lot of work to do," Vince said.

"Losing Jon underscored my belief that we have to follow our vision and set up a structure that will hold successful for the future of Fitzgerald International. It's the least we can do for the people that work for us. Besides, you are the logical choice to run the company if I was no longer around, and you should start learning to look after it."

"You and Sophia will be around for a long time," Vince said.

"Regardless, it's time for you to assume your place in the company. You are my only brother and I want you—better yet—I need your support," William said.

Vincent shook his head.

"You don't have to convince me. I'll turn in my resignation tomorrow and find out what's the minimum notice I can give at work."

Jon felt gladness as the conversation transpired. He often wished his uncle would join the company, but his father never pushed beyond the standing offer.

Vince put his arms around William and gently patted his back as tears rolled down his face.

"Brother, it is okay to let you're pain show and it's okay to cry. This sorrow is a testament of our love for Jon. Because we love him so much, in the same measure, we grieve for him. Let's be glad for our pain, because it says how great a gift he was to us. Pain is the price for love," he said to William with a voice choked full with emotions.

William nodded as tears rolled down his face too. "You're right. I'd rather hurt as I do because of how much he meant to me, than to feel not pain at all," said William.

Jon's dad had always said that Uncle Vince was the gentlest, yet strongest, man he knew. He was glad about that because William was going to need his love and support more than ever. Listening to the conversation, he could feel his dad being comforted and it made him glad. Jon put his arms around his dad and uncle and wished he could convey his sense of wellbeing, for he loved them both very much. In retrospect, he wished he had let them know more often how much he loved them while he was alive.

"Alive is a relative term, Jon, because if you exist right now, are you not alive?" Apollo asked him, interrupting his thoughts.

"I'm more alive than ever, it's just that there's a lot I need to learn and get used to," Jon said.

"Indeed," Apollo said, and in an instant they were whisked back to paradise and he was gone.

CHAPTER 4

RESTLESS SOUL

Jon found himself in his grandparents' heavenly mansion after his expedition to his funeral services. From the outside, it looked like a small castle made of glass, but after getting inside he found himself surrounded by things that were very familiar. Every room had a door leading to another area of the dwelling, each space filled with what his grandmother called "heavenly treasures." There was a room that when he entered it, took him back to his mother's childhood with her sister Ingrid. He felt as if he was in the middle of a movie or a time window where he could see and feel part of events unfolding around him that happened long time ago. But he could only be an invisible and silent observer, nothing more. He entered the next room where saw himself as a toddler petting and hugging his first dog, a white Labrador retriever named Rex. He was trying to ride him, happily giggling as he failed to stay on the dog's back time after time. He could see himself chasing the dog around calling him with his baby talk, "Come to me, Wex!" as the dog wagged his tail, trying to get away from him.

In yet another room, he saw his grandparents meeting for the first time, falling in love, and getting married; he saw their happy memories and things that happened before he was born. He pondered for a moment and it made sense to him. These were all blissful chapters in their lives, which were their treasures, a part of their heaven or paradise. He opened one last door, which led to the backyard garden where his grandparents were playing with a group of dogs. Jon recognized his pets Rex and Roxy playfully wrestling each other. When Rex saw Jon, he ran up and happily greeted him.

"Hello, Jon!" The dog said.

Jon smiled. "Hi boy," he said to Rex, "Long time no see."

Rex wagged his tail and looked at Jon with a quizzical look, asking, "Huh? What do you mean?"

"Jon, dear, time as we understood it in our physical life doesn't exist here. For Rex it seems as if he just saw you a little while ago." Grandmother Holmes said.

"I keep forgetting that. There is so much to learn and get used to," Jon said to her.

"It will all come to you at the right time," his grandfather said.

All of them referred to his home in paradise—his place in this plane of existence—yet Jon still felt like a stranger. There was no sense of belonging. He thought of Max and found himself instantly in his presence. Max's face was radiant with total joy and contentment, smiling like Jon had never seen him before. The feeling of total bliss and abandonment to this complete happiness was impossible for Jon not to sense.

"Jon," Max said softly, "isn't it all incredible? I never could have imagined such joy. It's not humanly possible to do, I suppose."

"No, I guess it's not. Perfection is humanly impossible, and that's what this world should be for me—perfection, but yet—"

"Oh Jon! Are you having trouble adapting to this? I didn't think that was possible. I mean, who could reject the gift of paradise?" Max asked.

Jon felt embarrassed and ungrateful.

"Don't tell me you rejected heaven!" he said to Jon incredulously. "Wow! I didn't think that was possible."

"I haven't rejected it, but for some reason Apollo doesn't think I'm ready for it."

"What about you? What do you think?" Max asked.

"I don't know what to think! He said that everything I need to decide was told or revealed to me in my mortal life. I'm sure it's a choice I had to make, but how do I know what it is if he won't tell me?" Jon said with a sense of frustration.

"Apollo already told you where to find the answers. It's up to you to find them."

"Don't you miss the loved ones we left behind?" Jon asked trying to make sense. "Did you see your parents and mine at my funeral?" Jon asked.

"Yes, I did. But their pain is only a temporary and inevitable part of human existence. No one is physically alive forever, but spiritually speaking, that's another story."

"I need to search within me," he said, knowing that he had a lot of reflecting to do.

"You need to seek Apollo's advice," Max said.

"I will," Jon said, and his spirit flew away.

He felt himself flying about an extraordinary world. He could see planet earth in the distance, reflected in the glass walls of heaven, and when he focused more, he saw the reflection of what looked like the most extraordinary canyon. Looking closer, it reminded him of a combination of Bryce Canyon and Zion National Park rolled into one, with breathtaking beauty thousands times greater. Its granite columns pointed straight up to the heavens, and the formations resembled skyscrapers etched out of glass rock in countless shades colors of every possible hue with incredible richness and beauty. He wondered if he was looking at a vision of heaven's outward appearance.

"Heaven on earth?" he asked himself. "Maybe in a different dimension."

He explored his environment, marveling at everything he saw. As he moved toward familiar surroundings, he found himself at the bridge portal where he and Max had first met Apollo. When he looked beyond, he noticed a mysterious obscure hallway off to the side. Curious, he moved toward it just as Apollo appeared.

"Why do you want to go backwards?" he asked.

"Do I?" Jon asked.

"Come on, Jonathan. I know you better than you could imagine. Here's the bottom line: you were told how to get to heaven while you were a mortal; you just weren't paying attention. Now you need to look back and find the answer."

"How can I look back at something I don't remember?" Jon asked.

"You're thinking like a human again," Apollo said.

"How can that be? Am I not a soul, a spirit being?"

"You are a spirit who happens to feel a strong pull from your human existence. A part of you still hasn't come to grips with the concept of giving up the physical control you thought you had," Apollo said.

"What's wrong with me?"

"You're confused. It happens rarely, but sometimes when departure from the physical body happens ahead of time, like in your case, it takes time to adjust to your new existence."

"Why does it take time if time itself is irrelevant in heaven?" Jon wanted to know.

"It's still relevant to you, because your soul is not in heaven yet." Apollo went on to warn him, "Stay away from that door. It is not for you to seek out. The consequences of breaking this rule can be destructive."

And with that warning he was gone, leaving Jonathan mystified.

***

Back in Alexandria Bay life had to go on for the Fitzgeralds. Pained by the loss of their son, Sophia decided to go back to work with William to keep him company, hoping that the distraction would take her mind off the tragedy. She also wanted to be close to her husband for mutual support.

On their first day back after Jon's funeral, a meeting was set up to let management know of the changes to be made in light of his death and the likelihood of Max's death as well. William announced that for obvious reasons his retirement was not going to happen as he had planned and that his brother Vince would be taking over Jon's position as Chief Financial Officer. Max's position as Director of Finance, he said, would be filled later on after they (Vince and William) had evaluated the immediate needs of the company.

"You all know that Jon and Max were invaluable to the company. They are irreplaceable to us, really," William started with his voice choking with emotions, "but until we know how it will all be structured, Sophia will be with us and will use Max's office for the time being. She's going to help us with some of the responsibilities he had, but the rest of his work will be shared by Vince and me until further notice."

Sitting in the small crowd, Bradley was none too pleased after hearing that he was not the automatic choice for Max's job. He assured himself that in time it would all come to him; after all, nothing was lost when his next coveted position had not been filled yet. In his self-absorbed mind, he considered himself too smart for Vince and Sophia to catch on to anything he was doing. Still, he managed to fake sincere gladness at having her there.

"I would like to welcome Sophia and Vince and tell you both that you can count on my full cooperation. I am sorry for the reasons that have brought you here. Jon was my friend and I miss him too. I would like to help in any way I can."

"Thank you Bradley. That's sweet of you, and I'm sure I'll need your help a lot. It's been many years since my time here," Sophia said sweetly. "No doubt things are quite different now."

"Like I said, count on me for anything," Bradley reiterated.

"I thank you for your kind words, Bradley," Vince said.

"Well, that's about it," William said. "Everyone is free to go, except for Lori and Jess. I'd like to see the two of you in my office."

Lori Cummings and Jess Parker were Jon's and Max's assistants respectively. Efficient and loyal, they had developed a kinship over the years, and as close as Jon and Max were, likewise the two assistants had developed a similar friendship. Next to Jon, Max and William, no one knew more about what their bosses did than their assistants. William was aware of that and knew how valuable they had become.

As they were filing out of the conference room, Bradley, infuriated at being left out, tried to comfort himself.

"You have to be smart about this," he thought to himself. "Right now, they're too wrapped up in their grief to be aware of things you don't want them to know. Just keep doing what you are doing now, Bradley boy. First the money, then the power." And with an inner smug look, he walked to his office.

At the other end of the building in William's office, Lori and Jess walked in, their grief obvious on their faces. Sophia and Vince were also there.

"Mr. and Mrs. Fitzgerald—" Lori struggled to speak.

"Please don't. I know," he said to her.

Sophia came to them and gave each of them a warm hug.

"Thank you for taking care of the boys all these years," she said to them.

"They were such a pleasure to work for; I'd do anything for them." Lori said.

"I know, and we're grateful for that. Now we're asking you and Jess to work with Vince closely. You two know his job better than most and he's going to need your help." William said.

"You can count on us." Jess said and Lori nodded in agreement.

The weeks following Jon's death were the hardest for William and Sofia. Dealing with the holidays was especially painful in light of their loss. They welcomed being swamped with work because it took their minds off the pain, but they were also reminded of how much they missed him every time they came across documents bearing his writing. Then slowly, without realizing it, days turned into weeks and then into months.

"Dearest William," Sophia said as she stood behind his chair and gently massaged his shoulders. "I read somewhere that something of ourselves remains wherever we have been. If that is true, there is a lot of him in this office. I couldn't imagine our lives without ever having him, even if that meant sparing us from this pain. Our son was worth all of it."

"Sophie, you are my rock and I love you for that and so many other reasons," he said. "I couldn't imagine my life without the two of you. Tell me, how is it that you somehow always manage to see the good even in the worst of circumstances?"

"I think about his life and his love for us, and I remind myself of how much joy he gave us by being our son. Besides, I know we will see him again. I am certain of that. I have to be," she said.

"Me too," he said closing his eyes, taking his wife's hands to his lips and softly kissing them. "But he also would have wanted us to go on with life, loving every day. I couldn't imagine my life without you now or any time ever."

"Neither could I," she said, looking lovingly at her husband. Then, with her face lighting up, she asked, "How about a getaway for a few days? It's been a while since we did that."

"That's a wonderful idea, and we sure could use one. I think Vince would be all right for a couple of days; he's been with us—oh goodness, almost four months! Besides, I am sure Bradley will help him, if he needs it, which I doubt Vince does," William said. "Let's go somewhere warm, I'm ready for spring weather."

"So am I, dear. The Florida Keys would be nice this time of the year."

"Splendid!" William said. "Let's make reservations."

"I'm on it, honey," Sophia said as she kissed him on the lips and went back to her office.

"This will be good," he thought as he closed his eyes, alone in his office. It felt good to see his wife slowly going back to being her normal self, and going away was always the best way to relax and recharge, especially romantically. His love for his wife was just as physical and passionate as it ever had been. He was sure she was the most beautiful woman he had ever seen. Just thinking about it made him feel a rush of anticipation.

"Oh yeah!" he said as he leaned his chair back and displayed a wide smile.

Day-to-day business operations slowly went back to normal at Fitzgerald International. Vince was absorbing everything fast and getting more comfortable with his new position, showing his low-key leadership qualities. In fact, he was more than qualified to assume the demanding responsibilities of his new position. With William going away for a few days, it would give him a feel for being in charge, and a few days was a good running start.

Since coming to work at the company, Vince had made it a point to get to know the personnel well. He always had an ability to read people, but there was something about Bradley that seemed detached and aloof. There was no transparency, which made him hard to read. Something didn't seem to click. Consequently, he rarely asked him for help.

Things were uneventful at work during William and Sophia's short vacation, but they had a magical time. An ocean-view room, long walks along the beach, romantic dinners, and of course some golf was the perfect getaway for them. By the last day, they both felt energized and revitalized, even if the memory of Jon was never away from their thoughts.

One unfinished task they had been putting off for months was Jonathan's will. They were not ready to handle it before, but felt that now was the time to face it and put it behind them.

Stanley Gold, their friend and attorney, performed the reading to which Max's parents were also summoned. Madison was there as well as Vince and his wife Laura. Predictably, Jonathan made his parents beneficiaries of his life insurance policy for seven million dollars and the bulk of his personal estate. He left both Lori and Jess, his and Max's loyal personal assistants, a stock-and-bonds combination valued at a quarter million each. To Max, his best friend, he had left his condominium in Aspen, as well as his airplane in which they perished. Given the circumstances, any assets left to Max would go to his rightful heirs, his parents Sarah and Patrick Adams.

Jon bequeathed Madison his suite in the Daytona Beach Atlas towers, which he purchased at her insistence just before his passing. Along with that he also left her a hundred thousand dollars cash. Half a million dollars of his fortune was earmarked for Children's Charities Funds, an organization focusing on helping underprivileged children in countries where Fitzgerald International conducted its business.

At the conclusion of the reading, William and Sophia waited after everyone was gone to have a word with their lawyer.

"Stanley," he said. "There is an item missing in his will. Three weeks before his death, when Jonathan was promoted to head Fitzgerald International, I gave him a five million dollar bonus, which seems to be unaccounted for."

"There is no mention of that in the will at all, William," Stanley said.

"That's odd. It wasn't like Jonathan to leave out something that important," William said.

"If this was shortly before his death, maybe he didn't have time to amend his will. At his age, you think you have all the time in the world. At any rate, the remaining amount and assets of his estate all goes to you, and that includes this bonus you're talking about. I'll double check my files for you, but I'm sure this is Jon's last will and testament."

"Thank you," William said.

William and Sophia walked out of Stanley's office mystified. They couldn't shake the feeling that something was amiss with Jon's will and testament.

***

Back in his new world Jon was curious after Apollo's last warning about the dark door.

"What is the big mystery about that door?" he asked himself.

He shrugged his shoulders, and just as the thought came to him, he found himself with his grandparents, who were in the company of another couple whom Jon didn't remember meeting before. They were intently watching a scene taking place in the physical realm as if it was a one-way mirror from where you could see the events unfolding on the other side. Their attention was directed at a group of hikers and climbers as they were going about their outdoor fun, but more specifically at a young couple standing atop a nearly five hundred feet high, dome-shaped rock. There was something familiar about the area that he recognized as Sunset Point in Bryce Canyon, with the majestic Queens Garden in the background.

The couple seemed swept away by their beautiful surroundings, immersed in conversation. Strangely, Jon's grandparents seemed just as fascinated by the pair as their friends. He wondered what the attraction about these two people was. Sensing his thoughts, his grandfather turned to him.

"The young woman is the granddaughter of our friends," he said.

"Did you know them before?" Jon wanted to know about the couple with them.

"No," said the grandfather.

Jonathan looked at him inquisitively.

"Jon, you can make new friends here too. This isn't the end of anything, in fact, and it's a continuation of us, with lives richer than imagined. You'll understand in time."

"I'm sure you're right."

There was a pause, as Jon felt the familiar loving embrace from his grandparents who introduced him to their friends.

"Jon these are our friends Barbara and Jon Conley. Barbara, John, this is my grandson Jonathan," they said.

"We are pleased to finally meet you," the couple said at the same time, sharing a knowing look which Jon didn't fail to notice.

He observed with them for a while then went away and both couples turned their attention again to what was happening in the physical realm with the group of climbers.

Outside in Bryce Canyon Eve Anne couldn't stop admiring her surroundings. It had been more than a year since she had been there and that was a long time to stay away. Something within her was drawn to it, whether it was climbing, hiking, or just being there. The feeling of peace permeated her inner being and she could never get enough.

It was the end of May after a long winter season, and the canyons' snow levels were higher than usual in certain areas. Vestiges of winter were visible from where Eve and Ethan stood after their climb, as the wild flowers sprouted thru the snow covered ground, and the cool breeze scent gave them a slight reminder that winter was not completely over. In the distance they could see the canyons and mesas, trees with bright green new foliage, wild plants full of buds with the promise of new flowers. Not far away from them, they could see snow in the canyons between the soaring sandstone pillar formations.

Besides the fact that all nature comes alive in spring, for Eve Anne, it signaled the season's start for climbing and hiking. There was something spiritual about the experience that she couldn't deny; in fact, she embraced it. Her love for nature was evident the first time she went away to summer camp. She was six years old when a junior rock climbing and hiking trip was offered to Bryce Canyon. After that she never looked back and it remained her sentimental favorite.

"When are you flying out?" Ethan asked, bringing her back into reality.

"Sunday," she said.

"That gives you just about a week. What's the report about, this time?"

"I'm going to Romania for a follow-up article on the plight of orphaned children afflicted with HIV."

"Sounds like a noble cause."

"It is," she said. "Judging from the research I've done, the signs are encouraging. I feel very optimistic about it."

"How long will you be gone?"

"That assignment should last four to eight weeks. But from Belgrade I'll be going to Paris for a week before my next project. I haven't been there in a few years and want to go see the Louvre again."

"So would I!" Ethan exclaimed. "While you are there, visit Les Invalides for me."

"Of course," she said. "You can't do one museum and not the other!"

"Say hello to Napoleon for me too," he said chuckling.

"I will do that," she said.

"Where are you going after that?"

"Central America. The black market of mahogany is thriving and the forests are being depleted in places that should be protected. The fact that these areas are designated as a part of a worldwide biosphere doesn't deter the poachers from making a quick buck if they can."

"What a shame!"

"Yeah. It is."

"It sounds like you will be gone for a few months," said Ethan.

"Around four at the most, I hope," she replied. "The mahogany piece shouldn't take more than two months, if all goes our way and the weather cooperates."

"That would have you back around the end of summer. Good time for some hiking and climbing."

"Yes, the timing looks good on paper, but you know how these things go sometimes," she said.

"Yes, change of plans is often part of your job," Ethan said as he stared into the distance.

A long time ago he had realized that Eve Anne loved her work because, more than a job, it was her cause. She wanted to make a difference in the world and was driven by a sense of purpose. For his part, he felt relieved and free that he didn't pine for her each time she went away, like he used to. For him, it felt good to love again.

Sensing her friend's reflective pause, she took his arm and gently squeezed it.

"Let's talk about you," she said. "Where are you going this summer?"

"I'm not sure, but a sun-drenched island with great beaches sounds pretty good."

"And someone to share it with would make it idyllic." She paused and looked at him for a moment and smiled as if she had just read his mind.

"Wait a minute! Is there someone new in your life?" she asked, excited.

"Well," he smiled, giving himself away, "there might be."

"That is wonderful! You sly fox! When were you going to tell me?"

"I'm telling you now," he said.

"Tell me all about her."

"I met her six months ago. She works for Legacy International, which is the parent company to a number of hotel chains. They are interested in two architectural building designs I entered in a bid competition eight months ago. She came by my office to discuss possible changes to one of them. They've narrowed their search to two entries, mine being one of them. They want to use the winner's design as the model to a new chain of upper-scale hotels worldwide."

"Ethan! That could be big. I'm so happy for you," she said with excitement.

"There's more. They want to hire the winner to consult onsite projects and their offer looks very tempting, if my design wins. But I would have time to decide."

"What would happen to Foster's Architecture?"

"This is a great opportunity, but I need to be absolutely sure it's what I want. Even if I just sold them my plans it would be very profitable for me."

"It sounds like a win-win situation for you. What would keep you from accepting their job offer? Oh! The girl," she said. "What about her?"

His face lit up. "Her name is Julia and she is an architect, too. She is beautiful, smart, and funny. We've only been out on three dates, but—" he shook his head.

"You're in love!" she exclaimed.

"That sounds a little strong."

"Aw, come on, you act like you're pretty smitten, just accept it. I've never seen that look on your face when talking about a woman before."

"She's special."

"No doubt she is if she caught your eye. I'm happy for the both of you. I can't wait to meet her."

"She'd like to meet you, too."

"Oh my God! This is serious if you told her about me," she said laughing.

"Time will tell if you are right," he said. "In the meantime, the summer vacation I mentioned could be a combination of business and pleasure."

"Potentially, you could get the girl and the job. That is fantastic. I hope she is the one," she said sincerely.

"Thanks."

"What about the lead you had from that company on the east coast?" she asked.

"I haven't heard anything from them, which is odd. They seemed very interested at first but I didn't get any feed back one way or the other."

"If it's meant to be…" she said.

"That's what I thought," he said.

They fell silent and admired the landscape.

"Phew!" she said, breaking the awkwardness of the moment. "It looks like we might not have to get married after all."

They burst into laughter that echoed in the canyons.

"Oh yeah!" Ethan said. "That's when we thought that turning thirty was the sunset of our lives, imagine that!"

"I thought it was a silly deal to make, but I just didn't want my best friend to end up alone," Eve said.

"And I won't," he assured her.

"This will change our friendship a little, and that's okay. Seeing you happy makes me happy too," she said.

"Come on, you make it sound as if you are never going to find somebody. Who knows, it could happen to you on this trip. Stranger things have happened."

"I guess it would be nice to have something like that happen to me," she said.

"As I am sure it will, and sometime soon. You are a beautiful woman that any man would want. That's why I've often wondered what happened to us, why things didn't work out," he reflected.

"Maybe because from the beginning Julia was the one meant for you, not me," she said. "Or maybe because we were always meant to be friends. I wouldn't change anything because I value your friendship greatly. But just to make it official, let's release each other of any prior promises, especially if we made them while at a high altitude. Our brains could have been deprived of oxygen, which would explain the silliness of it," she said.

"I agree. Life changes, and we have to grow up, and that's okay too."

"What does Julia do for fun? Is she into sports?"

"She plays tennis and has done a little hiking."

"You should bring her up here sometime," she said.

"For sure! Once here, how could she resist this?" he said making a sweeping motion across the landscape. "I will tell her that words or pictures don't do it justice, it's a place that she needs to come and experience," Ethan said.

"Once you get her here, she'll be hooked. You have to get her up here!" she exclaimed.

"I think we should be getting down and join the rest of the group. It's time to go back," he said looking at his watch.

"Oh my goodness, you're right. I didn't realize it was so late! I always lose track of time when I'm here," she said.

"I know that all too well," Ethan said.

She slowly turned and looked at the view all around her, as if taking a mental photograph; then picked up her gear and started to put it over her shoulders. As she was negotiating the straps of her backpack, she could see some snow below in the canyon beyond the edge of the cliff. She took a last look and closed her eyes for a second, taking a deep breath. The fragrance of spring flowers was in the air, and the crisp wind blowing across her face felt good. When she opened her eyes, she felt she was about to lose her balance, and realized that she was standing too close to the edge. She flailed her arms trying to steady herself and keep from falling into the precipice below.

Just as this scene was unfolding before the eyes of his grandparents, Jonathan's exploration had led him back to the hallway Apollo warned him to stay away from. He slowly approached it and looked into the void, dark space. At the end of it was a faint light shining in the distance. When he came closer, he saw a very tall dark door, with a round clear window at the top where the light originated. He looked for a knob, but there was none. Then his spirit elevated to the height of the window and tried to look beyond. Unable to see the other side thru the luminosity emanating from it, he willed his mind, forcing himself through the wall of light that separated both dimensions. As he felt his spirit passing through, there was an explosion of light across the sky. For some reason the occurrence had triggered a huge burst of brilliance al over the canyons.

Eve Anne, who was trying to keep herself from falling at that moment, was blinded by the light, and the impact knocked her backwards. Her foot slipped on a loose rock and she fell down a steep slope into a large, icy crevice, from where she slid down a slope for what seemed to her like an eternity. At the end of it, she could see a sheer drop coming fast and started to believe that this was the end of her life.

"Oh God, oh God!" was all she could scream as she was shot out of the side of the rock into the snowy canyon she was admiring earlier. Her freefall was broken by the branch of a fir tree and cushioned by her backpack still attached to her. But by the time she hit the snow, she was badly bruised and unconscious.

For his part, after bursting through the forbidden door, Jon immediately felt a difference in his spiritual state. No longer did he feel the same lightness as a spirit before. Instead, he was reminded of the cumbersome feeling of a physical body. He looked around and found himself in an enormous garden area outside the door. Beyond it was a pathway paved with smooth white river rocks and trees lined up the road that stretched a long distance before seemingly fading into the canyons.

"Hello!" He yelled, looking around for sign of others. "Anybody here? Anybody!"

Apollo appeared wearing a white tunic and a faint halo, with a somber look about him.

"Jonathan," he said with disappointment in his voice. "You ignored my warning."

"I'm sorry," he said contritely.

"Being sorry now does not change anything. You have crossed the line of dimensions—out of the afterlife and back to earth."

"What do you mean?" he asked.

"You can't go back to paradise because you just rejected the very existence of it. The fact that you are here confirms it."

"Can I go back to earth?" Jon asked with curiosity.

"That's a bit complicated. You could technically go back to it, but it would not be easy. It could be a huge mistake that would affect both worlds in a dramatic way. I wouldn't advise it."

"Give it to me straight. What options do I have?"

"Very well, you have two choices. One is: you remain a spirit in this realm until the damage of your breach has been determined. How long you remain here will depend on the level of damage caused by what you just did."

"Is time relative or not in this…halfway dimension I find myself in?" Jon asked.

"It's a little of both. You noticed as soon as you came through the door that you felt the heaviness, a bit reminiscent of carrying a physical body."

"That's true. Are there other souls like me?" Jon wanted to know.

"I cannot say."

"Okay, what can you tell me, then?" Jon asked with frustration.

"Don't take that attitude with me. What you really want to know is the future, but I can't do that for you. Remember, you rejected living in that world. That's why you are here now. You can't have it both ways," Apollo said, resolutely.

"I'm sorry, but surely you can understand if I am confused and overwhelmed. It seems that I violated some big universal law, all out of curiosity. How can you hold that against me?"

"It's not held against you. It's just that every act has its consequence, good or bad. No one did it to you; you did it to yourself. I don't think you realize the scope of what you just did, and the possible repercussions in the big scheme of things. But if your actions didn't have much of an impact in paradise, your stay here could be relatively short," Apollo said.

"Then what?"

"You get a new opportunity, but don't ask how. You should know enough to trust me by now."

"I do," Jon said with humility in his voice, "and I am learning to appreciate your guidance more by the second. What is the other option you mentioned?"

"You must find a suitable body; preferably one recently deceased because it would be less traumatic. You have a four-hour window from the time you decide and the time you achieve your goal. If you don't find a body to inhabit, all that's left is to face the consequences for your choices. But be warned, if you should decide on this and are successful in possessing a body, no one can see it happen. I can't stress that enough."

"Are there any other things I need to know?"

"Yes. You may never seek to speak or communicate with anyone you ever knew in your past life. It is imperative that you realize the seriousness of this. Do not take it as something light. The consequences will be swift and severe," Apollo said with a grave tone in his voice.

"I understand from the tone of your voice that this is an absolute rule and I will honor it to the best of my abilities," he promised.

"It's not a matter of doing it to the best of your abilities, it must absolutely not happen. I can't stress it enough. You have been advised and warned. I hope you choose wisely. If you need me, just call. I'm never far away," Apollo said, and was gone, leaving Jon feeling lonely and confused, wondering if he had just made a big mistake.

"Some things are best put behind," he assured himself as he followed the tree lined path leading away from the gate, into the canyon.

When he got to the end of it he realized the vision he'd seen from the portal was real. He found himself floating around the canyon area he had been observing with his grandparents from the other side. The man who was with the young woman earlier was hurrying down the canyon alone, with no sight of his companion.

After roaming about the area for a while, he recognized coordinates. If he was correct, he was not far from the area where his plane crash happened. He retraced his flight plan in his mind and spotted the towering tree he believed was the one where the plane first made impact. Following the possible trajectory of the plane's rear half, he thought of his friend's body lying somewhere under the snowy mountain below.

"Max!" he said softly.

Just as he said it, he spotted an indentation in the shape of a body in the snow. When he hovered over the spot, he saw Eve Anne's body resting in the small valley below. He got closer and sensed that she still had a pulse.

Startled by the light like the rest of them, Ethan had just enough time to see Eve Anne sliding down a large crevice through the icy rock resembling a frozen waterfall. A short time later, he saw her shooting out of the rock opening but didn't have the angle to see her landing. He hiked down as fast as he could while the others waited anxiously at the bottom. After what seemed like an eternity, he reached the rest of the group.

"What happened?" they all asked at the same time. "We heard Eve Anne scream and you calling her. We couldn't call emergency without knowing."

Ethan proceeded to quickly relate what happened as he was calling for emergency help. By now Jon was aware of both scenes taking place at the same time. He could hear Ethan's emergency call and wondered how long the young woman could hang on.

"It will take about thirty minutes," he heard Ethan say with an agitated voice. "They're sending a helicopter and an ambulance with a rescue unit familiar with this area. They should be here in less than a half hour."

"How long will it take to get to her?" Craig, one of the friends in the group asked.

"I don't know." Ethan said, wringing his hands. "But I can't just sit and wait for them. We need to do something. Lucas, come with me. Craig and you guys stay here to tell the rescuers what's going on. I am going to try to reach Eve Anne. Every minute counts right now."

The group agreed and soon Ethan and Lucas were following a trail around the base of the rock in a northeast direction.

CHAPTER 5

BE CAREFUL WHAT YOU WISH FOR

"Every minute counts."

The phrase triggered something in Jon's consciousness. First he thought of Apollo's timeline warning about his second option, and suddenly it hit him: If he could find Max's body in time, he could live another life as his best friend.

His choice was made instantly. He couldn't have wished for a better scenario than this.

"Living another physical life as Max is worth trying," he thought to himself.

At that moment, he glanced up at the sky and saw the cloud patterns unmistakably showing the starting time of 4:00 which started descending in sequence. His race with time and the rescuers had begun. He needed to search the area around where Eve Anne had landed before anybody else. If that was the area where the rear of the plane came to rest, and the searchers found the wreckage before he did, his prospect to come back as Max would be lost.

Jon quickly scanned the area but there wasn't a sign of what he was looking for. Beyond his location was a small snow-covered mountain with trees sparsely scattered about. He looked around the trees first, and then the surrounding area. After not detecting anything, he continued his search slowly down the slope on the other side. Nestled halfway down on a ridge, he saw an object sticking out of the snow. He took a closer look and to his astonishment discovered the plane's tail section with its identification number partially showing. His mind was racing with exhilaration!

"Could it be?" he asked himself excited. "It's too good to be true!"

With countless thoughts going through his mind, he hurried to inspect the immediate area and he was elated with what he saw.

There in front of him was the rear of his plane, with the number N4755H clearly visible. Unable to physically move anything, he willed himself inside the hollow of the aircraft, which incredibly remained in one piece. He could see pressure cracks as the weight of the snow pushed the structure almost to its breaking point. Thankfully for him, it managed to stay together. He only hoped that Max had faired as well.

Further exploration yielded signs that were encouraging. Max and Jon's small carry-on luggage, some golf clubs, and an open briefcase with business papers were scattered about the area under the snow. And then he saw him. Buried beneath three feet of leftover snow, Max's body had come to rest in a fetal position, cocooned by the tail end of the plane. He took a closer look. Max looked peaceful, like in a deep sleep, but the cuts and bruises on his face and body testified to the dramatic end of his life. As Jon got ready to enter the body, his thoughts flashed back to the young woman lying in the snow on the other side of the mountain.

"She still had a pulse," he thought as he found himself by her side.

He couldn't tell how long she was going to hang on, but he hoped that she would be found and rescued soon. He wanted her to survive for some reason. After all, he was curious about this mysterious girl that had his grandparents and their friends so interested.

"Talk about six degrees of separation!" he thought.

About this time Ethan and Lucas' voices could be heard in the distance. He felt relieved knowing they would be finding her soon. But now he needed to physically become Max and devise a plan to get out of the area without being seen. Instantly he found himself back with Max. His spirit embraced his friend's dead body, slowly emerging into him, and as he did he became a bright white light permeating through Max, fusing spirit and body together creating an array of never ending rainbow colors. As Max's body was regenerating itself, Jon felt renewed too, but at the same time burdened to experience again the restrictively familiar human body.

When the process was complete, he stood up, stretched and then retrieved both pieces of luggage and the one briefcase that had survived in good condition. Gone were the cuts, breaks, and bruises from his body. Instead, he felt as physically fit as his friend was before they both died.

At that point, he considered going to the injured girl to help her, but realizing that his footprints would be hard to explain, he opted for walking the moderate distance to the top of the mountain to see how close her rescuers were. When he got there he saw they had made their way halfway around the dome shaped rock where Ethan and Eve were admiring the surroundings earlier. The rescuers were coming down to the small valley by now. Following the direction they had taken, and judging by the sound of their voices, it was a matter of a short time before they would find her.

Reassured of this, he walked back down the slope, picked up his luggage items and started walking down the mountain, making sure to conceal his trail. He couldn't afford to be seen by the rescuers or the helicopter that would probably be there soon. Realizing he didn't have a lot of time, he felt the urgency and hurried through the snow and soon he could see the highway in the distance. Just as he stopped at the base of a cluster of pinnacles and spires, he heard the sound of the helicopter approaching. It was heading in the direction where the party of hikers was and Jon seized the moment to hurry and find somewhere to hide from view before it came back.

In the meantime, Ethan and Lucas were getting closer to Eve Anne. Ethan estimated she was somewhere between the rock they had been climbing and a large tree that stood out in the landscape a short distance away. Soon they were close enough to detect the indentation in the snow ahead and raced to it. They found Eve sprawled in the snow with her face down, not breathing. Ethan gently turned her over, cleared the snow from her nose, and proceeded to give her mouth-to-mouth resuscitation. He paused to take her pulse and wept with joy when he felt it. He started talking to her in between resuscitation efforts, gently patting her cheeks.

"Eve Anne, hold on, hon. I am here…I'm here for you. Stay with me."

He breathed into her mouth again, put his jacket on her and gently rubbed her arms to generate warmth. He checked her pulse again and it felt a little stronger.

Hopeful, he gave her mouth-to-mouth resuscitation for the third time.

"Eve, come back," he said to her, gently stroking the hair off her face.

It lasted a few minutes, but to Ethan and Lucas it seemed never-ending until they saw her chest move and she coughed, spitting out a small chunk of snow.

"Oh my God!" Ethan exclaimed when he saw her react. Then looking up to the sky, he uttered, "thank you," with tears of gratitude.

By now, they could hear the faint sound of the approaching helicopter. From their respective locations, Eve Anne's group started screaming and waving their hands in relief. The helicopter pilot hovered over the large group, and with their help was able to locate Eve Anne and her rescuers by following the direction in which they were pointing.

The small valley where Eve Anne's unfortunate accident came to a stop was surrounded by rocks that stood over a thousand feet high, making it impossible for the pilot to land safely and retrieve her.

"Is the victim conscious?" the pilot asked over the speaker while he circled the site, and through a series of signals, they communicated her condition to him.

"I will have to lower down a stretcher for you. Put her on it and make sure she's safely strapped. Then take her to the first clearing past the site where the rest of the group is. We will land there and wait to see if she needs to go with us or the ambulance."

Within a few seconds, the stretcher was coming down a line hanging from the chopper and soon was dropped about twenty-five yards away from them. Lucas quickly went to retrieve it while

Ethan tended to Eve Anne, who by now was breathing deeper and trying to open her eyes.

"You heard it; you will soon be out of here," Ethan told her. "Lucas will be back soon and we will put you on the stretcher and hurry on out of here. We have a straight way out now that we know where we are."

She managed to smile weakly.

"You have no idea how good it is to see you open your eyes." Ethan said, relieved.

He gently and slowly put his arms around her, careful not to make any movements that would jeopardize her condition, trying to keep her warm. The two men carefully laid her down, strapped her to the medical cot and started their way to the designated meeting point. The distance to their rendezvous with the helicopter was less than a quarter of a mile of snow-covered terrain, with levels decreasing to nothing as they got closer to the highway.

Twenty minutes into their silent journey, they heard the sound of the ambulance sirens.

"Sounds like music to my ears, man," Lucas said.

"It shouldn't be long," Ethan said, making small talk.

"No more than ten minutes. We're almost there," Lucas said.

Ethan turned to Eve Anne, who had been silent through the trek, but seemed slowly becoming more alert.

"How are you doing, kiddo?" he asked her.

She blinked her eyes and softly said, "Okay."

The two men were elated to hear the sound of her voice. It put a spring in their steps, giving them a rush of energy.

"Okay now, you've got to stay awake, Eve Anne," Lucas said.

They talked to her constantly all the way there, trying to keep her awake and as alert as possible. Before they knew it, they had reached the rest of the group. With the helicopter on the ground but still running, the medic in the passenger side jumped out and hurried toward them. They set her down and he immediately started checking her and taking her vital signs. Although she looked confused, to his surprise, her pulse was nearing normal and her eyes were open and following the events happening. She had bruises on her face and body but there was no visible sign of bleeding. He was pleased with the way she looked but would not take chances.

"Internal bleeding and concussion are my concern, not to mention broken bones. We'll fly her to the Oswell Hospital in Cedar City, which is a twenty-minute flight," he informed them.

Within a few minutes, she was hooked up to an IV and loaded into the helicopter. The ambulance had arrived to the scene just in time to be informed of what was happening.

"Do you need help in getting to the hospital," the ambulance driver asked.

"If you just give me general directions I can find it. I'm familiar with the area," Ethan said.

"O.K. then," the medic said and proceeded to tell him how to get to the hospital. "It should take about thirty minutes," he said.

The whole group hurriedly started their way toward their parked vehicles not far from the ambulance and drove away.

In the meantime, not too far from the scene, Jonathan had heard the helicopter pilot earlier and the ambulance later on. He decided to take advantage of the commotion going on with the group to rapidly reach the road. He would hitchhike his way out of there and figure out the whole mess later. Not long after the helicopter took off, he could hear the sound of the traffic and determined that the group would be too preoccupied to be paying any attention to him.

"Your assumption is right," said a familiar voice.

"Apollo!" he exclaimed. "Am I glad to see you!"

"I believe you are," he responded.

"What now?" Jon asked.

"Now you go out there and live again. But remember, you are not the average mortal, consequently you are subject to a different set of rules."

"Yes, like staying away from the people I know and love. Some life that will be."

"Not only of the people you love, but now you must also avoid Max's friends and loved ones for obvious reasons. They cannot see you or know about your return. As it is, you have changed the course of some events, and heaven only knows how that is going to affect both worlds."

"I'm very sorry," Jon said sincerely.

"I know you are, but now you will have a lifetime to reflect on it. I hope for your sake that nothing too significantly negative will come about because of your choices."

"So do I, Apollo, so do I."

"As the occasion requires, I will be available to you when you need me, depending on the circumstances. In view of the fact that your wish was to come back to human life, it shall be granted to you that you will live another life. You are, however, forbidden to reveal that which you have seen in the afterlife. Furthermore, you are not permitted to take your own life, nor will you be able to. Now you'll have to wait until it's your time to go back just like everyone else."

"I doubt that suicide would ever cross my mind," Jon said.

"You lived a good life your first time around. With a few exceptions, you were spared of personal tragedies. Losing your grandparents was the worst thing that happened to you. Still you were too young to understand the finality of it. Life can be overwhelming sometimes, but at least now you know for a fact some incredible things await beyond physical existence."

"How much of life after life did I experience?" Jon asked with curiosity.

"A small part of it. You could say that you existed in pre-paradise, where you only got glimpses of what was yet to come," Apollo said.

Jon felt a mild shiver down his spine.

"Could I have been a little hasty in leaving?" he asked.

"From now on you can only move forward in time. Make good use of your life and remember the rules."

And after his last words, he was gone.

Jon came back to reality, and at that second everything around him, which had been frozen in time during his conversation with

Apollo, continued on as if that window of time had not existed. The helicopter was in the same position as before the heavenly appearance, but for Jon it was a life changing conversation ago.

The early evening shadows were setting in across the canyons and he was feeling cold and tired. He hurried, pulling his and Max's luggage and briefcase, which he managed to stuff into one of the small suitcases. How glad he was that they both traveled light!

A short time later, feeling warmed up from the trek, he reached the highway and prepared himself to begin a new life in his old world. He set his bags down by the side of the road and proceeded to hitch for a ride going southwest. A short time later he saw the ambulance followed by two sports utility vehicles heading his way. As they approached him he recognized two of the hikers in the first vehicle as part of the group with the injured girl. Without even noticing him, they hurriedly drove past him, but the second vehicle with two other young men stopped and picked him up.

"Hi. I am Josh and this is Tim," the driver said.

"I'm Jon… but that's my nickname, my name is Max," he said, catching himself.

"Okay, Max," Josh said. "I hope you don't mind going to Cedar City. A friend of ours just had an accident and was airlifted to a hospital there and we're on our way to join the rest of the group.

Jon was thankful they were too busy thinking of their injured friend to pay much attention to him.

"Absolutely, I appreciate the ride. Not too many cars come by at this time of the day," he said.

"We're glad to help," Tim said. "We wouldn't leave you stranded. This is not a main highway where you have cars going all the time. Out here there's no traffic going through at night."

"So, what's your story?" Josh asked.

"What do you mean?" Jon tried to buy time by stalling.

"I mean, what are you doing in the middle of nowhere, with no car in sight and two pieces of luggage?"

Jon had to think fast. He looked at his hands and saw Max's wedding band.

"Well, my fiancé and I had an argument," he said.

"It must have been a big one if she left you where she did," Josh said, chuckling.

"It was something stupid, really. We were having the 'kids talk' and I said that if at all possible, a mother needs to stay home with the children at least the first two years, and she flipped out on me. She took it as a chauvinistic remark on my part and from there, things just escalated. She can be volatile, which is why my family doesn't like her."

"Maybe they have a point. You should evaluate the relationship more carefully."

"Most definitely," Jon said. "After this episode, it's over for good."

"Where were you going?" Tim asked.

"To Aspen for spring break but obviously, my plans have been changed."

"You shouldn't have started an argument, especially when she was driving," Josh said.

"I shouldn't have let her drive my car," Jon said.

"Maybe you're right," Tim said.

The rest of the trip was silent as they all meditated on their long and eventful day. Unknowingly and strangely unified, the three men were all giving thanks for Eve Anne's survival. As Josh was getting off at the next exit, Tim interrupted the silence.

"Where would you like to be dropped off?" he asked.

Jon felt a strange fascination that compelled him to stay with them.

"Don't worry about me. I don't want you to waste time. The hospital is as good a drop-off place as any."

"Very good, then," Josh said.

When they arrived to the hospital, the rest of the group was sitting on benches and chairs along the hallway of the emergency area. Separated only by curtains, the area was partly visible as the doctors went about caring for emergency arrivals. In some cases, loved ones were at their bedsides comforting them.

After getting checked out by the doctor, Eve Anne was sent for x-rays. As she was wheeled out and away she waved to her friends with a smile.

"Hi boys," she said softly as she went by them.

Jon felt his heart skip a beat when he saw her beautiful hazel-green eyes and heard her voice.

"Eve, how do you feel?" one of her friends asked her.

She nodded and gave thumbs up.

"Eve is her name?" Jon asked, curious.

"Her name is Eve Anne Vinson," Lucas said.

His words blurted out before he could realize it. "She is beautiful."

"Yes, she is. That's our buddy, our Eve Anne," Ethan said as he joined the group after talking to the attending physician.

"The doctors don't know how to explain it. She had a concussion, but there are no signs of internal bleeding or damage. After the x-rays results, we'll know if she can go home with us." He shook his head in disbelief. "Incredible!"

"Speaking of incredible, what was that light that filled the sky?" someone in the group asked.

"I have no idea, but in a strange way, I think it saved Eve Anne from a freefall. I don't think she would have survived that. Just before the light hit, she was losing her balance. I thought she was falling forward but the lightning impact blinded and pushed her backwards. She slipped on something icy and fell down a slippery slope."

"Well, thank God for miracles," Josh said.

Listening to the conversation, Jon couldn't help wondering if his return had anything to do with her accident or if he'd changed the course of something that was supposed to happen. He decided it was time for him to go.

"Well guys, thanks so much for the ride. I really appreciate it," he said, getting up to leave.

As he started to walk away, Tim called him back.

"Max, don't go yet. Come and meet the rest of the group. The x-rays shouldn't take too long. After that we can then give you a ride wherever you want. Unless you're in a hurry to get somewhere."

"What hurry? I accept your kind offer, thank you," he said as he was introduced to the rest of the group.

"Strange," he thought. There was something about the group that felt familiar, despite just having met them for the first time. A few minutes later a nursing assistant brought Eve Anne back, with the technician holding the x-rays following behind. Ethan went to her bedside as the rest of the group including Jon, congregated outside the door. The doctor took a long look at the x-rays and turned to her.

"Young lady," he said, "you must have nine lives. I don't know how you survived that fall with only an apparent concussion and bruises. Now, don't misunderstand me, a concussion is not a minor thing, but considering what could have happened to you, it's a miracle you're alive."

"Yes, I was very lucky this time," she said.

"You can go home, but have to stay awake for the next twelve hours and if there is anything abnormal, especially headaches, you get yourself to a doctor right away. Can you handle that?" the doctor asked her.

"We'll make sure of that," Ethan assured him as Eve Anne nodded in agreement.

Jon quietly walked down the hallway and stood around, waiting. He was surprised to be drawn to a woman who was a stranger, and yet not entirely so.

"Okay. Max, where to?" Tim asked him, interrupting his thoughts.

"A motel, please. Something close by would be nice."

Having discussed earlier with Ethan where to meet after Eve Anne was released from the hospital, her friends planned to drop Jonathan off at a motel on their way.

As they walked to the vehicle, Jon realized he had to come up with a way to pay for a room for the night. He checked his pockets and to his relief Max's wallet was still in his back pocket. He pulled it out as they got in their vehicle and drove off.

"Did she take your money, too?" Josh asked, referring to Jon's phantom girlfriend.

"No, no. I'm just checking," he said as he finished going through the wallet, "and it's all here."

"Good thing," Tim said. A few minutes later Josh made the turn into the driveway of a small hotel and stopped at the front door.

"Guys, I can't thank you enough," Jon said as he got out and pulled his luggage.

"No problem Max, good luck," they both said to him and drove away.

Jon waved goodbye and walked to the reception desk. He paid in cash, using a fictitious name and address.

As soon as he was in his room, he went through the wallet again, this time slowly checking its contents. Inside was Max's driver's license, a photograph of Elise, three credit cards, and other miscellaneous types of personal identification such as health insurance cards, and a gym membership. Neatly tucked in the side pocket, he found five one hundred-dollar bills and change.

He put the luggage pieces on the bed and opened them. He checked his carry on bag first, the contents of which he already knew: the usual personal items with three days worth of clothes. Inside it he had stuffed the briefcase that amazingly survived the crash. He then proceeded to go through Max's suitcase. It had clothing items, a pair of sneakers, and his passport. Tucked in its pages, he found another four hundred dollars in cash. He couldn't believe his fortune, but then again, Max told him more than once that he never traveled without his passport and some hard cash. He was the proverbial Boy Scout—always prepared—and was Jon ever so thankful for that! Lastly, he opened the briefcase. His heart beat faster at the prospect of having Internet access in private when he saw his computer notebook. But his hopes were dashed when he checked it out further and found cracks and fractures.

After he finished the inspection, he decided to get out of his clothes and take a shower. When he turned the bathroom light on, he was startled at what he saw in the mirror. Staring back at him was not himself, but Max, with his slim build of six-foot-one, light brown straight hair, blue eyes, and chiseled features. He was wearing brown slacks, black pullover sweater, and a rich brown Swede leather jacket. Truly reflecting the life beyond, the pain and melancholy permanent in Max's eyes after Elise died, was now gone. Instead they now seemed to look forward with apprehension to a new chapter to be written in his life.

The next day he got up early in the morning. The first thing he did after getting ready was call Max's credit card providers and try to find out if any of them were still active, anticipating that he would need one to rent a car. Having to come up with Max's mother's maiden name, among other things, wouldn't be a problem. Everything else he needed to know was in his wallet. Besides, he knew his friend's life like he knew his own. To his amazement, the first card he checked turned out to be still active. He decided to use it but made a mental note to get a post office box the next day to forward the monthly statements to himself, at least until he figured out possible plans for his new life. After having breakfast, he would have a few hours to think while he made the southbound drive.

As he entered the highway heading toward Las Vegas, he thought of beautiful Eve Anne and her friends. How did she fit in the whole puzzle of his new life, if at all? Strangely, he felt a yearning to see her again, and now he could kick himself for not finding out more about her.

It was a clear and mild day, perfect to reflect on what he was going to do. For starters, he thought Las Vegas, with its transient element, would be a great city to get a post office box. In the time it would take to get there, he hoped to have a clearer idea of what he was going to do.

By late afternoon, he was settled in his room at a major casino hotel, making plans about what to do next. He would like nothing better than to see his parents again, even if only from far away. He also needed money and a place to live, which in itself would not be easy given his circumstances.

Trying to remember the documents stored in his broken computer, he recalled that his last transaction on his Swiss bank account was the deposit of his bonus check. Sometime soon he needed to access it before he ran out of cash and that wouldn't be too long.

The next day he opened a post office box at a strip mall and arranged the forwarding of two of Max's credit cards there. He was told by the credit card companies that it would take about a month for him to receive a new card, since the last statements had just been sent out. After that, he took his computer to an electronic repair shop, where he was told that they could restore it but some of its data might be lost. However, the clerk pointed out to him that the electronic memory stick inside seemed undamaged and handed it to him.

"I can't believe I forgot about that," he said, shaking his head as he walked out of the shop. It would take at least three days to get his laptop back. He planned to use the time going to the public library and surfing the Internet to get caught up with current events. He considered reading the memory stick at the library computer, but the risk of leaving a trail behind, however small, was something he couldn't afford to do. On the upside, the free time would also give him a chance to look up real estate rentals and sales all over the country.

"A month will give me plenty of time to get a few leads for an ideal place to live," he thought. "But I can't do anything until I get the new credit cards and go to Europe."

Eve Anne, on the other hand, still hadn't been allowed to sleep by her friends. After being released from the hospital the previous night, the group drove to her family vacation home in the town of Springdale, eighty-five miles away. It was located five miles outside of town, isolated and private, facing a view of Zion National Park and a river stream running just beyond their backyard. Her grandparents had willed it to her, knowing how much she loved being there. They were very aware that it was a spot that always nurtured her talent for writing. Since the passing of Grandma and Grandpa Conley, the house had become the family's vacation home.

As soon as her parents were told of her accident, they wanted to come to her aid but she convinced them that after getting some sleep, Ethan would drive her to their home. By late afternoon most of the group had left, leaving Ethan and Josh with Eve. Not long after, she was finally allowed to go to sleep.

The next day, feeling better after getting much needed sleep, her friends drove her to her parents who were anxiously waiting. Once there, she went to see the family physician the next day. She hoped he would evaluate her and clear her to leave for Europe in time for her assignment. After pleading her case, she convinced the doctor to allow her to leave as planned. He allowed her to go on the condition that she would come back for a follow-up appointment before the week was over, and she agreed.

Thanks to her determination she would depart as planned to France, where she was to meet Matthew Morell, her photographer and cameraman. From there the two would fly to Bucharest, Romania to work on the story. Except for a wrist guard and a splinter on her left index finger, there was nothing to indicate her recent ordeal as she boarded the plane.

***

Jon filled the time he had to wait gambling a few hours at a time, winning just enough to help pay for his room, which was more than he expected. At this point, the last thing he wanted to do was attract attention.

Three days later, after picking up his repaired lap top computer, he anxiously hurried to his room to see what information had survived. He connected onto the Internet, using access available in the room, and quickly was looking into his personal documents. Approximately a quarter of the information was lost, but the combination of what was left and the memory stick was enough for him to recover the data he needed.

"So far, things are working out just as I would have wanted," he thought to himself, and for some reason that fact made him uneasy, but he shrugged it off. Now he needed to concentrate his attention on finding a place to live, which after a lot of research, he had narrowed down to Alaska.

"There's no chance of running into anyone I know. In fact, I could get lost there," he said to himself. However, there was one thing he wanted to do more than anything before he disappeared from the world. Five weeks later, after securing a place to live, pending his visual approval, he booked his plane reservation to La Guardia Airport in New York, en route to Alexandria Bay. He couldn't wait to see his parents.

Meanwhile, back at Fitzgerald International, finding Jonathan's missing bonus was proving elusive for William, thus he decided to enlist Sophia and Vince's help in the search. He couldn't afford to throw all his time into it and neglect the rest of his duties in the company.

It was Thursday afternoon and the three of them met in William's office behind closed doors, a fact that didn't go unnoticed by Bradley. It didn't matter that the meeting didn't pertain to him; he wanted to be aware of everything that had to do with the company. Still, there was nothing he could do about it and that frustrated him even more.

The three Fitzgeralds sat around the table of a mini-conference room adjacent to William and Vince's office, accessible to their two offices only.

"Something doesn't seem right. Five million dollars can't disappear just like that. It's a lot of money," William said, shaking his head. "All I've been able to track down was the deposit into his personal account and the cancelled check. The day his bonus check was processed, which was the day after Thanksgiving, the sum was electronically transferred somewhere else."

"Well, only Jonathan could have done that," Sophia said. "He would need personal and password information known only to him. Besides, he would have known if something was amiss.

He kept a close check on his accounts and would have told us if something was wrong. There was enough time for him to have noticed it before his death."

"Where was the money transferred to?" Vince asked.

"That's one of the problems," William said. "On his bank statements the transaction is recorded as a withdrawal, with no forwarding trail."

"That's unusual. It's as if he was trying to conceal it, and that's not like Jon," Sophia said.

"Is it possible that unbeknownst to you, he might have invested it back into the company?" Vince asked.

"Vince, that's a good idea to check into. Considering that he wasn't eager to accept his bonus, it's a possibility. I told him it was only fair he should get it. After all, hiring someone else would have cost a lot more. But I wouldn't put it past him. It's not the first time he put his bonuses back in company stock."

"Okay, that's worth pursuing," Sophia said.

"Very well, then," William said. "Let's divide the activity report of stock sales for the last six months into thirds and go from there."

"I'll request a copy of the report. It should take about two hours to get," Vince said.

"Let's get to it, then. Oh, by the way, for the time being I don't want anyone else involved in this project," William said.

"As soon as I have the report I'll let you know," Vince said and went back to his office.

Sophia and William looked at each other mystified.

"How could the bank show the transaction as an electronic transfer/withdrawal without forwarding entity? What does that mean?" Sophia asked.

"I don't know. We'll look into that after we see the stock sales and we can verify whether the money is invested there or not," William said.

"I hope we can solve this puzzle soon."

"So do I, Sophie."

Late in the afternoon, Vince received the stock sales report he requested. It was divided among the three of them, and each took their section home at the end of the day. They worked late into the night as they combed through their section of the accounts, looking for five-million-dollar purchases.

The next day they compared notes and submitted a list of the transactions to their company broker for verification. After their research, their broker confirmed that all the transactions submitted to be checked out were verified as purchases of clients on file.

The news was discouraging, but Vince wasn't ready to give up. Something was not right and he wanted to get to the bottom of it.

"Let's go through it again, but this time let's look for amounts recorded around the same date that add up to the amount we're looking for. I saw a few of those while going through the report last night," he proposed.

"Fine. We'll do that, but not until next week. This work will be here when we come back on Monday. Let's enjoy the weekend," William said.

But he knew that neither of them would be satisfied until they found out what happened to Jon's bonus.

The next week they each worked on their report for a few hours for two days and on Wednesday they met again, each with their list of the potential amounts and names.

The activity generated in the search was not lost on Bradley, who had been noticing that for the past week the Fitzgeralds had been working closely together without including him. He wanted to be aware of all the company decisions; after all, he said to himself, "Who better qualified than me?"

The name Vince came to mind following the thought of someone better qualified and it irritated him. He unquestionably hated him. In his unrealistic sense of self-importance, he saw Vince as an intruder who took a job that should have been his. Seeing the three family members working so close together made him uncomfortable. It was time to find out what was going on, so he walked to William's office, which had the door ajar and knocked gently.

"We're in here," William answered from the adjacent room.

Bradley walked to the door and stood glancing at the work on the conference table. He noticed that each person had reports which had notes that he couldn't read from where he stood.

"Good morning," he said. "I just came by to offer my help. It looks like quite a project you are working on."

"Thanks dear," Sophia said, "but this is more of a personal thing. We know you have a lot to do in your office."

"I appreciate it Bradley, but like Sophia said, it's not a work-related matter. It's actually something to do with Jon. But if we need any help, I won't hesitate to ask you," William said.

"I just wanted to let you know that I am here to help."

"You have enough on your plate with your job, but it's good of you to offer. I would rather not keep you from your duties which are essential to the company. Thanks anyway, Brad," William said.

"Okay," Bradley said as he turned around and left.

Vince sat silently watching the conversation exchange. It was obvious to him from the beginning that Bradley was not pleased with his presence in the company, and although he tried to disguise his true feelings, he didn't do a very good job. And if there was one thing Vince was good at, it was reading people and Bradley was only too obvious to him.

"Where were we?" William asked. "Oh yeah, Vince, would you please close the door? We'll get more done without interruptions."

Vince did as requested and the three of them continued to compare notes. Each one of their lists had a number of entries with possibilities, which they combined and again sent to their stockbroker for further verification. At the end of the day all but one of the combination entries were verified.

"I have a guess as to which combination is the only one pending: Serengeti Corporation," Vince said.

"How did you know?" Sophia asked.

"Oh, just a hunch. I went back and checked beyond the six-months report to a whole year and found a few other purchase transactions made by the same name. The corporation has steadily been increasing their shares acquisition in the business."

"How much did they buy last year?" William wanted to know.

"Roughly eight million," Vince replied.

"Hmm…if someone is investing that much money in our company, we need to know who they are. Have you heard of them before?" Sophia asked.

"Not until now. How long will it take to get their profile information from the broker?" Vince asked.

"We should have that by tomorrow. But it still doesn't answer our question. It seems like we're getting a little off track here," William said.

"We'll pursue the bank option. You just can't move around that kind of money without leaving a trail." Sophia said.

"Yes, we'll do that. Vince, would you get the account history on Serengeti Corporation as far back as you can? While we wait for the background information we can find out what we have about them in our files."

"We can look that up from your desktop if it's not an extensive file," Vince said.

"Let's check it out now," William said.

"William, you're not worried about the company, are you?" Sophia asked as they walked over to his desk in his office.

"Worried is not the word. I'm curious about who is secretly buying large amounts of our shares. In a stockholders meeting, that amount of shares translates to votes. I also find interesting that last year they bought the maximum shares Fitzgerald International allows for the buying period. Beyond that amount, we would conduct an audit on the solvency and background of the buyer."

"How does that affect the willingness of big investors to buy into the company?" Vince asked.

"Well, they mainly don't like the policy. Nobody likes audits, but they understand the need for transparency when securing their investment."

"Do you find any of them reluctant to cooperate?"

"Not really. Those who are willing to work with us are usually people of character, which is my preference. Ideally, I would rather make profits for the smaller investor and run it as a family-owned business."

"Well said, brother. I'm proud of you for that, as I'm sure Mom and Dad would be, not to mention Jonathan."

"Our son," William said with a wistful tone. "Sometimes he feels so close."

Sophia came up behind his chair and gently massaged his shoulders.

"Ah! That feels good! But let's focus here," he said and proceeded to search for the account history for Serengeti in his desktop computer.

"Eureka!" he said upon locating the account. "Its first purchase was two years ago for fifty thousand dollars and after that the amounts have steadily increased with every purchase."

"How much stock have they bought so far?" Sophia asked.

"They have bought a total of approximately fifteen million, honey. And that is too much for us not to know who they are. We need to approach them and inquire about their interest in our company, that is, after we've heard from Scott."

"Your broker?" Vince asked.

"Yes."

"I wonder," Sophia said, "do you think we should get Bradley involved? After all, as the controller he needs to be aware of it."

"He should have been aware of it," Vince said.

"Let's wait to have all the facts." William advised. "In the meantime, we should do some work around here."

Sophia and Vince agreed and went back to their offices. They spent the rest of the day immersed in work accumulated because of the time taken away from their duties by their side project. But in the back of their minds, the name Serengeti lingered with perplexing thoughts.

In the meantime, Bradley was not about to be left in the dark. After leaving William's office, he called the head systems analyst and requested a copy of the report that was printed for Vince the prior week.

"What report was it?" the analyst asked Brad.

"I'm not sure, but you have a way of looking it up, don't you?"

"Yes, but it will take time and I'm very busy right now. If you give me the name of the report, I can get it to you a lot quicker," the analyst said.

"I told you what I want. I don't care what you have to do, but that report should be on my desk by tomorrow morning!" Bradley demanded and hung up the phone.

That next day would prove an eventful one for all involved. When Bradley arrived at his office, the report he had ordered was sitting on his desk. His pulse accelerated when he saw the name on it. Immediately, he flipped through the pages, stopping to take a long and detailed look at the Serengeti account. Then he got his personal laptop out of his briefcase and he surfed through the account for up-to-the-minute activity information. Nothing about it stood out, but then he wondered why Vince, Sophia, and William were spending so much time going through the list of accounts.

"I'm just being paranoid," he told himself. "But you can't be too careful."

Still, he couldn't help himself from checking the number of shares he owned. He smiled as he stared at the account balance, and leaned back in his chair.

"Fifteen million dollars and counting," he whispered under his breath with satisfaction.

Later in the afternoon William received some of his answers from Scott, their broker.

"Serengeti International was incorporated in the state of Nevada with an address in Reno three years ago," he began telling Sophia and Vince. "They are not our clients and the nature of their business isn't too clear. Import and export was the only description given."

"That's not very informative," William said.

"I'm afraid you're right. They seem very low profile but we'll check further if you like," the broker said.

"Let me think about it. I need to get all my facts together and get back to you on this. Good bye Scott," William said and hung up the phone.

"So what's next?" Vince asked.

"The next step would be to investigate the business location. We want to know as much about them as we can before approaching them," William said.

"Who's going to do the legwork?" Vince wanted to know.

"I think it would be best to hire an investigator."

"I like that idea," said Sophia, who had been silent up until then.

"How do you go about finding a good man or woman for the job?" Vince asked.

"We have two private investigators we deal with. One is a man and the other a woman. They are both extremely good at what they do. The circumstance of the job many times dictates the gender of the private eye."

"Good then, let's print the statistics of the account and make the call," Vince suggested.

Sophia sat back and observed the two brothers working together. It was always her manner to remain in the background, but behind the scenes she was William's biggest asset. Her analytical nature compelled her to look at this new development and wonder what it had to do with her son, if anything at all.

"What is the icon on this space? I didn't see it when we checked the account before," she asked, pointing at the computer screen.

Vince got closer to it and his eyes got wide.

"That tells you that between the last time we accessed the account and now, someone else has been looking at it from our side of the company."

They turned to each other with a surprised look, their mouths open.

"Can we tell who did it?" Sophia asked.

William got up from his chair and gave his seat to Vince.

"You'll be much faster than I am," he said.

"This inquiry didn't come from our system. The account was accessed from an outside source," Vince told them

"We know it's not us. Who else has that kind of clearance in the company?" Sophia asked.

"I'll have Lori get the list of the people who are authorized this kind of access," Vince said.

"How long will it take?" William wanted to know.

"Not too long," he said as he got on the phone to request the list from Lori, who was now his assistant.

"You know, Bradley was the only one who saw the report we were working on yesterday and he has access to just about everything as a controller," Vince said.

"It's not Bradley, I'm sure," William said emphatically. "We've been friends with his parents since before he was born. Jonathan grew up with him and Max. They all knew each other and have been friends since they were children,"

"Okay, I'm not pointing fingers at anybody. I'm just stating facts and trying to make sense of this whole thing, which is fast turning into something totally different than we were looking for."

"Boy! That's for sure," William said, as his phone rang.

The voice of Jess, William's assistant informed him, "Mr. Fitzgerald, Scott Holland is on the line for you."

"Yes, Scott," he said as he got on the phone. The rest of the conversation consisted of William listening for the most part, interjecting with a few comments now and then.

"I understand. I'll talk to you tomorrow," he said at the end.

"Apparently Serengeti Corporation has aroused their interest too," he started telling Sophia and Vince. "They did some further checking and discovered some interesting facts. Serengeti was previously known as Onyx Enterprises, a part of BioSynergy Research Corporation. As a division of Fitzgerald International, BioSynergy was founded exclusively to study green energy. It has seven branches and each studies a different source of clean power. The objective is to produce eco-friendly energy compatible with the geographical locations of our home construction sites."

"Is this group coming up with new technology?" Vince asked.

"They are in the early stages of something new, but up to

now they've mostly worked on energy transport and storage. Right now we have four patents pending approval of units capable of condensing and storing energy which would expand when released for use. This will increase the amount of kilowatt-hours you can store in the same space by 500 percent. Basically this unit of the company has been very successful at fulfilling its purpose and beyond. It has great potential, given the encouraging results from its research," William said.

"I can see where it could be a very profitable business, provided the technology is affordable to the average person and delivers what it promises," Vince said.

"We had the technology years ago, but the price to the consumer was too high. We needed to cut production costs to make it an attractive alternative, and we have done that. Our aim was to make it cost efficient enough to be a feature in all the houses we build, and we have achieved that."

"Why hasn't there been any news coverage about this?" Vince was curious to know.

"We've managed to keep it pretty quiet. At first we were just looking for ways to incorporate our findings into our construction business—not for mass production on a large scale. But the findings have modified a lot of our original plans. For reasons which I will fill you in later, we will wait for confirmation of patents before issuing any announcements. I don't need any media circus right now."

"I understand," Vince said.

"But we're getting a little off track here; we're talking about the Serengeti Corporation. And by the way, apparently all the purchase transactions made by them were done electronically and without leaving much of a trail," William said.

"Well, in light of all this, we need to take major steps to protect the integrity of the company. The sooner we uncover what's happening the better," Vince said.

"No doubt about it," William answered. "Given all the possible implications, it's imperative that we call the appropriate government agency to come in and conduct an investigation.

This is not the way we conduct business, and if there is someone conspiring against us, we need to find them out."

"We should do that as soon as possible, but we need legal advice before acting on it," Vince said.

"I was about to suggest that," Sophia said to William.

"And as usual, you are right, dear," he said.

William marked the end of the meeting by placing a call to Stanley Gold, their attorney, and setting up a meeting at his office first thing on Monday morning.

CHAPTER 6

WITH FRIENDS LIKE THESE...

It was early Friday evening and everybody had gone home for the weekend, except for Bradley, who was in his office hiding, waiting for the Fitzgeralds to leave. As soon as he knew they were in the elevator, he walked over to make sure the display showed they were going down to the parking lot. When he was satisfied, he quickly walked over and using their security codes broke into William and Vince's office. He went through everything in their desks and computer files, searching for things to give him a hint of what the three of them were working on. The fact that the reports they had been working on were missing gave him a bad feeling.

Just before he left the office, he called Madison and they agreed to meet at an intimate nightclub not far from his high-rise condominium. There was a kind of kinship between the two, one born out of a shared spirit of malice and an exaggerated sense of self-worth. They were drawn to each other not because of noble feelings, but rather their mutual embrace of the opposite, lacking any sense of accountability.

Bradley needed someone to talk to about the dealings going on in the company, and she was the only person he felt would understand him. Although it involved a risk confiding in her, he knew what it took to keep her quiet and he was ready to give in to her.

They met at nine o'clock and started dancing and drinking until past midnight. Afterwards they each drove their car to Bradley's place. Once they settled in his living room overlooking the bay, he poured her and himself a glass of champagne.

"Do you think that Jon's been dead long enough that we can be seen together in public?" he asked.

"I think six months is an acceptable mourning time. After all, we weren't married and no one can blame me for going on with my life. To our friends and family I will be the sad fiancé that is forced to go on," she said, faking a sad face. "Why do you ask?"

"In case you didn't notice, it's been six months since Jon died."

"I notice the things that are in my best interest. I was just waiting for you to say something," she said.

"Good," he said. "How do you feel about telling our friends about us?"

"Which part do you mean?"

"The part where we were so torn by the grief of losing my best friend (and your fiancé) that we were drawn to each other and fell in love without realizing it."

"Ah Brad, baby, are you telling me that you fell madly in love with me?" she asked making fun of him.

"I was thinking that we have been together longer than many people I know. We compliment each other well, best of all, we understand each other. Given our personalities, that is hard to find."

"I would agree with you, and the sex is great," she said, raising her glass for a toast.

"That brings me to my next question: Madison, will you marry me?" Bradley asked point blank.

For once, he seemed to catch her at a loss for words.

"Do I detect by your stunned look that you will consider it?" he asked amused.

"I hadn't thought of us being married. Our arrangement has been so convenient. I liked it just the way it was, but marriage could be a good thing. I will most definitely consider it."

"How long will it take you to make a decision?"

"How's five minutes? The more I think about it the more I think it's a great idea. Yes! I will marry you," she eagerly said, throwing her arms around his neck and giving him a long, wet kiss, which he reciprocated.

"Okay then," he said reminding himself of the decisive reason for their union. "Let's toast to us."

They raised their glasses again; this time in celebration of what seemed only fitting for them, a partnership of lust and greed.

"I am glad you have accepted my proposal. It just came to me tonight while at the club, and that's the reason why I don't have a ring for you. But to make it up, I thought the ring should be your choice. Anything my future bride wants."

"Oh Brad!" she cooed, "See what I mean? The idea sounds better every minute. Your wife will have the most beautiful diamond," she said looking at her ring finger.

Listening to her, he knew this would turn out to be a good proposition for him, after all.

"Of course, timing will be a consideration. When do you want to do this?" she asked him.

"Whenever you like. A year after Jonathan's death is enough time. Anything after that would be good. We're halfway there, which means in six months we could do it."

"Six months is not enough to plan a wedding, especially when you don't want people to know until the last minute."

"You're an event coordinator. You should be able to pull it off."

"Organizing business events is a little different than coordinating a wedding, especially my own. Besides, what's your hurry? Don't you think it would look suspicious for me to marry you so soon?"

"Come on! People aren't paying attention to us. I believe that if you set your mind to it, you could do it. But it's your day and you should have the ultimate say in it."

"Thank you, darling," she said in a syrupy voice.

"It's just that after two and a half years together, an extra year is a long time to wait," he said.

"Yes, three and a half years is considerable time, but when did you become the marrying kind? I didn't think the idea ranked high in your agenda."

"It's time to settle down. I don't think I'll find anyone more compatible than you. We understand each other very well."

"That's true," she agreed.

"So…when will you let me know?"

"Do you mean a possible date for the wedding?"

"Yes," he said.

"I'm going to have to see how fast I can make it happen, and you know I have specific ideas of what I want."

"Don't remind me. I hated the idea of you marrying Jon," he lamented.

"I know, but as you see, things worked out for the best for us. Besides, I didn't have any intention of giving you up. It's what I liked about our relationship. No moral hang-ups, just looking out for number one," she said.

"Together we'll be rich, and I will get what should have been mine from the beginning," he said. "Fitzgerald International will make me a wealthy man and you'll be there to share it with me,"

"I like the sound of that," she said.

"Speaking of getting rich, there's something I've wanted to share with you for a long time. As my wife you will be entitled to part of it."

"I know you," she said pointing at him with a smile. "What are you hiding?"

"Let's just say that I found a way to supplement my salary at the expense of the Fitzgeralds. You're marrying a millionaire, my dear."

Her mouth dropped and her eyes got wide.

"Fantastic!" she exclaimed.

"I thought you'd like that."

"I always knew you had potential. Otherwise I wouldn't have accepted your proposal. I am not exactly low maintenance, but you know that."

"So you agreed to marry me based on my earning potential?"

"Don't take it the wrong way," she said snuggling up to him. "Think of it as my vote of confidence, my way of saying that I believe in you."

"Oh, I didn't take it in a bad way. I like that you can be frank with me."

Just as he said that, he realized the extent of her honesty was very small, going only as far as it took her to get what she wanted. Fortunately for him, he knew her very well.

"How much are we talking about?" she asked.

"A few million," he said nonchalantly.

"How much is a few?"

"I'm not sure," he lied. "The last time I checked the account it was around six million."

"That's a big raise!" she said.

"Nothing I shouldn't be entitled to. Half of that company should be mine."

"How did you do it?"

"I used my position and intellect to come up with a way," he said mysteriously.

"Don't lie to me; I want the same honesty I give you," she demanded.

"I will tell you all about it after we're married. For now you will just have to trust me, and to show you I am good for it, I will put all of my six million dollars under your name. Now that's a lot of trust."

She was speechless for a moment, her head spinning.

"How can you do that?" she asked incredulously.

"Because I want you to trust me, just as I am willing to trust you with my money. Besides, it'll all be ours anyway," he said.

"I trust you," she said with a little girl's voice.

"Good! Next week we will start transactions to open a corporation in your name and deposit the money into it."

"That's pretty quick, isn't it?"

"If you'd rather wait…" he said, knowing that a six-million-dollar carrot was something she couldn't resist.

"No, it's just all kind of overwhelming. The idea of going from clandestine lovers to an upstanding wealthy couple is a big change."

"It was about time."

"Yes!" she said. "And we should celebrate."

With that they fell into each other's arms and lustfully sealed their impending union. She had visions of spending lavishly going through her head, while he was pleased to have her as a partner in his ill-conceived venture. For the moment, he was only going to tell her what she needed to know.

The next day they started putting their plans into motion, beginning with the process of establishing a business identity to hide the money he had managed to steal from Fitzgerald International. She decided on a high fashion business that she would call what else? "Madison's" of course. He agreed.

"How much of this money can I spend?" she asked.

"It depends on whether you want a house right away or if you want to wait."

"I like your place. It's a great location. We can live there after we're married and later decide," she asserted.

"It sounds good to me. How about some jewelry shopping now?"

"I thought you'd never ask."

Bradley realized that she put aside the idea of buying a house until later not because she was fiscally responsible, rather because it allowed her to spend more. But he wasn't at all bothered. Her partnership and complicity were worth that much. Lucky for him, money was her weakness and he could afford her.

***

The beginning of the following week was a busy one for everybody. William and Sophia had a meeting with their attorney Stanley Gold at his office on Monday, where they related to him the events that brought them there that morning.

"William," Stanley said, "I will take care of dealing with the authorities. I am familiar with the agencies and will get this investigation going as soon as possible. I must stress, however, that this information should be kept confidential. Nobody else should know about it for now."

"My brother Vince and Sophia are the only ones aware of this. Ah, you might want to touch bases with Scott, our broker, too. He's been very helpful."

"I will speak to him about the need for discretion in this matter and alert him that the authorities might get in touch with him too," the attorney said.

"He's a professional. I am sure that won't be a problem," William said.

"I know Scott from a previous investigation and you're right. In fact, he would be a good ally in uncovering the truth behind all of this," Stanley assured them both.

"I am glad to know that," William said, standing up to leave.

Stanley Gold shook his hand.

"I'll call you later today to let you know who will be investigating this complaint. Again, please don't share this information with anyone, and let me know if anything new comes up."

"I will," William said, "and you do the same."

"I most certainly will," the attorney said as the couple walked out of the office.

Their drive to work was mostly silent. William and Sophia could read each other's thoughts, and neither one of them knew how to react. But they were sure that something very wrong was going on.

"I can't wait to find out who is doing this to us." Sophia said breaking the silence.

"It's hard to understand it. I mean, we don't have enemies. Well, at least up until now I thought we didn't."

"That's the most unsettling part about it. At least if we had enemies, we wouldn't be so shocked," Sophia said.

"We'll know it soon, I hope. In the meantime, I don't want this whole thing to influence our lives too much. I have confidence that the investigators will uncover the perpetrator. Life is too short to spend it worrying about something that isn't a life and death situation."

"You're right. It's just that I don't like having to put our employees under a cloud of suspicion," she said.

"Dear, we are not doing that. We don't even know if this is coming from within. It could conceivably be an outside source."

"You're right. Thinking too much about it can make you crazy."

"Let's change the subject," he said, reaching over to hold her hand. "How about dinner tonight? We'll leave work a little early."

"That sounds fun," she smiled.

"We're here," he said as they pulled into their parking space. "We should get more work done today. You know, it's a tremendous relief having Vince take on some of the burden of all of this."

"I know what you mean," she said as they got into the elevator.

"I hate to think of how I'd be able to handle this by myself," William said.

When they walked into the office mid-morning, everyone was working away. Vince had been catching up with the work that had accumulated and Bradley, taking advantage of William and Sophia's absence, worked on the incorporation of Madison's company. When Sophia and William walked past his office, he quickly put his personal material away and acted busy. But out of the corner of his eye, he was watching when they went into Vince's office, which of course, annoyed him to no end.

"Oh! If I could just fire him or set him up for a fall," he angrily said under his breath, grinding his teeth with anger, his jealousy of Vince bubbling over.

Meanwhile, inside Vince's office William was filling him in on what transpired at the meeting with the company attorney.

"More importantly, this has to stay between us and we must carry on as usual. We don't want to give anything away to alert the culprit, and until further notice our meetings should be conducted outside of here."

"I couldn't agree more. It's an eerie feeling to think our enemy or enemies could be watching us. There's no need to give them any reason to be suspicious," Vince said, specifically thinking of Brad.

Now more than ever he felt that Bradley should not be above suspicion, but he wouldn't suggest it to William any further. He hoped he was wrong, but only time would tell.

Later that afternoon, Stanley Gold placed a call to William. He informed him that, because the interstate status of Serengeti, the

FBI would be handling the investigation. A meeting was discreetly set up with the three of them for early afternoon the next day with agent Nelson O'Neill, and Stanley present.

After relating the events that had transpired and answering his questions, agent O'Neill reiterated caution and confidentiality.

"I appreciate your time, Mr. Fitzgerald. We're glad to have your cooperation," he said to them.

"I wouldn't have it any other way. Integrity has always been the cornerstone for my business and personal life. No one is more interested than I am in bringing this matter out in the open and finding out what is going on," William said.

"We're starting the preliminaries today. There is a good possibility that we will need to conduct an audit if we're not satisfied with the results of our other avenues of investigation."

"Do what you must, Mister O'Neill. You have our full cooperation."

"Thank you again for that," the agent answered.

The three Fitzgeralds and the attorney shook his hand and left. On their way to their cars, Vince suggested they stagger their arrivals at the office, as if to make it appear that they were not together. William agreed. The meeting was intentionally set up at a time when it could have been mistaken for a long lunch, and indeed that's what Bradley assumed. Vince arrived first, while Sophia and William stayed behind grabbing a cappuccino before going back.

On the surface things seemed to have returned to normal, but behind the scenes a flurry of developments were going on. By the end of the week, the FBI agents checked the location of what was supposed to be Serengeti headquarters and found it to be a 10,000-square-foot warehouse with nothing in it but some sporting equipment and two all-terrain vehicles. They also put electronic surveillance on the Serengeti Corporation activities, as well as the company's bank accounts, which contained a large amount of money.

After trying to reach someone in the company at the telephone numbers listed, they found themselves in a maze of electronic menus that never connected them with anyone. Instead, the caller was urged to leave a message, which would of course be promptly returned. All of these findings confirmed what everyone involved could plainly see: There was something illicit about a company with an empty warehouse as headquarters and an unresponsive business phone number. There were no visible assets to justify such a hefty bank account.

The next step for the agents would be to follow the money trail to the source. Accountants were sent to BioSynergy headquarters. The second day into the audit they focused their attention exclusively on the Serengeti evolution from a subsidiary to an independent, profitable corporation without any visible manufacturing or production activities. Throughout all facets of the investigation, William was kept abreast of the events by the authorities. Everything was moving smoothly so far and he felt encouraged.

For his part, Bradley felt a little reassured when the Fitzgeralds stopped having their meetings in the office. Nevertheless, his scare made him face the reality that he couldn't do it all alone and he trusted no one—except maybe Madison, and even she could only be trusted to a point. For that reason he made a drastic decision to sell his shares in the company and put some of the money in their business venture. What he didn't tell her was that the biggest portion of his loot was attached to her corporate account but accessible only to him. Now he was just waiting on the approval of the corporation filings, then the sale transaction would be complete and the funds transferred.

He had approximately one more week to wait and already it felt like the longest week of his life. He tried to keep busy doing his job and regularly monitored the Serengeti account, but didn't notice anything unusual. Little did he realize that things were working out so well for him by design, not by providence.

The one thing that didn't sit well with him was that Vince had been regularly working longer hours and requesting more information reports. He seemed to be on a mission to learn even the minor details about the company and all subsidiaries, and that didn't make Brad too happy. But he promised himself that after his stock transactions were processed, he would turn his attention to Vince. He would like nothing better than to eliminate him from Fitzgerald International once and for all.

But Vince was not blinded by the affection that his brother and sister-in-law had for Bradley. By now he was more convinced that he definitely had something to do with Serengeti. His suspicions were fueled by the fact that the start of the Fitzgerald International stock purchasing activity coincided with Bradley's promotion to controller. Based on this conclusion, he decided to pursue the angle of the money trail. He loved his brother and Sophia and that's why he couldn't sit passively; instead he decided to follow his instincts. Aware of the audits being conducted on Serengeti, he was also able to work with federal auditors because he was the only other individual aware of the goings on. It would prove to be a fruitful collaboration between him and the authorities.

After three weeks of investigations, the parties involved came together in a conference room in the Fitzgerald building top floor, accessible only to the Fitzgeralds themselves and away from prying eyes. The group was comprised of William, Vince, Sophia, and Stanley Gold. Agent O'Neill was accompanied by two other agents. Everyone sat around the conference table with notes aplenty.

"First of all, I would like to say that this is one of the most efficient assignments I have conducted in a long time, in part due to your cooperation. This fraud could have continued for a while, had Mr. Fitzgerald not come across the information that led us to this. I wanted to meet with you now because we expect to conclude our active part of the investigation shortly. We are now at a point where we'll wait for the suspect to make his next move, which judging by the paperwork, should be soon."

There was a mild sigh from the family.

"We discovered that two years ago, Onyx, a branch of BioSynergy Corporation was registered as sold and renamed Serengeti Corporation. The transactions' signatures seem to be that of Jonathan William Fitzgerald, but there's no record of payment exchange for the sale."

The Fitzgeralds were stunned.

"It is my suspicion," he continued, "that the signatures are forged, and I am sure that it will be confirmed when we get back the lab results of Jonathan's signature comparison. What makes me believe this theory is that even after Jonathan Fitzgerald's death, there were a small number of document transactions signed with his name."

"How long after Jon died was this happening?" William asked.

"Until the end of last year," Agent O'Neill answered. "After that, virtually all transactions have been performed by someone named Oliver Goldwyn, the president and apparent owner of the company. The activities of the Serengeti bank account occur between the fifteenth and twentieth of the month. At that time, it receives a number of electronically processed deposits and at the closing of each month, a withdrawal is made for the received amount. With the exception of a small operating balance, all of it goes into stock purchases, mostly Fitzgerald International."

"Where is all that money coming from?" Sophia wanted to know.

"We have one theory we are working on with Vince, and it looks like we guessed right. But let Vince tell you about what he found so far."

Vince took his turn.

"After analyzing the deposit patterns, I noticed that the time frame is the same as our Mortgage Receivable schedule. After Agent O'Neill gave me some of the deposit amounts, I went through the reports of the last two years. I found that those amounts were equal to a number of mortgage account payments previously carried by our mortgage company. Further research led me to discover that more than two years ago, a number of accounts totaling more than five hundred thousand dollars a month were directed by someone at Fitzgerald International to submit their monthly payments to the Serengeti Corporation account. After the changes were made, these customers were deleted from the Fitzgerald customer data base entirely."

"Who is Oliver Goldwyn? I've never heard that name before. The only Oliver I know is Bradley's father and he is no Goldwyn. Have you checked for the user identification of the person who performed these transactions?" William asked.

Nelson O'Neill fielded his question.

"I'm afraid it wasn't that easy. All the IDs used to perform these tasks had previously been assigned to employees who were no longer with the company. We ran a background check on them and they were all clean. In fact two of them have been living out of state for a year now. For the time being, we are going under the premise that someone in the company has been keeping active password combinations that should have been canceled long time ago. We have put in a request to your IT department to find out who requested the reinstatement of user IDs under investigation. We expect to have that information sometime tomorrow. In answer to your question of who is Oliver Goldwyn, we would like to know that too. A background check on that name didn't turn up anything, which tells me the name is an alias."

"Nelson, do you have any suspects?" William asked point blank.

"Yes. We have a few individuals in mind that could fit the profile. I can't give you names right now because I have a strong leaning toward one in particular. But time is running out for him or her. Besides, it would be unfair for the innocent to be labeled as suspects. We have the Serengeti accounts monitored so that we know immediately of any activity and where it's coming from. Something should be happening soon on that front, and if my suspicions are right, I will be giving you names with proof to put them away for a long time."

"How long will it be until then?" Sophia asked. "The suspense is killing me."

"And I am very curious too. Soon we'll all know, Mrs. Fitzgerald. According to my date calculations, in two days at the most Mr. Goldwyn will make his usual account transaction and we'll get him then."

"Two days," Vince said in a low voice.

"One last piece of information. All accounts related to Serengeti Corporation are frozen until the investigation concludes and ownership of assets is determined. The financial loss to Fitzgerald should be nominal, since the majority of funds were diverted back into the company stock, which to me is puzzling," O'Neal said.

"Who knows how a criminal mind works? It takes a different set of marbles to think that way," Vince said.

"Well, I'm hopeful that we'll get answers to our questions soon," William assured his brother.

"You have now been briefed about our findings. As soon as I have further information I will let you know. And I want you to do the same, should you come across anything you think I need to know."

He shook hands with the Fitzgeralds and left followed by his agent partners and afterwards by Stanley Gold, leaving the Fitzgeralds to digest the information. They looked at each other, shaking their heads.

"So it is someone from the inside!" Sophia said.

"It sure looks that way," Vince said to her.

"I don't want to accept this, but it looks like someone we trusted stuck a knife in our backs," William said. "But enough work for today. Let's get out of here, and Vince, call Laura and ask her to join us for dinner. In spite of what's happening, I am happy that the matter is being resolved swiftly and I would like to toast to that with my family."

Vince got on the phone and called his wife. Later on they met at their favorite Italian restaurant and together they toasted to Jonathan.

"If not for him, it could have been a very long time before someone would have uncovered this theft, and by then, who knows how much we could have lost," William asserted.

Underneath the celebration, however, feelings of a trusted person's betrayal occupied their thoughts. The worst part for William and Sophia was that the list of possible suspects included Bradley. The whole idea that he could be involved was hard to believe and would hurt them deeply. But they tried to assure themselves of his innocence by thinking that he was not the only one to fit the suspect profile.

Vince, on the other hand, was becoming more convinced that the evidence pointed to Bradley as the investigation went on. But he also knew it was going to be a painful blow for his brother and Sophia, who considered him like family.

The next morning, Bradley went to William and unexpectedly requested the rest of the week as vacation.

"Are you going away for some fun?" William asked, trying to act normal.

"No," Bradley said. "I'm doing some construction in my place and want to make sure things get done the way I requested."

"You've been living in that place a long time," William said, trying small talk to see if he could get any clues.

"About seven years now," Brad said.

"That's a long time."

"Yes it is. It has a great location and it's big enough for me. It's almost doubled in price since I bought it."

"Mm…good for you. Well, enjoy your days off."

"Thanks, I will."

Soon after Bradley left, William called Vince.

"Guess who is taking the rest of the week off?" he asked.

"Our controller?" Vince replied.

"You got it. I think he should be catching the elevator about now," William said.

"Then now is a good time to tell you. I have talked with the IT department and asked them to immediately flag his e-mail and let me know everything he does."

"Vince, you have morphed into Sherlock Holmes," Big brother William said.

"I take it that you approve."

"I trust you implicitly. You are my brother."

"The feeling is mutual, Will," Vince said.

By now, Bradley no longer felt comfortable conducting his personal business at the office. He believed that William was not likely to grow suspicious of him but Vince was another story. For that reason he decided to take time off and finish the transactions of his corporation with Madison as soon as possible and away from them.

He spent the rest of the afternoon with Madison shopping for her engagement ring, which he suspected would be pricey, judging from the list of stores she wanted to check. But that didn't faze him. He reasoned with irony that you get what you pay for, and the price would be worth it if it helped his plans succeed. After much debating, she decided on a rare three-karat blue diamond in an opulent marquis cut that set Bradley back a considerable amount.

Looking at Madison's glee with her ring, he felt assured more than ever that she would be easy to manipulate, as long as she believed in his sincerity and his wallet. And even though they had not gone public with their romance, she couldn't restrain herself from wearing her ring to the dinner celebration later that night.

"Darling," she said gazing at her finger. "Isn't it beautiful?"

He took her left hand and kissed it.

"It's magnificent, like you."

"And it matches my eyes," she said.

"I noticed," he said.

"Speaking of noticing, when are we going to come out and announce our engagement? I can't wait to start showing it off," she said, pointing at her ring.

"Have you changed your mind about waiting?" he asked her.

"I'm not sure now. Maybe we can wait a little longer. But really, what do we care about what others think?" she said.

"I will make the funds transfer tomorrow. As soon as the transaction is complete and your business is a reality, we can announce it to our friends."

"Oh, good!" she said, rubbing her hands in anticipation. "Now, let's eat. I am famished."

The next afternoon, he went online using the computer at his apartment and requested the liquidation of all the stock that Serengeti Corporation owned in Fitzgerald International. Six million dollars were to be transferred into his and Madison's corporate venture, and the balance of nine million would go to one of his separate personal accounts.

As soon as the electronic request came in, the trading company notified Agent O'Neill and he was elated.

"Be sure to verify that there's a freeze on all accounts related to them, but don't flag them yet. Let Oliver Goldwyn find out when he checks the status of their transaction tomorrow. As soon as they do that, call my office while they are online and leave the rest to us," he instructed the bank.

He couldn't contain his satisfaction after getting off the phone. He could have requested a list of user identification numbers two days earlier when the pieces of the puzzle came together, but he opted instead to monitor the accounts' activities, which turned to be a good call that saved him days of work. The timing of the transaction was extremely convenient, which fueled O'Neill's suspicions even more.

"This is so much better than I expected!" he exclaimed. "But is it possible they could be aware of the investigation?" he wondered. "All the more reason to try to wrap up the business at hand as soon as possible," he concluded.

He was confident that within the next twenty-four hours, the embezzler's identity would be revealed.

For his part, Bradley, assuming that the processing of his transaction was taking place, had started preliminary concepts for his next scheme to keep ripping off Fitzgerald International and eliminate Vince from the company. For now he was happy to have Madison distracted with the wedding planning. Everything seemed to be going according to his plans, or so he thought.

CHAPTER 7

GREETINGS AND FAREWELLS

Jonathan, in the meantime, had caught a flight Tuesday morning from Las Vegas to New York. His heart was beating so fast he felt like his chest was going to explode. It had been a little over six months since his crash, yet more than a lifetime had happened since he had seen his parents and Madison, while still alive.

"Madison," he thought. Somehow she didn't seem that important anymore. It would be nice to see her, he thought, but strangely he would rather see Eve Anne. For a reason he couldn't explain, he hadn't been able to get her out of his mind.

"Apollo, what is the connection between her, our grandparents, and me?" he asked rhetorically.

There was no answer—not that he expected one. He was hoping, more than anything.

After his flight landed he stepped out and took a deep breath as he went into the terminal. Although he had taken care to disguise himself, he couldn't avoid feeling edgy about being back in his familiar surroundings. He didn't know how he would react at seeing his parents. It hurt already knowing he could only see them from afar. He wanted so much to embrace them and tell them how much he loved them!

He rented a car and drove to Woodmere, a suburb outside Alexandria Bay, where he checked into a small secluded hotel aptly named Woodmere Inn. He used an assumed name and paid cash for three days. He didn't anticipate it would take much longer than that to do what brought him there. To begin with, it was risk-taking for him to be there and for that reason he needed to make this visit as short as possible.

That evening he drove into town, parked his car, and went for a walk around old familiar grounds. With his disguise of dark hair, mustache, and beard, he was completely unrecognizable. His eyes were the only feature he hadn't changed that night because they were tired and dry from wearing contact lenses all day in the plane. He decided on wearing glasses, instead.

He strolled around the Rockville Plaza, looking at the shops and restaurants, many of which brought memories of a past life, filled with friends and loved ones. When he walked past Belladonna, his favorite restaurant, he couldn't resist going in for dinner. It was the best Italian food in town, he thought, and was filled to its capacity of seventy-five every evening. Tonight was no different.

He asked for a table close to the back, from where he could see the whole restaurant and was seated next to an older couple he didn't recognize, which was a relief. His only dilemma was that they seemed to be at the end of their dessert and soon another party would sit there. He hoped it would be nobody he knew.

His dinner was being served when the next customers were seated at the newly available table. Madison and Bradley didn't even notice him. They were too busy acting petulant and complaining about their table location. For the first few seconds, Jon didn't know what to do; he quietly sat observing and listening to their conversation for a few minutes. It didn't take long to discover that they were together, and judging from their talk, he would soon know a lot more. Typical of their superior attitude, they had their backs turned to him, oblivious to everything but themselves.

"How are the preparations coming along?" Bradley asked.

"Coming along well. But we each need to make potential guests lists to have an idea of the size of the location. It all depends on how big a wedding we want," she said.

"It wouldn't look good to have something too extreme barely a year after Jon's death," he said.

"Yeah, I guess you're right. Even in his death he seems to dictate how we live our lives and that pisses me off!"

Jon was shocked at the unexpected revelations and callousness of her words.

"The other solution is to wait longer until you can have what you always wanted," he suggested.

"Do you realize that if we wait until the proper mourning time we would be close to celebrating four years together? I don't want to wait that long, and I think we should come out and announce our engagement now," she demanded.

"Four years!" Jon thought. He quickly did the math and realized that she had been cheating on him with Bradley all the time they were together. It was as if the light was suddenly turned on. Looking back at the way they used to behave around each other, it all made sense to him now.

"How could I have been so blind?" he asked in disbelief.

Strangely, he didn't feel hurt—only complete disappointment.

"I died at the right time. Otherwise I might have ended up married to her." He shuddered at the thought and for a change, he was grateful for the turn of events.

He looked upward and, putting his hands together as if to pray, said, "Thank you God, for sparing me."

By then he'd heard enough, and for the rest of his meal he tuned them out, their conversation blending into meaningless background chatter. On his way out he turned to see them both. How different they looked now that he could see them as they really were!

The next day he got up early, and after getting into his disguise, he drove his rented car to the flower mart. It was a ritual of his mother to buy flowers every Wednesday, even though she had more than her share in her garden. "You can't have too many flowers," she would often say.

He parked half a block away and walked in, bursting with anticipation at the thought of seeing his parents. It was early morning and the crowds of shoppers had not started to fill the warehouse yet. Looking at the profusion of flowers, he couldn't help but think of his grandmother and her garden in paradise. How minute this whole warehouse seemed in comparison. He smiled in the knowledge that, even in another plane of existence, in some form, flowers were still a part of life

"William, look!" Sophia said, lifting up an orchid plant.

Her voice jolted Jon out of his thoughts. It had never sounded so sweet to his ears, and being there was even better than he hoped for. On this day, his father was with her. He watched from a short distance, trying hard to stop the bittersweet tears that just kept coming. He took a deep breath, exhaling slowly.

"They look wonderful," he said softly, tears running down his face, but he knew he had to get himself together before someone noticed a grown man crying for no apparent reason. He chuckled. Who cared! After all, seeing his parents happy despite their circumstances was the most incredible feeling he had in a long time. They were close enough he could almost touch them, yet the separation was never greater.

William and Sophia chose an array of freshly picked flowers ranging from orchids to tulips, roses, and daisies, complemented by bells of Ireland. Mom loved those. Lastly they picked two potted plants filled with gardenia blooms and buds. Sophia smelled them as she closed her eyes.

Jon wished he could tell her…. "Tell her what?" He asked himself and sighed. He couldn't even answer his own question. There were so many things…but none he could share with them.

From a safe distance, he watched them load their purchases into their car and followed them home until their car disappeared behind the mansion's gate. He then drove back to his hotel and absent mindedly watched television for a while. After having to see his parents from afar and overhearing the eye-opening conversation between Brad and Madison the previous night, he realized he no longer belonged there. However, it warmed his heart to see the ever-present love his parents had for each other and how it helped them weather losing him. For that he was very grateful. But now he had to come back to reality and plan his future away from them. He got online and booked his flight to Nome, Alaska with his final destination being Hooper Bay. He needed to be there to sign a lease on a house isolated and remote, his ideal setting. He then proceeded to reserve a round-trip ticket to Bern, Switzerland.

He reasoned that, as he grew old and his appearance changed, he would be more likely to blend in without being recognized. But aging was years away, and for now he would like to just hide for a while and Hooper Bay sounded like the perfect place. However, he promised himself he would see his parents again one last time before he left town as a treat to himself, an oasis in the middle of his lonely life. His flight to Alaska was scheduled for Friday morning at 8:05 a.m., giving him one more day in Alexandria Bay. He intended to see his mother and father once more before leaving, if possible. There was no better way to spend the day before flying out.

***

The next Wednesday morning, while Bradley was having his first cup of coffee, he signed on to his computer to access the latest of Serengeti's account transactions. He wanted to confirm that everything was going as planned and his request had been processed. When he went into the account, the message on the screen stunned him.

"Whaaat?" he screamed, dropping his coffee mug on the floor, breaking it and spilling the beverage all over.

"REQUEST AND ACCESS DENIED – EXPLANATION: LACK OF FUNDS" was the message staring back at him.

His blood ran cold and his heart was racing. He tried frantically to restart the application, thinking it had to be an error, but to his horror, the same message kept popping up. He tried to collect himself and handle the problem calmly. He called the bank customer service and tried to find out was happening with his account. Much to his chagrin, he was told that he needed to come in person to resolve the matter with the branch manager.

"Would you like me to set up an appointment for you?" the representative asked him.

"No," he said, grinding his teeth with exasperation. "I'm coming by right now."

"Very well, Mr. Goldwyn, thank you for calling. Goodbye," said the friendly female voice on the other end of the line as she hung up.

Bradley slammed the phone.

"Thank you for freaking calling!" he ranted. "Where's my money!?" he screamed as he paced back and forth in front of his living room window. His fists were clenched and his neck veins were clearly visible and bulging. He went into a fit of rage, screaming obscenities and threats against the bank. Unable to see straight or put his thoughts in order, he started smashing items on the floor and against the wall, starting with the telephone. But after getting over his ranting, he started to look back and noticed the signs he should have picked up at the office: the printed reports, the secretive meetings excluding him, Vince working long hours. It all made sense now!

"Of course! Vince! That son of a bitch! I knew there was a reason why I hated him the first day he came to work at Fitzgeralds," he angrily shouted trying unsuccessfully to compose himself.

All of a sudden, he started to panic at the thought of being investigated and having to face the possibility that he had lost the Serengeti wealth. If he suspected right, it was a matter of time before the authorities tied him to it. He still had his personal account with legitimately earned money for close to a half million dollars. But that was a very small amount for him, considering how hard he had worked to establish the Serengeti Corporation. Now his immediate priority was to hide the very little money that was left. He thought of Madison. Could he trust her with the money he had left? Quickly he decided he couldn't.

His suspicions soon gave way to fear when he signed on to the Fitzgerald International network but could not gain any access. His mind started to unravel and he began to panic at the thought that soon the law could be knocking on his door to arrest him and he wasn't going to stick around. He decided at that moment that his only choice was to leave the country and escape preferably to South America, where he had always wanted to go, and avoid his punishment. There, he could find somewhere to blend and fade away. A place where he couldn't be tracked down by government agents of any kind, and if it turned out to be exotic, even better. But hiding for the rest of his life would take a lot more than the half million dollars he had to his name, especially since he didn't want to give up the lifestyle he was used to. He needed to come up with a way to make a lot of money fast.

After pacing back and forth in his living room a few more times, he went to his notebook computer again, but this time he went on the Internet and searched the miscellaneous solicitor services website, an underworld group that would perform "just about any job for the right price."

Long before he found himself in his precarious situation, he came across the website and was intrigued by the apparent ease with which you could order dirty jobs for the right price. Driven by his greed, he came up with a plan to get his hands on a considerable amount of hard cash. Feeling backed into a corner, he decided he needed to come up with something immediately.

"Maybe I can't get my hands on the Serengeti money," he thought, "but I'm going to get it from Fitzgerald International one way or another."

He followed directions on the website, selecting his request from a series of menus with ambiguous but unmistakable meanings. Then he got an electronic message that directed him to make a partial payment if he was serious about doing business. Without hesitation, Bradley went into his personal bank account online and did as he was told. After that was done, he was instructed to call a number he was given to make detailed arrangements with the "agents" who would be doing the job.

After calling the number, he reiterated his request to the man on the other line who questioned him on the specifics. Bradley put it bluntly.

"I want you to take an old woman hostage and hold her until I tell you otherwise."

"Mm…abduction," he said.

"I don't care what you call it. Can you handle it?" he asked impatiently.

"What are the details on this woman?"

"She's old and you can easily find her alone," Bradley said.

"It's an easy job to do, if what you say is true. However, that's not always the case. If it was, we wouldn't be in this business. Things need to run smoothly and timing is essential. Besides that, we have time considerations. We can't hold her indefinitely; five days is the maximum."

"What happens if I need more time?"

"Then it would cost you a lot more," the voice on the other side said.

"How much more?"

"The longer you want to hold her, the more risk we run and the price rises accordingly. As far as specific numbers, that would have to be decided by my boss."

"Fine! I'll have to stay within my time schedule. You're costing me plenty already. But you better keep your end of the deal," Bradley warned.

"You don't have to worry about our end of things, we are professionals at what we do. Is there anything else you need our help with? Ransom set up, pick-ups, you know, the stuff that goes with this job."

"No, thanks, I'm pretty sure I can handle that!" he said rudely.

"Okay. I need a photograph of this woman, as well as any information you can give me on where I can find her. Maybe you know her address, where she works, or somewhere she goes regularly—things like that," the man on the line requested.

"I don't have a photograph of her, but I can give you all the information you need to find and recognize her."

"Whatever it takes to get it done."

Bradley then proceeded to give him the Fitzgerald address, a detailed physical description of Sophia, as well as everything else he was asked, including what car she drove and where she worked and shopped.

"I'm Jake, and Leo will be my partner. Tomorrow, as soon as we have her, we'll call your number and let it ring twice. That will be your clue that we have her and will be contacting you later for further instructions. Then you can start making your arrangements, because time starts ticking tomorrow, when we get her."

"Do you need my phone number?" Bradley asked.

"Only if it's different from the one you're calling from right now," Jake said.

"How soon can you do it?" Bradley asked.

"As early as tomorrow. But it depends on the opportunities we get," the voice on the other side answered.

"All right. I'll wait for your call with the news that you have Sophia."

"We'll have her when we call you; you can bet on it," Jake said and hung up, leaving Bradley deep in thought.

Just as he was hanging up the phone, the doorbell rang, giving him a jolt of reality. Anxiously, he peeked through the porthole of the door and was relieved to see that it was only Madison.

"Ah! Madison!" he thought to himself, realizing that he hadn't even thought about her when he put his plans into motion.

He opened the door, hurried her in, and quickly closed it.

"Hi, lover," she said, letting him kiss her cheek and sitting on a plush chair.

Bradley walked over to the bar and poured a drink for both of them, handing one to her. She smiled seductively as she looked at him and crossed her legs.

"I am glad you are here," he said, taking a deep breath. "Madison, we have to talk."

"That phrase never precedes anything good. What is it? Give it to me straight," she said impatiently, knowing intuitively that she would not like what he was about to say.

"The transaction for the transfer of funds to your business account was declined."

"What do you mean declined?"

"It means," he said, "that I've had a feeling for a while that there may be some kind of investigation going at work. All the assets I was going to deposit into your account are frozen and I can't get access to them."

"You had a feeling!" she screamed. "How long have you known about this investigation, Brad?" she asked, furious.

"I only suspected it two weeks ago," he said sheepishly. "That is why I was going to liquidate all the Fitzgerald International stock I owned as Serengeti Corporation, in case they were on to me."

"And how much was that?" she asked angrily.

He hesitated for a moment before answering, feeling unsure of how much he should confide in her. Sensing his apprehension to come clean, she exploded with rage.

"You son of a bitch! It was more than you told me, wasn't it?"

"What does it matter now?" he said, trying to downplay the whole thing.

"Well, it matters to me! Maybe you forgot the little detail that you got my name linked to your scam when you established that business corporation! Now when they trace everything to you, they will find my name too."

"It didn't matter to you when you thought you had six million dollars to spend as you pleased!" he yelled back.

"Yeah, that was before I knew that I could go to jail for it. You lied to me. Oh yes! It all makes sense now. You wanted to marry me to launder your money under my name. I should have known that it was out of character for you to be so generous or even want to get married, because you have no moral fiber!"

"Look who's talking! You only agreed to marry me because you have dollar signs in your eyes. You never cared where the money came from as long as you got what you wanted. You knew it was all coming from Fitzgerald International."

"That was before I realized how stupid you are! You're not even smart enough to pull this off. You're pathetic!" she said disgusted.

"Don't flatter yourself thinking anything coming from a money hungry whore like you could bother me. I was just buying you for six million dollars."

"Why else would I have married you?" she retorted.

Realizing they had no future together, he decided to tell her exactly how he really felt.

"Well, we both had a lot to gain from it, so don't flatter yourself thinking you're that important to me. It was just a business deal!" he yelled in her face.

"Don't even dream to get your ring back, and don't ever look for me. I hope you get run over by a truck. Goodbye!" she said walking out and slamming the door behind her.

"That went about as well as I expected," he said as he took a sip from his drink and stared into the distance out of a window.

At the moment he had more important things to worry about than Madison. There was a lot to be done in what he called "Operation Sophia." Knowing William as well as he did, he knew it would be easy to squeeze ten million dollars for his wife, because Sophia meant the world to him.

"It's going to be the easiest money I ever made. In fact, ten million might be a low figure. I'm sure he'd be willing to pay a lot more than that for Sophia," he thought. "Love is on my side," he smiled sarcastically as he planned the implementation of the rest of his plan.

He didn't know how much time he had, but he suspected it wasn't a lot. Unsure if he could access his personal accounts on-line, he drove to his bank just before closing time. To his elation, he was able to transfer part of his personal funds to an alias account he had opened prior to establishing Serengeti as a business entity. He took out a large quantity of cash for himself and put the balance in a money market account, under another one of his aliases. As soon as things settled down a little around him, he planned to take his money out and close the accounts, thus erasing any trails leading to him. He was ecstatic that his personal accounts hadn't been confiscated. That made him think that perhaps in his haste, he had jumped to conclusions and exaggerated the reason for the incompletion of his stock transaction; maybe it was just a mistake on the bank's part after all. Furthermore, he could not believe that he had overreacted to the point of not even thinking to access the Serengeti account for the latest activity, which would also give him a better idea of what was going on.

Feeling more confident, he drove home and turned on his computer as soon as he got in. Armed with a dose of wishful thinking, he signed on to access Serengeti's three corporate accounts. Much to his dismay, he was denied access to all three of them. He sat there frozen, staring blankly at the computer screen, convinced he'd been found out.

"What are my options?" he pondered. "If I'm arrested and tried, could a good lawyer get me off? If not, how much time of my life would I spend in prison?"

He thought about his family, especially his father, who would be devastated to see his good name smeared by the press—not to mention what it would do to him knowing that his son would do such a thing to his friend. The rest of his reality, however, also set in: He had set the wheels in motion for his despicable plan and couldn't go back now.

"Just as well," he told himself out loud, because he wasn't willing to go to prison when he saw an easy way to finance his unplanned early retirement.

"It's not like I'm killing anybody," he thought, shrugging off any sense of guilt or accountability.

Conscience, he believed, was a useless concept if you are in jail or broke. Besides, in the book of life according to Brad, the ends always justified the means and at the moment his objective was money, lots of it.

Convinced that he had very little time left as a free man if he stuck around, he went downstairs to the lobby of his apartment building, tipped the doorman lavishly, and instructed him to call ahead if anyone came looking for him. Having perceived Bradley as an affluent and security conscious tenant, the doorman agreed to do him the favor. Bradley went back up to his apartment and started packing. Knowing how much information his desktop computer could yield if left behind, he disconnected it and set it aside to get rid of before he left.

By now he realized the imminence of a law enforcement visit. Knowing that it wouldn't be long before the whole scheme was traced to him, the sooner he got out of there the better, he thought. He finished closing up two large, crammed suitcases and took the elevator downstairs to the underground parking to put the luggage pieces in the trunk of his car. On his second trip, he took his desktop computer and threw it down the garbage chute, hoping that it would be destroyed by the time it fell twelve stories down into the trash bin. He then went back upstairs to his apartment to wait. It had been a long day and now all he could do was wait for Jake's call the next day, hoping he would be on time, like he had promised.

Inside a federal building in another part of the city, Nelson O'Neill was nearing the end of his investigation. After receiving the call from the bank, the electronic tracer placed on all the Serengeti accounts yielded the web name as well as other pertinent information necessary to prove the identity of Oliver Goldwyn. He estimated that it would take a day to receive the report, after which he would issue and execute the order for arrest. However, before he did that, he felt he owed William Fitzgerald the courtesy of informing him of the facts and evidence that was uncovered.

"Tomorrow," O'Neill thought, "will be a real busy one." He finished his work for the day and headed home.

That night, before the fateful Thursday, Jon went to bed anticipating his trip the next day. Sophia slept well, blissfully unaware of the plot against her. Of course, Madison had to take sedatives to go sleep and Bradley could not rest, his thoughts vacillating between the fear of his arrest and the satisfaction of fading into the sunset with millions of dollars, courtesy of Fitzgerald.

The morning came and Jonathan was up and ready early to make the drive to his parents home before they left for work, hoping to catch a glimpse before leaving town. But in another part of city, Jake and Leo were also getting ready to drive to the Fitzgerald's and make visual contact with Sophia. The early spring day was clear with few hints of clouds in the horizon.

Not anticipating that he would be close enough to be recognized by anyone, Jon didn't bother to wear his disguise, opting instead to wear blue pants with a gray sweater underneath a navy blue jacket and plain gray sports hat that hid most of his hair and sunglasses. He arrived to his parents' address at 7:30 in the morning, followed closely by the Jake and Leo, who parked at a discreet distance.

At 7:45, William and Sophia left their gated home in their luxury automobile and started the familiar route to work, with Jon following them and Jake behind. Right away, the would-be abductors realized that William was driving the car, and with him in the picture, the plan wouldn't work. Still, they decided to follow them at a safe distance for a while.

Unaware of all the attention, William turned into the Fitzgerald building and disappeared into the underground garage, with Jon lagging behind. Knowing their designated parking spot, he stayed behind just far enough to see them get out of the car and walk into the elevator. Parked in a darkened corner, he watched their familiar faces from a safe distance as they made their way up to the office. After a few minutes, he left the parking structure and found a spot across the street, where he could observe the cars going in and out of the building.

Jake on the other hand, was out on the street weighing his options. The job that they were hired to do was a simple abduction of an older woman without involving anyone else. For now he decided to watch and follow her around to learn about her routine. Jon, on the other hand, was filling his time by playing electronic games on his cell phone and listening to music. For good measure he also had some magazines and a book to read. But they didn't have to wait as long as they expected, because two hours into their watch they observed Sophia driving out of the building alone. Both cars followed her at a safe distance, and ten minutes into the trip Jonathan realized that his mother was going to her favorite seafood market on the Alexandra Bay pier, where she would shop once a week for their daily fresh catches. Jon loved how his mother put her loving touch on everything she did for her family.

As they made their way on the scenic highway overlooking the ocean, he noticed that the car in front of him was the same as the one he had seen earlier on his way to Fitzgerald International.

"What a strange coincidence," he thought.

But as they entered a stretch of the highway that was sparsely inhabited, he noticed that the black sports utility was inching closer to his mother's car, despite the fact that traffic was light. Jon sped up alongside of them to catch a glimpse, but the darkened windows prevented him from seeing anything, so he stayed behind and observed them. Aware of the tailgater behind her, Sophia signaled and merged into the open lane to her right. Soon after, Jake pulled close behind her. At that point, Jon became sure that they were targeting his mother.

"But, why?" he wondered.

He didn't have time to speculate any further as he saw the black vehicle tap the rear of Sophia's car, enough for her to get startled, but not make her lose control. She pulled over to the shoulder at the end of the bridge and got out to check if there was any damage to her car. Jon stopped at a distance from them and just as he suspected, the utility vehicle stopped behind Sophia.

"All right," Jake said to Leo after parking a few feet behind Sophia, before getting out of the car. "You know the drill. It's simple enough. I'll try to make it appear as if I'm helping the lady. You pull up when I motion to you. I'll shove her inside and you peel tire, but be aware of the passing cars. Got it?"

"Don't worry about it. I got it and I'm ready," Leo answered, gripping the steering wheel so hard it made his knuckles white.

"Remember, there's no time to lose when I get her in the car."

"I know."

Jake got out and went over to Sophia, who was inspecting her car for scratches. The crooks were so engrossed in their plan that they didn't notice Jon's parked car.

"I'm sorry ma'am. Are you all right?" he asked her with faked concern. "I hope I didn't do too much damage."

"Just a little scratch on the bumper, young man. Not a big deal," Sophia said.

"I guess I wasn't paying as close attention as I should have. I'm sorry."

"You've got to always keep your eyes on the road," she said to him.

"I will try Ms…"

"Fitzgerald, Sophia Fitzgerald," she said.

"Well, Mrs. Fitzgerald, I would like to exchange insurance information with you to take care of the damage I caused to your car. I have my insurance card in my car," he said, motioning her to follow him.

"Like I said, it's not a big deal. I will take care of it myself, thank you," she said.

Jon was seeing it all from his car and noticed from the body language that his mother had refused the stranger's request. At that point Jake walked back to Sophia.

"Look lady! It's not a request, it's an order. You'll have to come with me right now," Jake said, forcefully grabbing and pulling her, motioning for Leo to come up.

Sophia pulled herself away from him and started screaming as Jake was trying to drag her into the waiting car. A driver passing by stopped when he saw the commotion, but Jake pointed a gun and ordered him to keep going. Intimidated and scared, the man sped away. In the meantime, Jonathan was now driving towards them, honking his horn and yelling.

"Leave her alone!" he screamed as he stuck his head out the window.

When Jake saw Jon getting out of his car and coming toward him, he threw Sophia to the ground and ran back to the waiting vehicle with Leo on the driver's seat.

"Let's go!" He motioned to Leo, opening the car door.

As he jumped in, Leo was trying to negotiate through the confusion and the traffic that was slowing to take a look at what was happening. Jake turned to him impatiently from the passenger side.

"I told you to gun it! What the hell are you waiting for!?" he yelled.

At the same time as Leo pressed the accelerator, Jake was trying to steer the car from the passenger side. Sophia had just gotten up and was rushing to get into her car. Her hand was reaching for the door when Jake pulled the steering wheel making the vehicle swerve, pinning her violently against her car. They quickly sped away just as Jon was running to her. She fell to the ground like a rag doll, bleeding from her nose and mouth, saturating her white silk blouse and the rest of her clothes.

Jonathan was stunned and in shock as he took off his sunglasses to get a better look at the fleeing car without license plates. They drove past the end of the bridge and made a U-turn into the median divider. They then merged into the traffic going the opposite direction they'd been traveling before, cutting off several vehicles, and finally rear-ending a small sports car. The impact caused it to flip and tumble over the rail, eventually coming to rest on a downhill slope under the bridge, facing the ocean. The sound of the screeching tires and twisting metal filled the air as the traffic started to back up at the accident site, while the men who caused it all sped away.

Jon turned around, knelt by his mother, and cradled her face in his arms. She weakly opened her eyes and looked into his, which were looking at her full of tears. Her face lit up and she smiled happily at him as she used the last bit of strength she had to lift her hand and touch his face.

"Son," she said, looking at him with a peaceful smile.

"How did you know?" he asked her, stunned.

"All I can see in you is my Jonathan. I love you, son," Sophia said.

She slowly closed her eyes as the life went out of her. He gently put her motionless body down as a line of blood started to trickle from her right ear and nose.

"Somebody please call an ambulance. Hurry!" he yelled at the top of his lungs, his voice breaking.

"Someone already did," he heard a bystander say.

He stood up and saw a small group of people across the

highway, at the second accident site. In the background he could hear the faint sound of the ambulance coming for his mother. The police would be arriving shortly, he realized, and he had to disappear fast.

By now the traffic in both directions was slowly coming to a stop and he had to go. Leaving his mother in such circumstances was the hardest thing he ever had to do, but he had no choice. Gathering strength, with his heart breaking, he walked away from her, blending with the rest of the crowd gathering around. Luckily for him, their attention was mainly directed at the second tragedy.

From the scene of the other accident, he saw the ambulance arrive and the paramedics treat his mother and take her away. It gave him hope to know that she would be getting much needed medical care soon, but deep inside he knew better.

The people's attention quickly shifted to the ambulance's arrival and Sophia's condition, temporarily ignoring the scene of the mangled sports car. Resting precariously on its side, it was a few feet away from the cliff. The lifeless body of the driver was clearly visible and his seatbelt still on. Part of the hard roof was crushed in, and a corner of it had been ripped open, allowing a view of the occupant. The sides also were crushed in, but there were no shattered windows, as the driver apparently was driving with them down.

There didn't seem to be any room to survive in such a tiny space, and the car looked like it might roll down anytime. Jon stared at it for a few minutes and then realized there was no time to waste. He needed to get back to his car, but before walking away, he looked back at the mangled car one more time. Just then, he noticed a bright light flash across the sky through the clouds. His heart started beating quickly as he noticed the lifeless body of the driver move.

"Oh my God! Is this possible?" he exclaimed out loud, shaking his head in disbelief.

His joy turned into bewilderment and then into curiosity when the lifeless driver of the crashed car incredibly started going through what he thought at first was a seizure. But soon the movements turned more into controlled actions. The man stretched his neck, moving it in a circular motion, and quickly glanced up through the torn roof, as if checking to see if he was being watched. He unbuckled himself and climbed out through the open passenger window. Without his weight to keep its balance, the car fell to the bottom of the hill. With only a few seconds to spare, Jon took one look at the crash survivor; his pants were torn on the sides and soiled with blood and dirt. The man quickly disappeared from sight into the area's vegetation as Jon was getting into his car.

The sounds of the tumbling car and the ambulance taking Sophia to the hospital faded and the attention was turned back to the sports car, which was now resting at the bottom of the ravine. Jonathan realized that he had overstayed his time when he heard the police and the second ambulance sirens blaring and getting closer. He shifted his car into reverse, driving back on the shoulder far enough to get off the highway's previous exit. Fortunately other people stuck in the traffic followed suit ahead and behind, helping him blend anonymously into the crowd.

When he found himself far enough from the accident, he stopped at an isolated spot on a residential street. Bewildered and crushed, he collapsed, his cries echoed by the seagulls' sounds coming through the car's partially opened sunroof.

After composing himself, he went back to his hotel and turned on the television news, hoping against the odds to see a good update about his mother. He knew that being well-known in the community, news of her accident would be reported.

***

Earlier in the morning that day agent O'Neill had placed a call to William. He recommended that Vince and Sophia be present during his conference call to them, but since Sophia had gone out to run her errands, it was just Vince and William behind closed doors.

"I'd like to inform you both that I am satisfied that our investigation relating to Serengeti Corporation is pretty much wrapped up. This courtesy call to you is the last step before enforcing the arrest warrant we've issued for Bradley Spellman."

"Who did you say? Our Bradley?!" William asked incredulously.

"I'm afraid so. Bradley Spellman, your controller," he confirmed.

William was speechless. His mind was having trouble trying to grasp the reality of what he was hearing.

"I'm sorry to be the bearer of bad news, but the evidence is indisputable. He is our man," O'Neill said.

"What evidence are you talking about?" William asked with the reality of the news still hard to believe.

"All kinds," O'Neill said. "First of all, he was the Oliver Goodwin behind Serengeti, from its conception as a separate identity, financed by your company. The forensic results conclude that Jonathan's signature was forged and Mr. Spellman wanted to transfer the funds of the stock sale to a new fashion business named Madison Incorporated. It's owned by someone named Madison Shelton, but with Spellman himself as a silent majority partner. Madison Incorporated is a new filing, recently created we believe, to divert and launder the money taken from your business. The accounting practices uncovered by your brother Vince make it clear that Bradley's intention was to systematically drain funds from your company. It could have gone undetected for many years, had it not been for you stumbling onto it."

William turned to Vince.

"What accounting practices? Oh never mind, you'll tell me after." He turned to the agent on the phone. "So what else is there for us to do?" he asked.

"Nothing for now. We'll be getting in touch with you soon to finalize the list of charges to be filed before the trial. I will be notifying you if there's anything we need from you."

"We're here to help," Vince said.

"I'm just pleased that this was uncovered before too much damage was done to your company; I'm glad for you and your family. I will be in touch with you."

"You know where to find us," William said.

"Thank you. Goodbye," Agent O'Neill said.

William stared at the speaker phone, shocked by what he'd just heard and then looked at Vince with bewilderment. For his part, Vince felt it was about time to tell his brother everything he knew.

"I found out while researching Serengeti that the mortgage accounts instructed to send their payments directly to them were set up that way by Bradley. He did it using passwords given to employees no longer with the company. Once the conversion of the accounts was complete, the same users deleted the accounts out of our central database. At the end of each quarter, the Fitzgerald mortgage numbers were naturally short. But Bradley fixed the account by making monthly adjustments to miscellaneous accounts he had set up as part of the scheme. That's how he balanced the reports. He could do it because you trusted him implicitly. I am sorry, but that's the way it is," Vince told William.

"No. I am the one who's sorry. I didn't even consider the idea when you suggested he could be a suspect. How could I entertain the thought? Brad grew up with Jon and was one of his best friends, or so we thought," William said.

"Who can blame you for not believing?" Vince said. "It's not the kind of behavior you expect from your friends, especially when you have known him all his life. He was Jonathan's childhood friend, for Pete's sake."

"Yeah," William said with a look of shock. "Well, it's just you and us now."

"For the time being. But it's better that than having a traitor in our midst," Vince said.

"Yeah, things could be a lot worse," William said.

There was a reflective moment that was interrupted by William's phone.

"Yes?" he said as he picked it up. He listened silently for a few seconds.

"What!?" he screamed.

Vince noticed William's face go white.

"It can't be! Are you sure?" he asked. He listened briefly and said, "I'm on my way."

He turned to Vince with a horrified look, his hands shaking. Vince had a feeling of something terrible had happened.

"Sophia," he said and started to walk out of his office toward the elevator in a zombie-like state.

Vince grabbed his keys and followed. He put his arms around his older brother and asked, "What about Sophia?"

"She was hit by a car and rushed to Brotman Hospital," he said in a state of shock.

"Where did this happen?" Vince asked.

"I don't know! I don't know anything except that I want Sophia to be alright," he said as they got in the elevator.

It didn't take long to get to the hospital, but to them it was forever. Upon arriving to the emergency area, they walked up to reception desk and anxiously asked about Sophia's condition. They were told that the doctor who had attended to her had been informed of their arrival and would be with them shortly. Vince had never seen his brother so shaken up and it was heartbreaking.

"She's everything to me, Vince. Without her, my life means nothing," William said, his voice breaking.

"I know, brother, but let's not lose hope. We still don't know how serious it is," Vince said, trying to comfort him.

"Oh, it's serious. I could hear it in the voice of the medic that called."

"Oh, William," Vince said, putting his arms around his brother, trying to protect him from the hard reality that was to come.

A few minutes later, Doctor Richard Ross approached them.

"Mr. Fitzgerald?" he asked, looking at them both.

"I am William Fitzgerald, Sophia's husband, and this is my brother Vince."

The doctor shook their hands and put a hand on William's shoulder.

"I'm sorry," he said. "We did everything possible but couldn't save her. By the time she got here there wasn't a lot we could do."

William fell on his knees as if the weight of the tragedy was too much for him to bear.

"No, God! Not my Sophia!" he wept, looking up to the heavens. "You know I can't live without her. It's not possible. Not my wife. Why my wife? Doctor, this can't be true. No, it's not true!" he cried out, breaking down in grief-stricken sobs.

Vince and the doctor picked him up by his arms and led him to a chair. William was inconsolable and completely lost in his pain.

"If it's any consolation, she didn't suffer. She didn't have time," the doctor said.

"The only thing that would make me feel better is to have my wife back," William said in between sobs. "This can't be happening. I want to be with Sophia," he said, his voice sounding suddenly calm. "Yes, to be with my Sophia. Come on, Vince. Let's go home," he said, walking out the door.

"William, don't you want to see Sophia before you leave?" Vince asked, following behind.

"We're going to see her now. She's at home, let's go."

"But William..."

William was not listening. Vince didn't know what to do, so he just went along, realizing his brother was in state of shock. Sooner or later reality would set in and his pain would once again be nearly impossible to bear.

"Hurry up Vince. I want to give my wife a hug and wake up from this horrible nightmare," William said adjusting his seatbelt as he sat on the passenger seat.

Vince made his way out of the hospital parking structure and headed towards his brother's house.

"William, I know that it is the worst nightmare, but I'm afraid that it's true, it's real," Vince said.

"I can't accept that she's gone any more than I can accept life without her."

"Nothing I say will make things better. Just know that I love you and I'm here for you."

"You're a good brother, Vince."

"I learned it from my big brother."

"Ah! As always, you're too modest," William said, turning his head away to look out the window.

As they got closer to the house Vince braced himself for what his brother was going to do when reality hit him.

"William," he said gently, "as much as it hurts to say it, you know that Sophia won't be home when we get there, right?"

William didn't answer and a few minutes later they were driving thru the gate of the estate.

"We're here," Vince said as they came to a stop on the circular driveway by the front door.

He looked over at William, who was clutching his chest and having trouble catching his breath. Immediately, Vince turned around and raced back to the hospital.

"Hold on William! I'm getting you to the hospital as soon as I can, but you got to stay with me brother, please!" Vince pleaded as he was speeding through the street. "Don't leave me here." By now William was unconscious and all Vince could do was his best getting him to the hospital fast.

When they arrived to the emergency room William was immediately rushed in and taken by a team of three doctors including Richard Ross, who was still on duty. The emergency personnel connected him to a heart monitor, along with an apparatus to measure brain activity. In the controlled chaos that ensued, they all worked frantically trying to asses William's condition to save his life.

"His heart stopped and there is no pulse," said one of the physicians, looking into William's eyes, which had rolled back. The doctor pressed on his chest to stimulate his heart, but William remained unresponsive.

"His brother said he stopped breathing about ten minutes ago," Doctor Ross said, exposing his patient's bare chest. "Nurse, the defibrillator," he called out.

The nurse handed the device and the doctor administered the electric shock to William's chest, trying to prompt his heart to start beating. William's body was jerked back by the electric shock but didn't react any further. After the second try, there was a faint heartbeat on the monitor but it faded soon after. The doctor tried a third time and was able to get the heartbeat back for only a few seconds once again.

"This man needs surgery immediately. Even then, things don't look good. Get him prepped immediately and I'll speak to his brother," Doctor Ross said and went out to the waiting room to speak to Vince.

As the doctor was walking towards the door, William went into convulsions briefly then fell limp as the lines on the monitors went flat. Dr. Ross ran out the door.

"Mr. Fitzgerald, your brother needs surgery right now," he said to Vince. "We're conducting some tests and I think he just had a stroke. I don't know how long his brain has been deprived of oxygen by the lack of blood flow to the area. His heart is not responding and we need your approval to do surgery," Doctor Ross said hurriedly.

"What's the prognosis?" Vince asked.

"Not too good, I'm afraid. At this time we're not even sure we can bring him back enough to operate. He's been unconscious for some time from what you tell us."

"I tried to get him here as soon as I could," Vince said.

At that time, the nurse assisting the doctors came out.

"Doctor Ross, we need you," she said motioning him over. "I think we lost him," she whispered as they hurried back to William, who was being wheeled into surgery.

"Mister Fitzgerald, I'll come out to update you as soon as I can. The nurse will bring the papers for you to sign. The waiting room is located in the second floor. I'll see you there," the doctor said disappearing behind the emergency room door.

Vince hurried to the elevator. A nurse at the station directed him to the waiting room nearby, where he nervously paced the floor.

When Doctor Ross came back to William, the other two physicians were laboring to get his heart going again, administering medication prompting it to function.

"There's no time to waste!" shouted one of the doctors, as they sprinted towards the surgery room pushing the gurney.

But all their heroic efforts were to no avail. William's heart didn't want to live and this statement was evident by the silence of the equipment tracking his condition. The massive heart attack had taken a toll and his body gave up on life. As the rest of the team worked frantically to revive him again, the doctor came back to Vince looking distressed.

"I'm afraid there isn't much more we can do. Your brother suffered a massive heart attack and doesn't seem to have the will to fight back," he said to Vince. "We're trying to get his heart beating again but we've done that twice already. Each time it takes longer and becomes more difficult to do. If he has a living will, now is the time to consider what decision you want to make next."

"My brother wouldn't want to be a vegetable, if that's what you mean," Vince said.

Before the doctor could answer Vince, one of his colleagues came and stood outside the door, still wearing his surgery cap and a look that needed no explanation.

"I'm sorry. We did all we could," he told Vince.

Vince sat down and held his head in his hands. He couldn't believe that he had just lost his brother and Sophia almost at the same time. He knew that William would not want to live without his wife, but knowing that did little to ease his pain.

"It's the way my brother would have wanted it, I am sure of it," he said to the doctor, his voice cracking with tears. "He is where he wants to be: with his wife and son."

And indeed, after passing away, his brother and Sophia were together in paradise only to find out that Jon was physically alive again as Max. Still, their souls were happy knowing that Jon knew with certainty that they were more alive now than ever. When Sophia's spirit was leaving her body after the accident, she felt

Jonathan's essence in Max's body. But her spirit only saw Jon's presence as he sobbed in sorrow after seeing her take her last breath. Yet she felt no grief, only a sense of deep love for her son.

When William arrived at the gates of paradise, Sophia greeted him.

"What took you so long?" she kidded him.

As they began to look around, they were in awe by the wonder of what they saw. It was beyond anything they could have ever imagined. They could see into each other's souls, overflowing with love for each other and everything around them. It was just the way they used to dream about it—that in heaven their souls would be as one, intertwined as they never could as physical beings. They felt a yearning to know more about the new world which they had waited for all their lives.

"Hello! Welcome. I am Apollo, your gatekeeper, and I will help you with your transition to paradise."

"We're elated to finally be here," Sophia and William communicated simultaneously.

Apollo smiled, which gave his countenance a radiant look.

"Welcome home, then," he said with joy as he proceeded to give them the tour of paradise and give them answers to all they wished to know.

Soon their spirits were experiencing heaven in the company of friends and loved ones who'd died before them. They experienced joy without measure and felt like children in a toy store with spiritual delights beyond imagination. They were home at last and they knew Jon would be soon, because to them time was no longer relevant.

In contrast, Jon's state of mind back in his hotel room couldn't be more opposite. Beside himself with grief, he paced back and forth countless times, flipping through the local television news channels trying to catch anything about his mother's condition. Although deep inside he knew the worst had happened, denial was a good way to buy himself some time. He thought about his dad and felt like he was being punched in his stomach. He knew that living without his mother would be no life for him, and that made him even more disheartened.

The voice of the reporter on television brought him back from his contemplative state. She was reporting on a news conference given by the Brotman Hospital spokesperson.

"We interrupt this program to bring you this report just in," said the anchorwoman, as they image cut immediately to the scene in front of the hospital.

"This is Walter Romero, reporting from the front steps of Brotman Hospital, where doctors just announced the tragic death of a couple much beloved in our community. Sophia and William Fitzgerald passed away tragically today, within an hour of each other at the same hospital. The double tragedy started when Mrs. Fitzgerald was hit by a vehicle fleeing the scene after what onlookers described as a kidnapping gone wrong. Apparently, William Fitzgerald was so distraught with grief after hearing the news of his wife's passing that he died shortly after of a massive heart attack.

"This comes as another terrible blow to the family, who was still recovering from the death of Jonathan Fitzgerald in a tragic plane crash six months ago," the anchorwoman said to the reporter on the scene.

"Yes, Christine," Walter said. "Perhaps you remember the family being in the news more than six months ago when the Fitzgeralds lost their only son Jonathan and his best friend Maxwell Adams, whose body has yet to be recovered. It was a major blow to the couple and their company, since the two young men held high positions at Fitzgerald International. It was their deaths that prompted Mr. Fitzgerald to convince his younger brother Vincent to join him at the helm of the company."

"Now the question is, can Vincent Fitzgerald handle the weight of the responsibility forced on him?" the anchorwoman asked the reporter.

"His brother gave the position of second in command only to him, which demonstrates his confidence in Vince's abilities.

However, it remains to be seen what kind of leadership he will bring to the company. Sources close to the situation share William Fitzgerald's confidence and think Vince will run the company much the way his brother did because of their similar personalities, with Vince being the more reserved of the two."

"Our deepest sympathies go to the Fitzgerald family. They will be deeply missed…" he heard the anchorwoman say.

As the voices faded in the background, he closed his eyes.

"I love you, Mom and Dad," he said, weeping. "How I wish I could be there with you, but I know that you are here with me, and I thank God for that."

His grief and sorrow had been transformed into deep loneliness and regret. He couldn't help feeling sorry for himself and wondered if his coming back to life had an effect on the latest events in any way.

"Someday I'll know," he said to himself confidently.

He thought about the big responsibility falling on his uncle and felt helpless at first, but then decided he would find a way to somehow help him.

"In this age of technology there has to be a way to do it all electronically without ever meeting face to face and I will find it. Mom and Dad would like that," he said with determination.

His eyes absentmindedly fixed on the images running on the television screen showing the site of his mother's accident, followed by footage of the mangled silver sports car still resting at the bottom of the cliff. The voice of the reporter narrating in the background caught his attention.

"And in an apparently related incident, the utility vehicle fleeing the scene of the Fitzgerald accident hit this late-model sports car. The impact sent it and its driver careening over the guardrail and onto the hill below. After teetering for a while on the slope, the vehicle's weight gave way and it plunged to the bottom of the cliff under the bridge. But in a strange twist, the authorities have not been able to locate the driver or his body, which witnesses saw inside the car following the crash. Even after an extensive search around the site, the authorities have not turned up with the missing driver."

Jonathan's thoughts turned to the man climbing out of the sports car just before it rolled down the hill. He seemed to be walking quite well for a guy who had survived a horrible crash and just minutes earlier seemed lifeless. Something about the whole thing didn't add up in his mind.

"Why would he run away from the accident? Did he steal the car? Surely, if that was the case, they would have said so in the news." Jon had so many questions. "Could the driver have lost his memory?" he wondered, as the reporter's voice continued in the background and the man's photograph was now displayed.

"This latest update just in. According to motor vehicle records, the car's registered owner is twenty-seven-year-old Sean Michael Stevens, an architect working for a national development firm. Anyone with information regarding these two accidents is encouraged to call the authorities at the telephone number on the screen."

The face staring from the screen looked like the man Jon had seen leaving the scene of the crash, but how could he tell anybody about what he saw? Apollo's warnings played in his mind. He couldn't tell anyone, but he could go back and see if what he saw really happened. Considering his state of mind after having to walk away from his dying mother, he was beginning to doubt what he had seen but still felt the need to go back and check. Getting distracted from the passing of his parents was a welcome change, however brief. It was just a shame that it should take another tragedy to distract him from his own heartache, if only for a little while.

Bradley was looking at the news announcements from his apartment, too, and immediately called Jake to demand an explanation for what had happened.

"It didn't go as planned," he said. "For being an old lady, your friend put up quite a fight and attracted too much attention."

"Why the hell did you run her over?" Bradley asked, screaming.

"That was an accident. Once in a while, these things don't go as planned," Jake said calmly.

"I don't care about her accident! What I want to know is whether anybody saw you!" Bradley said, exasperated.

"Not enough to recognize me. Oh wait. There was this one guy who rushed over to her rescue towards the end. I was getting in the car by then, but I'm not sure how much he saw."

"I thought that you guys were professionals. How could a simple kidnapping of an old lady turn into this?" he yelled at Jake.

"Look, man, you better cut that blaming shit. Like I said, these things happen! Besides, you came to us, not the other way around. And if we go down, we won't be doing it alone," Jake warned him.

"All right, I am sorry, man," he said quickly calming down. "It's just that this whole thing is out of control and I'm in shit up to my neck already."

"We don't intend to get caught, but there's strength in numbers. It's in our best interest to work together now," Jake said.

"Okay. There's no turning back now. Did you take a good look at the guy that you think saw you?" Bradley asked.

"Look, we've stayed on the phone way too long. We need to meet to close this thing out," Jake said.

"You're right." Bradley said. "Where?"

"Meet me at the Marie Kerr Park parking lot in the aquatic complex at two p.m. tomorrow."

"Fine. How will I recognize you?"

"I'm driving an old Subaru, blue station wagon," Jake said.

"I'm driving a BMW, red convertible," Bradley said.

"See you then," Jake said and hung up.

***

It was early afternoon the next day and Bradley sensed his time was running out. He gathered his notebook computer, packed it in its case and took a quick look around his apartment for the last time. The state of the dwelling didn't at all reflect the turmoil of his life because it looked orderly like any other day. Beyond the glass wall in the living room, he saw a beautiful afternoon in the making, with clear skies and pleasant temperatures.

He loved his place and hated leaving it. From his vantage point, he had a view of the main entrance to the high rise complex. For a moment, he stood and looked out for any police cars coming in but quickly realized that those looking for him would probably drive unmarked cars. Being on top, looking down on the world was his comfort zone. But knowing it was just a matter of time before he would have to give it up made it a little easier to walk out. Just as he shut the door behind, he heard his phone ring and it sent shivers up his spine, knowing it was the door man letting him know they were looking for him. When he was stepping off the elevator and walking to his car, Nelson O'Neill was getting into the lobby elevator on his way to Bradley's apartment. By the time he was knocking on the door, Bradley was going out of the parking garage and on his way to meet with Jake.

Just as Nelson O'Neill's expected it, there was no answer after knocking on Bradley's door. By now, he had to know that his time was up, the agent believed. After the seizure of his business accounts, and confirmation of Oliver Goldwyn's identity, the search for his personal accounts was initiated. All that was left to tie the whole case together was Bradley's arrest and the gathering of a few evidence items. He decided to seal the apartment off and come back later with a warrant to conduct a thorough search, feeling certain that Bradley was gone for good. In the meantime, he would release a photograph and press report about the case, hoping it would give him good leads.

For his part, Bradley arrived at the park's aquatic complex, where an old blue Subaru station wagon was parked with the driver in it. The two men got out of their cars and casually strolled toward a bench. They sat without looking at each other, staring straight ahead and started talking.

"Isn't that a strange choice for a car?" Bradley asked sardonically.

"Maybe," Jake answered. "It isn't the kind of car cops expect me to be driving, which is more than I can say for you. With your flashy cherry red wheels, you can be spotted miles away."

"Yeah, I know. I need to be less conspicuous. I'm going to get a rental as soon as I leave here. I didn't do it before coming because I didn't have time."

"Okay. We're here to discuss the job, and as far as our end goes, the deal is done, obviously. I'm sorry that it was one of those rare occasions that things didn't work out. Now we just need to make sure there are no witnesses, and it's to our advantage that we find out if there are any, because like it or not, we're in this together now."

"Are you saying that you think someone took a good look at you? Is it the guy that came to Sophia's aid?" Brad asked.

"I was wearing a baseball cap, so I don't know for sure. But I can tell you that he looked at me, I just don't know how well. It was just a fraction of a second," Jake responded.

"What now?" Brad asked, resigned to follow Jake's advice.

"We lay low, wear disguises when we venture out for a while, until the whole thing dies down."

"What did you do with the car? I assume you didn't use your wagon to pull off the job." Bradley said.

"Of course not! I wouldn't use Old Faithful for that," Jake said referring to his station wagon. "That's what SUVs are for. By tonight the one we used for the job will just be scrap metal in a junkyard. Now we just wait for things to cool down, like I said. That's all."

"Time is something I don't have," Bradley said. "I need to get out of the country fast."

"I don't know what to tell you, but if you are going to skip town be aware, if we need to find you, we can track you down anywhere. You can't hide from us," Jake warned him.

"I'm not trying to. I am running from the Feds, who by now must have me on their wanted list."

"What the hell did you do?" Jake asked him.

"Helped myself to some funds from the company I worked for."

"Where's the money?" Jake wanted to know.

"They found it before I could hide it away. They seized my accounts," Bradley said.

"I guess you didn't do a very good job of hiding it," Jake said chuckling.

"Yeah, well, I waited too long to cash out. It was a big mistake, but I can't change that now."

"How did they find you out?"

"I'm not sure. But since all my assets were frozen, I don't have to be a genius to know that they're on to me."

"If they did that, they must be looking for you by now."

"Exactly! That's why I got to split as soon as I can."

"I've got to talk to my boss, then," Jake said. "Before I let you go I need to ask him if that would be a problem with us."

"When will you speak to him?" Bradley asked.

"Later, when I'm done here."

"How am I going to know?" he again asked.

"You'll be with me until then, just to make sure."

"But I have to go to a car rental from here. I can't be driving around in that," Brad said, pointing to his car.

"I'll leave first and wait for you down the street. From there I'll follow you to get your rental car, and then we'll go by my place and call my boss."

"Sounds like a plan," Bradley said as Jake got up and started walking to his car.

Not long after, Bradley followed and they drove to a quiet street around the corner from the car rental office. He got out of his car and walked the rest of the way in an effort to avoid attention, while Jake followed from a distance.

After finishing with his rental transaction, which he put under one of his alias credit accounts, he went back to his car and transferred his luggage and other items to the rental car.

"I got to figure out what to do about this," Bradley said to Jake, referring to his car. "I can't leave it here."

"We'll come back and pick it up later, when it's dark," Jake said as he started the ignition in his station wagon. "Let's go."

Brad followed him to a secluded tree-lined street and a cozy looking two-story bungalow home. Jake opened his garage door and as he pulled into the three-car garage he motioned for Bradley to park in the spot next to him. They closed the door and went inside.

"Sit down," Jake told Brad, pointing to a chair.

"I'm too hyped-up to sit."

"Suit yourself," Jake said as he picked up the phone and dialed a number.

Bradley looked around, killing time while Jake talked on the phone.

"It's me. Yeah, he's here. What do you want me to do?"

Jake listened for a moment.

"Okay. What do you want to do about him? He says the Feds are looking for him."

There was a pause as Jake listened and stared at Bradley.

"I don't know. Can you find that out?" he asked to the other voice on the phone.

He listened carefully.

"Okay," he said and hung up.

"My boss says there is no problem, we don't need you to bring attention to us, but he needs some collateral in the event that this business of ours becomes more complicated." Jake said.

"Will you take my car? It's only a year old paid for and, worth a lot," Bradley said.

"Yeah, we'll take it."

"Slightly off the subject, I was wondering, could you help or fix me up with someone for a passport?"

"Yeah, I know somebody," Jake said.

"Great! Let's get the ball rolling on that," Bradley said.

"We can get that going after the boss clears you. He wants some time to verify that your story about the Feds is true. It's not contingent upon you leaving; it's just that he doesn't like people lying to him, even if it's a small matter."

"That's cool. How long will it take?" he asked confidently.

"A day or so," Jake answered.

"In the meantime?" Brad asked.

"In the meantime you find a hotel room. When my boss calls

me back I'll let you know and then we'll arrange the passport deal. Right now I am going to have a beer, and after that I'll follow you to your hotel."

"I'm not going to run away," Bradley assured him.

"I know. This is for my protection. I'd rather call you than the other way around."

"I see. This way you know where I am."

"You got it!" Jake said.

He went into the kitchen and came back with two beers, offering one to Bradley. He settled into his favorite chair and turned the television on.

"Do you mind if I use your bathroom?" Brad asked.

"It's down the hall, second door on the right," Jake said as he channel surfed, looking for the news. Suddenly he stopped.

"Hey, dude!" he called to Bradley. "Come quick. Check this out."

Brad came back just in time to catch most of the news segment relating to him.

"And in a bizarre turn of events, still relating to the Fitzgeralds, authorities are now looking for Bradley Spellman as a main suspect of embezzling funds from Fitzgerald International. He held high profile position with the company and was supposed to be a childhood friend of Jonathan Fitzgerald, son of the late William Fitzgerald." The anchorman went on as Brad's picture flashed on the screen, followed by one of Jon and Max.

"You may recall," the anchorman continued, "that just six months ago Jonathan Fitzgerald was tragically killed in a plane crash with his best friend Maxwell Adams. Mr. Adams's body has yet to be recovered from the accident site. Sources say the embezzlement investigation is ongoing and authorities expect to be making arrests soon. "

Jake jumped up from his chair excitedly pointing to the screen, unable to get the words out of his mouth fast enough.

"That's the dude! That's the guy that came to the rescue of the old lady!" he finally exclaimed.

"Are you sure?" Bradley asked incredulously.

"Yeah, man. He's wearing a baseball hat, but I'm sure that's the face," Jake insisted.

"I'll be a son of a bitch!" Bradley exclaimed, sitting down on the couch. "That's Maxwell Adams, and he's supposed to be dead! I don't get it."

"If you know who he is, you can help us find him and take care of the only lose end—him." Jake said.

"You saw the report. He's supposed to be dead. Are you absolutely sure of what you're saying?"

"I'm sure. That's him. It's either him or his identical twin," Jake assured him.

"I know where he used to live, if he was really Max, but since his death his family sold the house. But I know where his parents live," he said, feeling proud of himself.

"That might help. It's a start," Jake said.

"Wait a minute!" Bradley exclaimed. "If he is the same guy I think he is, he is bound to show up for the funeral services of the Fitzgeralds. We just need to find out where that's taking place, and if he is indeed Max, he'll show up for that."

"Great idea. We'll need to find out where this funeral will be so we can join him," Jake said.

"That's easy. I'm pretty sure it will be at the Lighthouse Memorial Park, where their son was buried. Now all we need is the day and time, which I'm sure we can easily find in the paper obituaries."

"Yes! Lucky for us they were upstanding members of the community. That way the press will keep us informed," Jake said.

"Yeah," Brad said, toasting with the last of his beer in celebration. "And now it's time for me to go," he said putting the empty can on the coffee table.

"You can't go out like that," Jake said as he disappeared in a rear room and came back with a box full of disguise items. "Pick one if you don't want to be a sitting duck. People in motels look at news too, you know."

Bradley did as Jake told him and a little later they left the residence and headed out to find his motel room for the night.

Back at his hotel, Jon waited until early in the evening before donning his disguise and started driving in the direction of the Alexandria Bay pier. A few minutes into the drive, he heard again on the radio, the same news television stations were broadcasting about Bradley earlier. He shook his head in total disbelief and disappointment.

"How could he have fooled us all?"

Twenty minutes later, he passed the bridge going in the direction the silver sports car was traveling. The traffic was flowing freely and the sun was setting over the ocean not far from the accident, yielding to the early evening shadows. The large and small tire marks of the vehicles, still fresh from the afternoon crash, pointed at the respective trajectory of the vehicles. The large marks veered across the lanes of the highway and straightened up, while the small car's tracks went straight into and over the guard rail. Jon briefly glanced at the area where he thought he saw the driver walk away from the wreck and wondered where he might have gone. Instinctively, he got off at the following exit while glancing at the site of his mother's crash on the other side in the rearview mirror.

After driving around aimlessly for some time, he took a road heading toward the ocean. He needed to get his thoughts sorted out and could think of nothing better than taking a walk along the beach. Before getting out of his car, he took his shoes and socks off and walked barefooted to the water. The sounds of the waves crashing on the shore gave him a feeling of peace, and as he remembered his grandfather in paradise, he felt his presence walking besides him. He smiled gratefully.

"It's good to feel you near, Grandpa," he softly said with a smile. "I know Mom and Dad are here too. I love you guys. I really messed things up, didn't I? A great deal of my last life was as not it seemed. Well, to be fair it was only Brad and Madison," he corrected himself.

By this time in the early evening, the beach was nearly deserted, with little more than a handful of people around and the lifeguards long gone. Two couples were strolling towards their parked cars hand in hand and a young woman was walking ahead of him, in a trance of blissful solitude. A few yards from Jon was a young man who was sitting off to the side, staring into the stars' reflection on the ocean. Jon rolled up his pants and walked towards the water. He stood with his hands in his pockets waiting for the next wave to crash against the wet sand. Feeling the cool touch of the water on his feet, his thoughts turned to Bradley.

"Wasn't it enough that he had a relationship with Madison during the time I was with her, and even proposed?" he asked, bewildered. "But why?"

He couldn't even begin to make sense of the whole thing. To say he was stunned would have been an understatement. A feeling of isolation and regret came over him. He had come back to physical existence just to witness his mortal world collapse around him. The very reasons why he had come back were gone. From the betrayal of Bradley and Madison to his parents passing on, for the first time he rued the choice he had made.

"This isn't much of a life. The people that meant the most to me are gone now," he thought to himself as his mind wandered to his grandmother and her garden in paradise. He sighed and smiled as he imagined his grandparents together with his parents. How he wished he could be with them!

"As you no doubt will," said Apollo's familiar voice.

"Oh, boy! Am I glad to see you," Jon said with elation.

"I thought you might be. And yes, in answer to your question, your parents are in paradise. No doubt you already knew that."

"Yes, and I can't wait to see them again," he said. "I'm sorry for messing things up. Is it my fault that any of this happened?"

"You cannot change what is predestined. You can only influence circumstances in which it is fulfilled," Apollo said.

"I take it that I am taking the long way to get there."

"That's well put. But you can't hide from fate, you know," Apollo said.

"Apollo, did you know about Brad and Madison all along?"

"Of course."

"Now what?" Jonathan asked.

"These events change nothing for you. You still must live your life, and abide by the rules you agreed to when you chose to come back."

Jon hung his head and dropped his shoulders in poignant resignation.

"I don't want my parents to miss me because of a stupid thing I did," he said contritely.

"You relate your parents' state of existence as physical like your own. Remember, time is irrelevant where they are. They're not tied to it. For them it doesn't exist and neither does grief or pain."

"Yes, I know, don't remind me," he said, clearly regretting the choice he made.

"Very well, then. I just dropped by because I thought you might need a bit of encouragement. Tomorrow at the funeral you must be mindful of people that don't seem to belong there."

"I will," Jon said as he saw Apollo disappear into thin air.

"Thank you," he whispered.

"You can thank me later," he heard him say as his voice faded into silence.

A calm feeling came over him as he started walking along the shore. Apollo seemed to have that effect, and for that he was thankful.

By now he was coming up to the young man who was sitting a few yards from the water staring ahead, rigid as a statue. Jon walked up to him giving a friendly wave. When he got close enough to make out the man's facial features, he seemed vaguely familiar.

"Do I know you?" Jon asked, with an inquisitive look.

"I don't think so," the young man answered.

"I'm sorry. You really look familiar, that's all," Jon said.

"Are you from around here?" the stranger asked.

"Sort of. I'm familiar with the area. How about you?"

"I've never been here before," he blurted out.

"It's a beautiful city. You should check it out."

"I wish it was that easy," he said under his breath.

By now Jon's eyes had gotten used to the evening shadows and could see that the khaki shorts were really slacks torn out at the knees. Traces of blood and caked dirt were barely visible in the increasing darkness, with only the faint moonlight coming through the evening haze. His unbuttoned, light-blue ripped shirt softly waved in the sea air, but strangely there was not a scratch on him that would attest to his obviously recent ordeal.

"Are you staying anywhere?" Jon asked, trying to keep the conversation going.

"No," he said running his fingers through his hair. "No, I haven't got around to doing that."

Jon decided to speak frankly with him.

"You look to me like the driver of the sports car in the crash earlier today, not far from here. I'd like to help you, that is, if you need it. My name is Max. You can trust me, really," he said, as he extended his hand offering a handshake.

The young man accepted the gesture and stood up. He needed somebody's help and decided to accept Jon's offer.

"Well Max, to be truthful, I don't even understand what happened to me after my car plunged down the hill. I don't even have a memory of who I am."

"Your picture was all over the news. They're looking for you or your body because they don't think you could have survived the fall. You have them all puzzled," Jon said.

"What's my name?" he asked.

"I think it's Sean something. Why don't you check your driver's license?"

"Then call me Sean," the stranger said.

"Okay, Sean. What happened to you after the crash?" Jon asked point blank.

Sensing Sean's apprehension and confusion he sought to help him.

"I saw you as you climbed out of the car. You looked around as if looking for witnesses before you left. Why did you run away?"

"I'm sorry, but I can't tell you," he said.

"Alright. Would you at least like a ride to a hotel? You have to sleep somewhere, and I hope you're not thinking of staying here all night." Jon said, deciding not to press him further.

"I have to see how much cash I have in my wallet," Sean said.

"You must have credit cards," Jon asserted.

"I can't use credit cards," Sean said.

"Why not?" Jon asked.

"You ask too many questions and I can't answer them. Are you sure you want to help me?"

"Of course I want to help you," he said as they walked toward the parking lot, which by now only had three cars left.

When they reached the concrete walkway, Jon stopped to shake the sand off his feet while Sean kept walking ahead to Jon's parked car. Without making a comment, Jon unlocked the passenger door and motioned him to get in, then turned the overhead light on for Sean to check his wallet.

"Sean Michael Stevens is the name on the driver's license and I have around two hundred dollars in cash, enough for a room tonight and a fare out of this town," Sean said, slightly upbeat.

"Where would you go? Isn't this supposed to be your hometown according to your license?" Jon asked curious.

"Well, uhm, I don't remember anything from here, so it doesn't matter where I go."

"What about your family? Don't you want to know about them?"

"Of course! It's just that I don't feel like I belong here," Sean said.

"It's all up to you. But if you don't mind, let me pay for your room tonight. I'm sure you'll need the cash later for other things," Jon said.

"Thanks. I'll accept your offer," Sean said after hesitating. "But I intend to pay you back some day soon," he assured Jon.

"That won't be necessary, really."

"I always pay my debts," Sean asserted.

"An admirable trait," Jon commended him. "By the way, do you have any preference for a place to stay?"

"Somewhere that won't take you out of your way will be fine."

"How about the place where I'm staying? It's a little secluded and I think they have rooms available," Jon said.

"That sounds perfect, thank you," Sean said.

Jon's mind was working fast, trying to put the pieces together. He noticed Sean looking at the landscape as if he was seeing it for the first time, which explained his memory loss. But his apprehension to use his own credit cards seemed strange, but then again, there were a lot of things that didn't make sense about this guy.

Jon's mind flashed back to the accident and recalled the apparent sky turbulence at about the same time as the crash. Slowly it was all beginning to make sense to him.

"Sean, does the name Apollo mean anything to you?" he asked. There was an awkward moment of silence. "Your hesitance says it all and it might also explain why you knew which car in the parking lot was mine."

"You got me there, I do know Apollo. But I knew your car because I saw you when you had arrived earlier. You were the last one to get there. And how do you know Apollo?" asked Sean with curiosity.

"I know that he is the guide when you arrive to the afterlife," Jon said.

"If you know that, then you must also know the limitations to what I can reveal," Marco said.

"To the average person, yes, but I don't see why we can't talk about things we both have seen. We're not sharing our experience with anyone outside of us, and we didn't know each other before. No rules are being broken. Maybe I was supposed to be here, to help guide you through."

"That's entirely possible."

"Why did you want to come back?" Jon asked.

"I didn't want to. I was told it wasn't my time yet. Why? Don't tell me you wanted to come back," Sean said incredulously.

"Believe it or not, I did. Pretty stupid, huh?"

"I'll say. How much did you get to see?" Sean asked with curiosity.

"According to Apollo, a very small glimpse of paradise."

"That's more than I saw," Sean said.

"So, what is your real name?" Jon asked.

"Marco Mendoza, what about yours? I'm sure it's not Max."

"You're right of course. My real name is Jonathan Fitzgerald," Jon said.

"Who's Max?" Marco asked.

"He's my best friend. We died in a plane crash together more than six months ago."

"Sorry about that, man."

"Sorry about you too. How did it happen?" Jon asked.

"I was serving in Iraq. Our helicopter was shot down and exploded in midair, killing all of us on board."

"I see now why you couldn't come back as yourself. That was going to be my next question," Jon said.

"So little of our remains were found scattered afterwards that it was impossible to even try to separate and identify us. We were all buried in a single tomb."

"You are a hero, man! I'm humbled by your selfless sacrifice. You're willing to do what many of us wouldn't."

"When fate calls you, there's little choice in the matter," Marco said.

"Don't be so modest. You deserve credit," Jon said with a sense of admiration.

"Thanks," Marco said, uncomfortable with the compliments. "My problem is, who am I now?" Marco asked.

"It seems to me that for the time being you can only be Sean Michael Stevens because you can't go back to your old life or the people you knew and loved. It's against the rules."

"What do you mean?" Marco asked.

"Didn't Apollo give you a set of laws that you must abide by when you came back?"

"I have no idea what you're talking about."

"What exactly did you see?" Jon was curious now.

"Maybe I just don't have much to tell. Unlike you, I wasn't there very long. It all happened so fast. When I left my body and went through a tunnel toward the light, I saw a light being that I believed was Jesus, but his vision quickly disappeared and I found myself in the most incredible garden. I remember thinking it had to be the Garden of Eden when Apollo appeared and told me that my arrival was premature and I had to go back. Next thing I know, I am in this car, hanging perilously close to the edge of a hill. I think you saw the rest."

"Your presence there was brief," Jon said.

"Like the blink of an eye," Marco said.

"I guess that's a good thing, because maybe it means you can at least have contact with your past, which is more than I can say for myself."

"Sure, I guess I can, but what would I say? Think about it; my situation is not much different than yours."

"That's true. But at least you can have some kind of contact with your loved ones, if you so choose."

They were now arriving at Jon's hotel and he was about to park in front of the registration office.

"I'll just wait here, if you don't mind—just trying to avoid anyone recognizing me," Marco said.

"You're right. Let's go up to my room first. I'll call the front desk and ask them to put another room on my bill. After that, I'll just go down to the lobby and get the key. How does that sound to you?" Jon asked as he drove to his secluded parking spot.

"Thank you, that'd be great. It's just that I need to get my head together and figure where my life goes from here," Marco said as they walked toward the empty elevator on the side of the building and took it to the third floor.

"If you're not Sean, who will you be?" Jon asked when they got to his room.

"I guess I don't have a choice about that, do I? Now I'll just have to find out everything I can about Sean Michael Stevens," Marco said, sitting down on a chair.

"For starters, you can watch and read the news. They seem obsessed with knowing what happened to Sean. Your mysterious disappearance has all of them baffled."

Jon looked at his watch and turned the television on. "It's almost eleven o'clock. The news will be coming on any minute," he said.

A few minutes later, they saw an expanded coverage from the earlier news version Jon had seen. It gave both of them, especially Marco, a small window into who he was supposed to be. Staring at the stranger's face on the screen, he realized that it was a look he was going to have to get used to.

"Aren't you curious to see what you look like now?" Jon asked.

"You're right. With so much to think about, it slipped my mind," Marco said, looking around for a mirror, which was over a dresser by the door. He stood in front of it silently for a few minutes.

Staring back at him was a man close to his age with a tall and slender build that looked very different from his old self. His buzz cut, brown eyes, and slender face had been replaced by short brown hair, deep blue eyes, and an inviting smile.

"Well?" Jon said.

"Well, I am still good looking, but obviously I have crossed the racial divide," he said, jokingly.

"That's funny! I'm glad to see you have a sense of humor my friend, you're gonna need it. Tell me about yourself."

"I'm twenty-five years old, from Flagstaff, Arizona. My parents came to America to get away from violence and unrest in Colombia. They were afraid that my younger brother and I would be forced to join the paramilitary groups, like it happened to a lot of families in our neighborhood. Young boys, and even girls as young as eight, were forced to join and then disappeared. Sadly, a high number of them ended up dead. So when I was eight years old, my family and I came here as tourists, but soon after that my parents got visas that allowed them to work. They quickly found jobs and started to build our new life. But my dad became a long distance truck driver when I was around twelve and was gone most of the time since then. After high school, I got accepted at the naval academy, where I found a sense of purpose. Of course, I also wanted to give something back for all the opportunities I have received here. I love this country."

"Do you have any children?"

"No! I'm too young. What about you?"

"No children for me either. I had what you would call an ideal childhood and life."

"What a bummer. I could tell by the news report that your family is well known around here, hence your disguise?" Marco said quizzically.

"Oh yes, I've got to keep it on until I get your room key from the front desk," Jon said as he dialed the receptionist.

"I need to get an extra room," he said to the clerk and paused to listen a few seconds. "Thank you," he said and hung up.

"Sorry. There aren't any rooms available, but if you like, you are welcomed to sleep on the couch. It turns into a bed," Jon said.

"Sorry for having to inconvenience you like this. I really appreciate what you're doing for me, being a stranger and all. I'll figure something out tomorrow. After all the excitement of today, I am confused, tired and would like to get some sleep. Maybe things will make better sense after a night's rest."

"Don't worry about it, it's not an inconvenience for me, I'm glad to help and you'll keep me company. But here's some food for thought. Why not go back to live Sean's life? All you have to do is tell them you have no memory of who you are, which is technically true. You can be an amnesiac who somehow made it home relying on the kindness of a stranger. That would make Sean's loved ones very happy. I'm sure they would rather have you back without your memory than not at all. It's a win-win situation for everybody."

"That sounds like a good idea and I am sure tomorrow it will sound even better."

"Yes. Tomorrow will be another day," Jon said philosophically.

"I have a question. What were you doing at the site of the crash?" Marco asked.

"I was following my mother when the attempted kidnapping happened."

"Oh yeah! That was your mother!" he exclaimed. "I am so sorry."

"You and I know that she and my father are enjoying total bliss where they are. We should be so lucky," Jon said as he handed some pajamas to his friend. "I hope they fit."

"Thank you for all that you're doing," Marco said.

"Don't mention it," Jon said.

They watched the evening news until they were too tired to stay awake. Exhausted by the emotionally draining day, they finally fell asleep sometime after one o'clock in the morning.

***

The next day, while they waited for their breakfast at the hotel coffee shop, Jon searched the newspaper obituaries for the funeral and service arrangements of his parents. It said there would be a graveyard service and internment the next day at three in the afternoon. He didn't need read where it would take place. His body was lying next to the grave where they would be buried. The new Sean Stevens sat across from him, wearing a borrowed baseball cap and sunglasses, engrossed by the report about him and his car crash.

"So I am an architect. I haven't the faintest idea how do that," he said.

"I can help you there. I was an architect before."

"How convenient for me. But I'm sure it's not that simple."

"You have your amnesia story going for you, which means that you can buy yourself considerable time while you learn to be an architect again, if that's what you choose. I'm sure if you have a good employer, he would understand your quandary."

"Let's hope you're right, but we'll see."

"Think of it as what it is—a second chance at life. Who knows! It could turn out to be a great adventure," Jon said, trying to cheer him up.

"I thought about what you said last night; there are a lot of people going through a terrible time because of Sean's disappearance, and finding him alive would bring an end to a lot of grief. There is no sense in prolonging their pain; I will go back to the address on the license this afternoon. Besides, this is as good a place to start my new life as any. At least here I'll have a family, sort of."

"I'd be happy to drive you there if you like," Jon volunteered.

"Thank you, Jon, or is it Max? What would like me to call you?"

"Jonathan or Jon is cool with me. In fact, I prefer it. Not many people can call me by that name now."

"Okay, then you can call me Marco."

"Well Marco, you'll have a whole new family, and you can still get in touch with the loved ones in your past. That's a pretty good deal."

"Yes, but only to an extent, because I can't tell them the truth, they'd think I'm nuts."

"Well, no! You can't tell them the truth. Who'd believe you? But isn't it better to enjoy their company as a stranger than not at all?" Jon asked.

"Absolutely. Without a question. When you put it that way, it's very simple."

"Time will no doubt determine what kind of role you will play in their lives and the other way around. But first you need to know who Sean Michael Stevens is and what he's all about," Jon said.

"You're right. My family already buried me; the idea of expecting them to deal with the truth would be unrealistic. Some things just can't be explained."

"I agree."

"We'll stay in touch, of course. I take it you won't be staying around too long, since you are originally from here. Where are you going to live?" Marco asked.

"In view of all that happened yesterday, I have to change my plans to be at my parents' funeral tomorrow. I had to postpone a trip I had booked to Hooper Bay to secure a place to live."

"Where's Hooper Bay?"

"Alaska," Jon said.

"That's far enough away and pretty much removed from here," Marco noted.

"Yes, but now I have to go to Switzerland to take care of my finances instead. I'll find a place to live when I come back."

"What are you going to do in Switzerland?"

"I have a bank account and made a sizable deposit shortly before I died, with Max as my second signature—an account which, luckily, only the two of us knew about. But I need to take care of this matter personally."

"I see. I guess that means right now you don't know where you're going to settle down. How am I going to stay in touch, then?"

"I'll give you my e-mail address and don't worry, I'll stay in touch. Besides, I'll have your address, that is, if you want to give it to me."

"Of course I do. Besides, I could sure use your input about a lot of things, it seems. I still need to figure out what I'll be doing for a living."

"What did you do before?"

"I went to Annapolis right out of high school. All I know is the Navy. My last position was in tactics and operations, flying surveillance missions, high tech kind of stuff," Marco said.

"You'll have to decide if you'd like to stick with what you know or take advantage of the opportunity to do something different. It isn't often that a man gets a second chance like you did."

"You mean, consider architecture?"

"Yes, among other things. Why not?" Jon said.

"But I don't know the first thing about it."

"You must know how to read blue prints as part of your job."

"Sure. We had to know our equipment inside and out, our lives depended on it," Marco said.

"Then, you already have a skill that is important to be an architect. It all starts with blue prints."

"I took an Introduction to Architecture class as a requirement, but that's about the extent of my knowledge. It's not much."

"Well, just let me know if you decide to explore that possibility," Jon said.

"I don't know how to thank you."

"It's not necessary. Helping to get you home is reward enough for me."

Marco smiled. The chances of finding someone else who had experienced the afterlife like him were very unlikely. He had no doubt that meeting Jon was no accident.

"By the way, how long have you been back as Max?" Marco wanted to know.

"Just a few weeks," Jon responded.

"That's not very long."

"Not in real time, but in terms of what's transpired, a whole lifetime of events has happened since. In just a short period of time, my world changed drastically and not in a good way. My mother and father are dead and the man I thought was my friend turned out to be a rat."

"That's rough. How long were you in the afterlife?"

"You mean in physical time? Close to six months," Jon said. "What about you?"

Marco looked at Jon, puzzled.

"I don't know. What's today's date? Never mind, I've got the paper here in front of me. Duh! It looks like I've been gone three weeks."

"That's not long."

"Not really," Marco said.

"When do you want to go to your place? I mean, Sean's home," Jon said.

"Whenever is convenient for you."

"I don't have anything to do. I'm just waiting for my Mom and Dad's services tomorrow before I go to Europe. But if you don't mind, early evening would be best for me. The chances of being recognized are far less."

"Okay then. Early evening sounds good to me," Marco said as their breakfast was served.

Jon nodded and the two fell silent as they ate their breakfast and reflected about their respective circumstances. For Jon, the feeling of isolation and loneliness was comforted by the knowledge that there was another being who understood where he was coming from. He was secretly thankful for a friend who could relate to his state of existence.

After finishing their breakfast, they went back to Jon's room, where they made small talk and watched a basketball game. Marco prepared himself mentally to face an unfamiliar new life and Jon braced himself for the physical farewell to his parents the next day. They exchanged e-mails and home address and agreed to stay in touch.

Later in the day, as the evening shadows began to appear, Jonathan drove Marco to the address on Sean Stevens' driver's license. The house turned out to be in a charming middle-class neighborhood, abundant in plants and trees, with an impeccable yard and a cozy New England look. Marco took a deep breath as he looked at what was to be his new home and he was pleased. Although it definitely looked unlike anything he would have been able to afford in his previous life, he liked Sean's choice.

His heartbeat accelerated as he opened the car door, anxious and curious about what he was going to find inside the house. He took a deep breath.

"Well friend, here I go," he said to Jon.

"I'm just an e-mail away and will be happy to help you any way I can. When I get settled, you'll be the first to know. Wait, you'll be the only one to know. You can understand why I don't see the need for a cell phone, at least for now. Besides you, I got no friends."

"Yes, I see your point. Hey man, thanks for everything. Your help made it all easier," Marco said shaking Jon's hand.

"I'm sure I'll see you in the news. Good luck, and remember, you can handle it just fine. You've been through much worse. In comparison this should be a piece of cake. I have total confidence in you," he said wanting to encourage Marco.

"That's true. I'll be seeing you, then?" Marco said as he got out of the car.

"You can bet on it," Jon said.

"I'll be checking out the news to hear about you, and your family too," he said as he went up the winding walkway to the front door of the house.

Instinctively, he checked into his pocket for a key but there was nothing, so he decided to try the doorbell. His summons was greeted by loud barking, and after waiting for a few seconds, he decided to check around the side, where he found an intricate wrought iron gate conveniently unlocked. Catching a look inside, he found himself face to face with a chocolate Labrador retriever, which after looking at him through the gate, started trying to climb over it, obviously happy to see him. Marco looked at Jon, who was still parked in front of the house, and waved goodbye giving him the o.k. sign. Slowly, he opened the gate ajar, just enough to put part of his hand inside to allow the dog to sniff his scent. After recognizing him, the animal started to lick his hand and arm excited to see him. He opened the gate waving good bye again to Jon, who was just driving off. The dog started sniffing him all over and soon was jumping on Marco and making noises letting him know how happy he was to have him back.

"So you're my boy! Or are you a girl?" Marco said to the dog, getting down to pet him and check the name on his collar.

"Brownie Stevens, huh? I guess that makes you a girl," he said, checking her gender as Brownie licked his face, showing her gladness.

"Yes, girl, it's good for me to be home too," he said to her.

Brownie happily led him past the basketball hoop area in the backyard and to the doggy door, where she stood and looked up at him inquisitively as her tail slowly moved from side to side. Marco thought about it for a minute.

"Let me check the doors to see if any of them are unlocked," he said to the dog as he went around the backyard and checked the two doors going outside, but they were both locked. He decided to listen to Brownie's suggestion and soon was wiggling his way through the doggy door and into a spacious but obviously bachelor's kitchen with new appliances but nothing else on the counters. After checking the first floor, Marco moved on through the rest of the house, walking up the stairs leading to the second floor with three bedrooms and three baths. One of the rooms was apparently being used for storage as marked boxes piled the floor, an obvious sign of having just moved in. He went back downstairs and was going into what was obviously an office when he heard the sound of the front door unlocking. Startled, he froze, not knowing what to do when he heard the two women's voices.

"Brownie! Come girl!" one of them called as they came into the living room.

The dog stood looking at him as she was called again, wagging her tail at him as if asking for his permission to obey the call.

"Go on, girl," he said to her softly. "They're calling you."

By now, he could tell one of the women was coming in his direction, judging by the sound of her voice from the hallway.

"I can't believe we left this light on this morning!" she exclaimed.

"Considering what's happened lately, it's a wonder we can function at all," the second female voice said.

Seeing Brownie coming out of the office, she bent down to pet her.

"There's our girl!" she said to the dog, hugging her and gently rubbing her stomach as Brownie rolled over, showing her joy.

"Mom and Dad are devastated and I'm worried about them. Why did this have to happen to Sean?" she exclaimed in frustration. "It's not fair, Emily! He was such a good brother, our only brother. Why did it have to happen to him! I don't understand."

"I don't understand either, Susan. But let's hold out hope until they find him or his body, however slim the chances are, after all his body hasn't been found. It's all we've got to hold on to for now," Emily said, hugging her younger sister, trying to comfort her.

"I guess you're right," Susan said, wiping away tears from her face.

As the two women walked down the hallway, Brownie walked to the office door and stood in front of it, staring at the two of them. Marco realized the time had come to face the beginning of his new life and slowly walked toward the door. The dog barked once and wagged her tail at the sisters, who walked toward her as Marco emerged from the office and found himself face to face with Sean's obviously two younger sisters, who were in shock, staring at him in disbelief.

Emily and Susan Stevens were at first stunned and speechless but within seconds ran to embrace him, tears of joy running down their faces.

"Oh my God! Oh my God!" was all Susan could say, overwhelmed by the emotion of seeing her brother alive. She hugged him tightly and closed her eyes.

"Thank God you're alive! I just can't believe you're alive! Thank you, God," Emily exclaimed, looking up and hugging her brother and sister tightly.

"But you still had some hope. I heard you say so," Marco said

Emily didn't say anything; she just leaned her head on her brother's shoulder and cried tears of joy. Marco patted her on the shoulder, not knowing exactly what to do. Looking at her, their resemblance was remarkable. Her long auburn hair tied in a ponytail and blue eyes made him feel as if he was seeing a version of his new self. There was, at the very least, a physical connection to his new family.

After experiencing the sisters' elation at seeing him, Marco knew coming back and becoming Sean was the right thing to do. Seeing their outpouring of love and joy at having him back made him feel privileged to be able to ease their pain and end their mourning. By the same token, he knew he had to be as honest as possible with his new family.

"I can't tell you how great it is to be back with my family, but there's something I have to tell you," he started.

"Whatever it is, it doesn't matter. You're back with us and that's all that counts. Why haven't you called?" Emily asked.

"Because I have no memory of who I was before the accident," Marco said, feeling a sense of relief.

"Then how did you get home?" Susan asked him.

"A kind stranger helped me find my way and drove me here. We got this address from my driver's license," he said.

"Do you remember anything from the accident?" Emily asked.

"No, I don't. I only remember waking up to the sound of the ocean at the bottom of a ravine. From there, I walked to the beach where I met Max, who put me up for the night and brought me here today."

"The only important thing is that you're with us. Besides, there's probably a good chance you could get your memory back. In the meantime, we'll make new memories. We're just so overjoyed and thankful for your life. I can't believe you're here!" Emily said as the three of them joined in a hug and cried.

"Let's call Mom and Dad right now!" Susan said jubilantly, running to the nearest telephone.

He stood there, not knowing how to address the young women.

"Wait!" he said." I don't even remember your names."

"Oh yeah, I'm sorry! I didn't think about that! I'm Susan; I just turned seventeen and I am your baby sister," she said with a big smile.

"A high school senior, huh?" he said.

"Yup," she answered, still smiling.

"I'm Emily, the middle child," she said, shrugging her shoulders.

"Our resemblance is remarkable," he said to her.

"We've been told that all our lives," she said.

"Our dad's name is Michael, hence your middle name, and our Mom is Nancy. Now, let's call them," Susan urged them as she dialed her parents' phone number.

"Yes, but if you don't mind, I'd rather talk to them in person," he said, feeling terribly awkward and unprepared for the meeting.

"Mom, I have great news. Are you sitting down? Never mind that. Sean is home!" she exclaimed.

"What are you saying?" her mother asked, in disbelief.

"Yes. We came by to feed Brownie and there he was, coming out of his office!"

"Oh my God! Let me talk to him."

Susan turned to Emily with a pleading look.

"Mom, here's Emily. She can explain," Susan said, handing her sister the phone.

"Isn't it great news?" Emily said to her mother.

"It' wonderful! But why doesn't he talk to me? Is he all right? Is something wrong with your brother? Please tell me."

"He's physically fine, Mom. It's just that he has amnesia and doesn't remember any of us. He would rather talk to you in person. But don't worry; he looks no worse for the wear."

"I got my son back! Thank you God! Hurry on home! I want to see him."

"Yes mother, we're on our way there. We'll be seeing you in a little bit. I love you," she said and hung up the phone.

"You heard her. Of course, they can't wait to see you," Emily told the new Sean as he nodded in agreement.

Within a few minutes they were on their way to their parents' home. With his heart beating with anticipation and curiosity, he tried to take advantage of the ride to learn more about his family.

"How long does it take to get there?" he asked Emily.

"About twenty minutes. When you were looking to buy your home you decided to stay within half an hour of our parents," she said.

"That's why the house looks as if someone had just moved in! How long ago did I move?"

"Less than two months ago. You've been gone on business a lot. That's why you weren't finished unpacking yet."

"I see. Who takes care of Brownie when I'm gone?"

"We do. It's one of the things you don't like about being gone. Just a couple of weeks ago you were talking about working for another firm that wouldn't have you traveling so much," Susan said from the backseat.

"What about you, Emily? What's your major?"

"Don't laugh. I'm going to be an archeologist," she said.

"That's awesome!" he said. "How about you, Susan?"

"I'm thinking about going into sports medicine, but that's a long way off."

"Wow, I'm impressed to have such intelligent sisters."

"You're not so bad yourself," Emily said.

"I hope I can live up to my old self," he said.

"Aw, come on! That's not even a question; it's still you in there," Susan said.

They were silent the rest of the way, and as they pulled into the driveway of the Stevens' home, Nancy and Michael were standing by the open front door waiting. When he walked toward them, it all became joyous pandemonium as his new mother and father showered him with affection. They told him that they loved him and how glad they were that he had survived the horrific accident without as much as a scratch.

The feeling of festivity went on until late in the evening. Feeling the love and support of his new family, Marco started to feel at home among them and acknowledged to himself that he would now learn to think of his old self as a past experience, from which he needed to move on and become Sean Michael Stevens. But he could never forget or stop being the man he was before. He needed to find an adequate balance of both, and he trusted his friend Jonathan to help and guide him through the maze of his new life.

Sean's father, Michael, decided it was best to wait until the next day to speak to the newspapers about the return of his son. He wanted to bask in the joy of having him back. For now he didn't want to expose him to the news glare, especially in light of his lack of memory.

For his part, after dropping Marco at the address of his new identity, Jon picked up dinner to go on his way and went back to the hotel. After settling in for the night, he turned on the television news and took out the disguise he would wear for his parents' memorial service.

The next day he left two hours early, feeling the need to take a walk along the beach before the funeral services, which he was anticipating with mixed feelings. He felt jealous of his parents because he imagined their joy, and felt glad that they no longer had to endure the cumbersome weight of a physical body and all that went along with it. Instead they now enjoyed the freedom gained by their loss.

Walking along the beach had always been his best therapy since he was a child. There was something about water, frozen or flowing that spiritually energized him. He felt comforted when he listened to the rhythm of the ocean, soothed by the sound of the even-flow occurrence that had been going on for millions of years. He loved to sense its overwhelming power, capable of giving life and taking it away, but more than anything he liked the feeling of just being when he was there.

Around two o'clock in the afternoon, he started to make his way to the cemetery, which was not far away. His parents loved the sea like him, and chose a final resting place with a view of the Atlantic Ocean. As he made the drive through the scenic road, he saw many familiar faces on their way to the service. He parked his rented car at an adjacent section of the cemetery, and casually walked toward the crowd gathering around the two caskets acting as if he was looking for a grave marker nearby.

No one could recognize him with curly black hair, a beard and a mustache, sunglasses, and baggy black pants worn over a pair of loose jeans. A blue shirt over a bulky sweater made him appear overweight. He stayed by a grave close by as if he was visiting it, completely unaware of the fact that Jake and Bradley were also there in disguise, looking for him.

The chairs set up for the outdoor service quickly filled up as the surroundings filled with the overflow of people coming to pay their respect to his parents.

Not long after that, Vince arrived with his family and took the front row seats reserved for them. He looked worn out but managed a weak smile for his wife Laura. His children—Cassie, Elise, and Dylan—were with him. Their eyes and noses were red, obviously from crying. How Jon wished he could share the peace he felt with them! If he could just spare some of their pain! But such as it was, he might as well be invisible.

Following behind Vince were Sarah and Patrick Adams, Max's parents, who with the rest of his family occupied the first row seats on the other side. Seated in the last row, covered up in black with a wide-brimmed hat and sunglasses was Madison, alone. He could not believe her nerve!

"How dare she show up here? She doesn't have a shred of decency. Is there no limit to her hypocrisy and greed? Unbelievable!" he thought, shaking his head in disbelief.

But he soon shrugged the feeling off. After all, she was the least of his worries. Instead, he concentrated on his loved ones and friends joined together to show their love for his parents.

Looking at Max's parents gave him a mix of spontaneous love and guilt. Logically, he felt inevitably connected to them in a way hard to describe. But just as he was surveying the event, likewise, Jake and Bradley were looking to blend in as part of the crowd of mourners.

"We have to look for someone who is most likely alone. If it's the guy you think, and he is hiding for some reason, he will come alone," Jake whispered to Bradley.

"Yeah. I don't know why Max would hide, but if he is the guy, I'm sure he's here right now."

"With everyone around wearing black, he won't be easy to spot without being obvious."

"We'll just stick around after it's over and see who leaves alone fitting his description," Bradley said.

"Whatever works," Jake said.

Their conversation was cut short as they joined in the crowd of mourners. Bradley looked around, scrutinizing men's faces while trying to be discreet, but he had a difficult time doing so when he saw his parents sitting on the third row, behind the Fitzgerald family. He almost felt bad for disappointing them, if he wasn't concerned only with himself. But kindness had never been his strong suit, especially when it was a matter of his survival. He always thought that some of his father Oliver's noble qualities kept him from being more financially successful, specifically relating to the success of Fitzgerald International. In spite of the fact that Oliver Spellman made a profitable living with his business, enabling his children to attend the finest schools and live in reasonable luxury, Bradley's blind greed prevented him from appreciating the good fortune in his life.

From his vantage point, Jon was taking it all in. He didn't know if he ever would have an opportunity to see so many people dear to him together, and he was enjoying it for all that was worth. But it was more special knowing that his parents' spirits were present and in the midst of it all. He decided to move off to the side, as to not attract undue attention and to slowly blend with the crowd standing behind the seating area.

***

It was three o'clock in the afternoon when the Pastor who was conducting the service made his way to the makeshift podium with a microphone.

"We are here to celebrate the passing of William and Sophia's souls," he began. "You know, I have a friend whose father has this inscription on his tombstone: The shell is here, but the nut is gone. Friends, I believe that, in a nutshell, if you pardon the pun, that's what our existence is. The best part comes after the shell is gone. Who among us, who likes nuts, would rather have the shell over the nut itself? I would venture to say not many. Likewise, when we leave this human shell, the best part of ourselves will be refined and God's glory will be revealed to us, as Sophia and William no doubt have experienced. I am sure that if they had the choice to go back into their shells, they would refuse it."

"And now, I'm happy to introduce to you a man of faith and integrity, a man that I am privileged to have known for many years. For those of you who don't know him, I give you Vincent Fitzgerald, William's brother, who will share with us his loving tribute to his brother and sister-in-law."

There was complete silence as Vince made his way to the podium, and Jon listened intently as his uncle approached the microphone.

"I would like to start by sharing with you one of William and Sophia's favorite scripture verses that comes from the book of Luke. It happened when Jesus was crucified with two criminals, and one of them made a request. This is what it says," Vince started. "And he was saying, 'Jesus, remember me when You come in your kingdom!' And He said to him, 'Truly I say to you, today you shall be with me in paradise." NAS. And I say to you today, don't despair for William and Sophia, because they are in paradise, experiencing the joy of being in the presence of God. Let us rejoice in knowing that someday we will be with them, praising the glory of our God."

Jon felt more proud of his parents than ever. He looked up at the sky and whispered, "I love you, guys. I know you're here with me as I was with you then. What a disappointment it must have been for you not to find me there. I'm so sorry."

Vince continued on,

"As I looked at the events in the last three days, I realized my grief is not so much for William and Sophia as it is for all of us who loved and lost two incredibly wonderful human beings. I know they wouldn't want me to point to their good deeds, because they believed it was their privilege to serve others."

Jon couldn't help feeling a knot in his throat and the tears, which came pouring out even as he tried to suppress them.

"I should be with them. Instead..." he thought regretfully.

"It is safe to say," Vince continued, interrupting Jon's thoughts, "that Sophia wouldn't mind a lot of flowers on her grave. We all know how much she loved them and what a great green thumb she had. But typical of them, they would like to be remembered by giving to those who are most in need, instead. A handwritten note from Sophia to all of us, signed by both of them says:

"Dear Friends,

Obviously, if you're hearing this, at least one of us has passed on. I love you all and always will, because love never dies. If you should find yourself wishing to remember me or us, with any gesture, we would consider ourselves blessed if you should reach and touch lives which need help and healing, whether it's a one-time thing like volunteering for any good cause that touches your heart or sponsoring children who are the neediest. I couldn't think of a better way to be remembered than serving those in need. "See you all in heaven."

"And it's signed by Sophia and William."

Vince paused to clear his throat and wipe his nose and tears, and then continued,

"That, friends, was the essence of the two lives we celebrate here today. To all of us who deeply loved Will and Sophie, as we lovingly called them in the family, let's not be twice burdened by the pain of losing them both at once. I assure you it's the way they would have wanted it to be.

The minister walked to the caskets and prayed over them before the mourners started to form a line and walk past William and Sophia, lying flowers as a sign of their love and respect for them. It was now the end of the service and some of the people who'd gone through the line started walking to their cars. As the crowd started to thin, Apollo's words resonated in Jon's mind. "Be mindful of people who don't belong at the funeral...." He instinctively looked around him.

Noticing two men off to the side by themselves, he realized that, like him, they too were wearing disguises. The mustache of one of them coming unglued on the side gave them away, and it didn't take Jon long to realize that these men were probably looking for him. He turned his back to them and pressed his own mustache and beard firmly to his skin, making sure they were in place.

Then he started to look into the faces of the people who were left, searching for someone he didn't know. After maneuvering himself around, he found a young couple he was sure he'd never met and decided to take his chances and sit in the row behind them.

William and Sophia's caskets were now being lowered into the tandem grave, with his first and her afterward. Jonathan smiled when he remembered the day that his mother cheerfully informed her husband that they could have a tandem burial plot.

As this was happening, Jon leaned over and struck up the conversation in a low voice with the young couple in front of him.

"Hi. How did you know the Fitzgeralds?" he asked.

"My parents knew them since college," the young man answered. "How did you know them?"

"I was a very good friend of their son Jonathan in college. Did you know him?" Jonathan asked.

"No," he said to Jon's relief. "But I've heard of him."

"He was a good guy," Jon said, casually.

"My name is Fulton and this is my wife Janice."

"It's nice meeting you," Jon said as he shook their hands. "I'm Keith."

He made small talk with the couple until the rest of the people started to get up from their seats and head to their cars.

"I'm from out of town, and I don't see my taxi," he said, pretending to look around for it.

"We'll be happy to give you a lift," Fulton said.

"I'd really appreciate it, if it's not too much trouble. Just to the bottom of the hill where I can catch a cab would be great," Jon said.

"You got it," Fulton said as the three of them walked over to their car.

When Jon got behind the tinted windows he looked back at the two men in disguise, whom he suspected were the same who tried to kidnap his mother, looking for him. A few minutes later he was dropped off at the bottom of the hill from the cemetery, and quickly went into a fast food restaurant on the corner to wait a while. He ordered some food and sat by a window strategically located to observe the traffic coming down from the memorial park. He sat there until he saw a dual-cabin silver truck with the disguised men he had seen at the funeral driving by. Ten minutes later, when he felt assured that the coast was clear, he walked out and went up the road to retrieve his car.

Later that night he called his airline and rescheduled his flight to Europe for the next day, Sunday at 11:40 in the evening. He felt the urge to get out of town as soon as possible because he knew now that his safety was at stake. There was nothing keeping him around except his uncle, but once again, his plans were being changed by the circumstances. He would stay in his room during the day and drive to the airport later in the evening to catch his flight to Paris and then to Switzerland.

Just before going to sleep, the phone rang with Marco's voice at the end of the line.

"Did I wake you up?" he asked.

"Not at all. I was getting ready to turn in. How's everything?"

"It's going really well. I couldn't have picked a better family to be part of, inconveniences aside. They are very nice people. And speaking of nice people, I read the paper and saw the articles written about your parents and they were pretty impressive people. I also saw the news report on their funeral this afternoon. Congratulations on being raised by such a nice couple."

"Thanks. They were pretty great; and I saw the news piece on you too. It was very good," Jon said.

"That was quite a crowd at the service today. There were a lot of people!" Marco said.

"Yes, including the guys responsible for my mom's death."

"What?! What were they doing there? What happened?"

"I think they were looking for me because they had disguises too. In fact, that's how I noticed them, because one of their fake mustaches started falling off."

"Why would they be looking for you?" Marco asked.

"Maybe because I was a witness to the whole thing. Although I didn't really see much of the driver, I took a really good look at the guy who tried to shove my mother into their car. I'll never forget that face," Jon said.

"How did they know to look for you there?"

"Maybe they figured that I was the Good Samaritan who wanted to attend her service. I haven't the faintest idea!"

"Did they see you?"

"I'm not sure. But I was able to shake them off and made sure they couldn't follow me," Jon said.

"I hope you're right. In any event, be careful and if there's anything I can do just let me know."

"The best thing I can do is to get out of town as soon as possible. I just rescheduled my flight for tomorrow night. I would love to leave sooner, but the next available flight was in the morning and I have to keep a low profile. Going out during the day would not be wise for me at this point."

"Would you like a ride to the airport?" Marco offered.

"No thanks. I have my rental and will return it there."

"In that case, I hope you have a good trip and will see you when you come back. Remember I will count on your help if I decide to stay an architect," Marco said.

"I'm a man of my word. As I said before, I'll be happy to be of help, man," Jon said.

"How long will you be in Europe?"

"I'm planning a week. It shouldn't be longer than that to take care of what I have to do. The transactions themselves will be done in a day or two, I think."

"Let me give you my telephone numbers so we can get in touch when you come back," Marco said.

Jon walked to the night table with the writing tablet and pen, and wrote down the phone numbers and address.

"Best of luck on your trip," Marco wished Jon.

"Thanks. See you when I come back," Jon said and hung up.

He watched television for a while, knowing that the next day was going to be a long one. He couldn't wait to get out of Alexandria Bay.

In another part of the city, Bradley and Jake were annoyed and frustrated at the lack of success during their outing that afternoon.

"Is it possible that he wasn't there?" Jake asked.

"Not likely. If the guy you saw was Maxwell, I'm absolute sure he would be there. Maybe he wasn't the guy you saw and just made a mistake," Bradley said.

"I did not make a mistake," Jake said angrily. "That is the guy I saw!"

"Okay then, if you think he was there, then he just got away from us, or he wasn't there alone," Brad said to him.

Jake paced in his living room back at home, the wheels of his mind turning. After a few minutes, he stopped in his tracks.

"Or maybe that green mid-size car that we saw nearby, when we were driving around looking for him after the memorial services was indeed his car. We figured that it was somebody visiting a grave, but come to think of it, I don't remember seeing anyone around or close to it."

"Neither did I," Brad said.

"Where does that leave us?" Jake wondered out loud.

"Well, assuming still that this guy is Max, we could stake out his parents' house. He might show up there. But I would say that we go back to the cemetery just to be thorough—to see if that car is still there."

"I think that's a long shot," Jake said.

"We can't lose anything but time," Bradley said.

"Okay, let's go."

They got into the Subaru wagon with its tinted windows, drove to the memorial park, and went to the spot where the green car had been parked earlier in the afternoon, but it was no longer there. When they stopped on the spot and looked toward the Fitzgeralds' grave, they realized there was an unobstructed view of the burial location; they looked at each other and knew.

"He was here!" Jake exclaimed.

"Son of a bitch! How did he do that, and why is he hiding? I don't understand it. I have to tell you, there for a minute I thought he might not be the guy you thought. After all, the plane he was riding in crashed in some Utah or Colorado mountains around seven months ago. The body of the pilot, Jonathan Fitzgerald, was recovered, but Maxwell Spellman—our friend—his body was never recovered," Bradley said.

"Well, for some reason he seems to have something to hide too," Jake said.

"Watching his parents' house might be a good great idea," Bradley suggested.

"Well, of course it is." Jake said with a smile as he turned around and drove off toward Bradley's hotel. "But I don't think you tagging along is a good idea. This is something that Leo and I should take care of."

"Look, I don't want to do this any more than you want me to, but I want to know what Maxwell is hiding. You've got to admit it's not every day that the dead come back to life. Just let me tag along with you tomorrow, I've got to get out of here soon anyway. Oh! That reminds me, how soon can you get me a passport?"

"One day, two tops. You'll need a passport picture."

"I can get that tomorrow."

"Then you should have the passport the day after," Jake said.

"How much will it cost me?"

"Ten thousand dollars."

"That's a lot of money."

"Not that much when you consider its worth to you."

"I guess, you're right, but they are first rate documents, right?" he asked, looking for assurance.

"The best money can buy."

"All right, then." Bradley said, breathing a sigh of relief. They were now pulling into the motel driveway.

"Sleep good; tomorrow will be a long day. I'm going back to pick up Leo. I was just thinking that if this Max guy doesn't want to be seen, night would be the time for him to come around, if he does," Jake said as he stopped to drop Bradley off in front of the stairwell that led to his room.

"Should I go with you guys?" Bradley volunteered.

"No," said Jake. "You get your sleep. We'll need you more awake tomorrow if Leo and I spend the night staking out the house. What I need from you is the address."

"If you think that Max would probably show up at night, what's the point in having the house under surveillance during the day? Isn't it a waste of time?"

"Because the family could also lead us to him," Jake answered impatiently.

"Okay then, tomorrow it is. Should I drive, meet you there, or should we go together?"

"I'll pick you up at seven o'clock."

"I'll be here," Bradley said, getting out of the car.

"Hey, the address." Jake reminded him.

"I have to get that from my room. Do you want me to call your cell phone or do you want to wait?"

"I'll wait," Jake said as he parked in the back of the hotel.

Bradley went upstairs and a few minutes later he was back with a small piece of paper with Max's information, which he handed to Jake.

"Tomorrow, then," he said as he started his truck and drove off.

Bradley nodded and waved.

That night Jake and Leo watched Sarah and Patrick Adams's house from half a block away until six o'clock in the morning the next day. They took turns watching while the other slept, but predictably, they saw nothing out of the ordinary all night. In the morning, Jake dropped Leo off at his place so he could get some rest. Afterwards, he got something to eat and picked Bradley up and they went back to watch the Adams's residence. Before nine o'clock, Sarah and Patrick came out of their garage down the landscaped yard. Jake and Bradley followed them until they went into their local community church, and then they decided to go have breakfast while their targets were in the church service.

An hour and a half later, they came back to their watch and not long after Max's parents came out and drove back to their home. But by the afternoon, Jake was beginning to think that it might take a long time to get results doing surveillance, if they had success at all. It wasn't the kind of neighborhood that you could watch safely for long; with the security cameras and the security company cars driving by periodically, there were only a few blind spots where you could be inconspicuous. Jake decided it would be wise to change cars, and sometime in the afternoon he switched to the truck.

"Assuming that this Max is the same person you think, we can't be sure he hasn't been in contact with them and met them away from here. We could do this for a long time and not get a bite."

"This is true, but what else have we got?" Bradley asked.

"We'll watch the house for at least twenty-four hours. In the meantime, we may be wasting our time worrying about this guy. If he is in hiding, going to the cops is the last thing he wants," Jake reasoned.

"You just have to be sure that he is hiding from something. I guess it all depends on whether he is Max or not."

"I think the circumstances speak for themselves. If he wasn't hiding, why was he disguised at the funeral? Because otherwise, I would have recognized him. Didn't he know the old lady and her husband?"

"Yes, very well. In fact, they were his best friend's parents. Didn't I tell you this before?"

"Maybe you did. But anyway, the way I see it, our job here will be done soon."

"I guess you're right. I got a little sidetracked myself. After we're done here I'm going to see if I can get my passport photos. Do you think I could have it by tomorrow?"

"No, man. You need at least another day if you want a quality document that will stand ID scanning."

"All right, then. If I get the pictures tonight, when would I have the passport in my hands?"

"Tuesday."

"For sure? I mean, sure enough for me to make plane reservations?"

"As soon as the man knows what your new name will be, he will let me know so you can start making your arrangements; and that should be after he gets the photos," Jake told him.

"Okay. Could you drive me by a store to get the pictures taken so I can give them to you before you drop me off at the hotel?"

"Yeah, okay. I guess," Jake said reluctantly.

"Thanks a lot."

Before they realized it, darkness started setting in and there had been no activity from the Adams's home. Jake decided to call it a day and took Bradley to get his passport pictures taken. By now it was eight o'clock at night and they were both hungry, so they decided to grab a bite to eat before Jake dropped Bradley off. On their way, Jake had some advice for Bradley.

"How long have you been staying at the motel?" Jake asked.

"A couple of nights," Bradley answered.

"You've got to move on to another place. Too much time in one spot can be hazardous for someone who is trying to avoid detection."

"Yeah, you're right. I need to find something that is out of the way."

"There are a couple of places within ten minutes from here."

"Do you mind if we drive by them before dinner?"

"I think we got ten minutes to spare, and there's a good little restaurant close to one of them." Jake said.

"Cool," Bradley said.

Within seven minutes of driving, they came to the first small hotel, which had a no vacancy sign. Jake made a couple of turns and a few minutes later they were on a secluded tree-lined street with apartments on both sides, beyond which was a discreet sign of the Woodmere Inn amid a landscaping heavy on the privacy.

"This one looks good!" Brad said.

"This is the one I was thinking of," Jake said.

"Good find, man."

"Let's go in to see if they have any rooms available."

They parked by the lobby and went inside. Bradley walked to the front desk while Jake looked around, making time.

"Good evening, sir," the receptionist behind the desk said.

"Do you have any available rooms?" Bradley asked.

"We have one that will be available in an hour. Our guest just checked out."

"I'll take it," Bradley said.

"May I have your last name?" she asked.

Bradley pulled his credit card and handed it to her and waited for his room key.

CHAPTER 8

THE CHASE BEGINS

For Jon the wait was finally over. After all that had happened, he couldn't wait to get out of Alexandra Bay. As if losing his parents wasn't enough, he was sure the two men wearing disguises at the funeral were the same ones who attempted to kidnap his mother. He was sure that somehow they had picked up his trail and were after him. Why else would Apollo warn him about the funeral?

He gave the room one last look checking for items he might have forgotten and made sure once again, that he had packed everything. Having checked out of the room earlier, he went down and got into his rental car. It was 8:15 in the evening, and he had plenty of time to return it at the airport before his flight at midnight.

As he made his way out of the parking area and toward the exit, he noticed the silver pickup truck, like the one he had seen at the funeral the day before, parked outside the registration office. His heart raced when he looked through the window into the lobby and saw Jake inside looking around seemingly waiting for something. As he drove past the office and out of the driveway, he couldn't take his eyes off him.

"I'll never forget that face," he thought to himself.

Just then, out of the corner of his eye, Jon saw Jake look out the window directly at his car as he drove past him. The man he believed was his mother's kidnapper started making gestures at someone at the front desk that Jon couldn't see. In his rearview mirror, he saw the two men run out the door to their truck. He quickly turned right as he left the motel in an attempt to lose them. He pulled into an alley of an apartment complex, turned his lights off, and waited for their truck to pass by. A short time later he saw them drive by, obviously looking for him and after waiting a few minutes, he came out and headed toward the airport in the opposite direction.

Bradley and Jake, for their part, were irritated by their inability to find Jon but were not ready to give up.

"He can't disappear just like that. Where the hell did he go?" Jake asked rhetorically.

"Did you see his face?" Bradley asked.

"No, he had a hat on, but I'm pretty sure that was the car at the cemetery."

"Did he see you?"

"I am not sure, but by the way he disappeared, I would say yes!" Jake answered.

"Now what?"

"Aren't you full of questions? You're supposed to be the smart one. Where do you think your 'friend' is going?" Jake asked Bradley.

"I don't know him that well. He's really not a friend of mine; more like my rival," he snapped back.

"Well, whatever your problem with him is, I don't care. We need to find him, and I think we're going in the wrong direction here. He wouldn't be going toward the beach if he just checked out of his room. That means that he should be going toward New York, which narrows down our choices," Jake said, turning around.

"I have a feeling he was hiding and we missed him when we passed one of those side streets. It's the only explanation. He couldn't disappear just like that," Jake lamented.

"Maybe you're right," Bradley said.

They drove past the motel, turning left into Royal Oaks Boulevard, the main street leading to the highway. As they were coming down toward the underpass, Bradley looked up at the freeway and started pointing wildly.

"There he goes!" he said. "Headed south toward New York, just like you said."

From where they sat at a red light, they were able to see Jon take the circular on ramp and blend into the rest of the traffic.

Frustrated, Jake cut in front of the traffic to his right, nearly causing an accident, and got into the line to the freeway, drawing honks and insults from the other drivers.

"Ah, go screw yourselves!" he screamed at them as he floored the gas pedal toward the highway, giving the complaining drivers his middle finger.

When they got on the highway, they had the advantage of sitting high in the truck, which gave them the ability to see Jon's car into the distance and maneuver to get ahead and closer to him.

Jon, on the other hand, was not taking for granted that he had lost them; thus he was trying to get to the airport quickly and staying close to other cars of the same color to confuse his followers. Twenty-five minutes later, he got off and drove to the rental return level at La Guardia Airport.

Trying to secure the gap between them, Jake and Bradley stayed close but lost Jon when he went into the lower level of the structure to return his car. They decided instead to go into the airport and look for him. They waited in a common area one level over the departing flights. From there they observed the passengers going through the security checkpoints before reaching their gates.

After returning his car, Jon quickly made his way to the electronic ticket counter, printed his boarding pass, and headed toward the security check for international flights with his two carry-on bags. He waited anxiously for what seemed like hours. Twenty minutes later, he was walking to his gate, after a welcomed security check.

"Sir!" the security agent called and Jon turned around. "Don't forget your computer battery," he said, handing the battery to Jon.

He put it in the outside pockets of one of his bags.

"That's him!" Bradley said loudly, clearly agitated. His unintended high-pitched shout was loud enough for Jon to look back at the direction where it came from. He recognized that voice instantly!

"Was that? It can't be," he said to himself, looking toward Jake and Bradley and quickly turning around.

He couldn't believe his eyes!

"Was that Bradley?" he wondered in disbelief. His hat and glasses were hardly enough for Jon not to recognize him. "But what is he doing with my mother's kidnappers?"

He pondered for a few minutes and suddenly things began to make sense.

"Oh no! He was involved in that too?" he asked, sensing that unfortunately it was true.

There was no doubt in his mind about Bradley's complicity in the death of his mother now.

"But why?" he asked himself. "The money?"

His mind was overloaded with questions he had no answers for. He couldn't help turning around again and looking at the spot where Bradley was standing, but he was no longer there. Jon sighed with great relief. He was so glad to be past security and on his way to his boarding gate! Moreover, he felt reassured that only ticketed passengers could go past the security checks.

For his part, Bradley was just as baffled as Jon. On one hand he'd felt reluctant to believe Jake when he pointed out Max's picture on the news, but he couldn't refute his claims now—not after seeing Max with his own eyes. Worse than that, he was sure Max had seen him.

"He saw us, man! Did you see him turn around?" Bradley asked in a paranoid voice as they hid behind a column.

They stayed hidden until Jon blended with the crowd of travelers and they could no longer see him from their spot. They took note, however, that Jon went toward the international flights gate, and that was helpful to them.

When they could no longer see him in the crowd, they went to the nearest television screen listing all the flights and wrote down the information on international departures. Afterward they walked back to the car without saying a word, each contemplating their predicament from different angles. As they were driving out of the airport Bradley broke the silence.

"It would have been good if we could have followed him past security. That way we could at least find out what flight he is taking."

"Yeah, but ever since the terrorist attack, you just can't go anywhere past the ticket counter without a ticket and a strip search," Jake said. "Besides, we really couldn't afford to be seen any more than we have already, but technology is our ally, my friend. It shouldn't be too hard to narrow down the flights he could have taken. Then we can access the database information of the airlines and hopefully we can find what we're looking for."

"I can help with that if you like," Bradley volunteered.

"Thanks, but I know someone who does this kind of work. We just give him a short list of possible flight destinations and he'll print the passenger information for those flights."

"Awesome. You have all kinds of connections," Bradley said.

"Our job is to come up with the list of the potential flight numbers and we already got that," Jake said.

"Now you just have to call your friend."

"We can do that before you change hotels. We got to find this guy and there's no time to waste."

"I'm with you on that. He's a threat as long as he is out there," Bradley said, knowing that if he was implicated with Jake and his business, it would be more disastrous for him than what he was already facing.

"I just got to call my boss and give him a heads-up and confirm what he wants me to do, but first, let's have something to eat," Jake suggested.

"Yeah, I forgot about that in the excitement."

They stopped by a coffee shop and Bradley picked up a newspaper from the rack before they sat down to dinner to check for any news about himself and the Fitzgeralds. In the second half of the front page was a news article about his embezzlement. Fortunately for him, there was no photograph included. But it was evident that they were looking for him and he needed to get out of town.

It was now midnight, and after debating whether to checkout of his hotel then or the next morning, Brad decided there would be less of a chance of being seen at night. He didn't think the front desk person would remember him from when he first checked in, nevertheless, he decided to wear his disguise.

"Hi!" he said, trying to be friendly to the receptionist, who at the time was making coffee.

She walked over to behind the counter and smiled at him.

"Checking in?" she asked.

"No. Checking out," he said, handing her his credit card. "Got to catch a flight."

"Where are you going?" she asked him, making small talk.

The question took him off guard. His eyes looked straight ahead to the rack of tourists' pamphlets on the side.

"Oh, I'm going to Chicago," he said.

"It should be nice this time a year," she said, handing him a transaction copy to sign.

"Yes, it should be," he said as he signed for his charges.

She tore the sections apart and handed him his copy.

"Thank you very much. Come visit us again," she said smiling as he turned around and walked out the door.

On his way to Woodmere Inn, he thought about the irony of running into Max at the hotel. Bradley was now sure that he was on his way somewhere outside the country, much like he would like to be, but without a new passport he couldn't leave the country. With the law after him, his own passport was useless.

"Two days!" he thought, wishing he could fast forward time.

He walked to his room and went to sleep right away. The next morning, the phone ringing woke him up early. It was Jake.

"Hey! What's up?" he asked, still half asleep.

"I talked to my boss last night and he doesn't want you involved in this job anymore. Professionals should handle it, and you are in enough trouble already. It doesn't help any of us."

"I understand. Did you have any luck with the flight list?" Bradley asked, wide awake by now.

"I'm waiting for him to call me. He'll post the coded information on one of our websites for half an hour, long enough for me to print it out."

"That sounds good. Can you let me know when you get it?"

"I guess so. Give me the complete spelling of this Max guy's name, will you?" Jake said.

"It's Maxwell Adams, just like it sounds, Maxwell with two L's. Hey! What about my passport? Did you check on that?"

"I'll get that going this morning, and then I'll let you know who will be your contact."

"Why's that? What's going on with you?"

"As soon as we get the information about Max's itinerary, I'm going after him and Leo is coming with me. That'll happen before your passport is ready. But don't worry. It's all been arranged and you will have it by tomorrow."

"I wish I could go with you guys."

"Well, you can't." Jake said emphatically. "We have to make sure he won't be back in the States to talk to the police, and you coming along won't help things especially considering your troubles with the law already."

"Whatever, man. Call me when you know more," Bradley said.

"Okay. Goodbye," Jake said and hung up.

In another part of the city, Vince Fitzgerald had called for an assembly of all the employees of the company. Cutting a strong figure, he stood up at the podium and addressed the packed conference hall full of concerned and mourning faces.

"Good morning, Fitzgerald International family. I want to thank you very much for all the support and love you have shown to my family and me in these difficult times. I can assure you that without you, it would have been much harder to face the responsibility that lies before me now. I would like to emphasize the concept that my brother always had: This Company is a family and you are its members.

"There is but one way to carry on the legacy of my brother. We must remain loyally committed as employees and family members of this company, but most of all we must be committed to our customers. In the coming months there will be many adjustments we'll have to make—promotions to consider, and positions to be filled. We have no intentions at this time to hire outside the company, but rather to allow those within who have proven their commitment to move up.   I believe that, under the circumstances, that's what my brother and Sophia would have wanted.

"Please be assured that there are no plans for changes, so there's no need to worry about your jobs. Fitzgerald International remains committed to its customers and employees the same way it was before. I will be available when needed, and you can also e-mail me with any concerns.

"I know that all of you must have questions about our legal situation regarding our former Controller, whose name I'd rather not mention," he continued. For now all I can tell you is that the financial damage is very minimal to the company because we were lucky enough to catch it early. Our financial and credit status are excellent and I foresee no negative fallout from this in the long term. Our stock value has declined slightly, but that was to be expected. Such a move is temporary. As soon as the authorities release the related information, we will pass it on to you, just as my brother would have wanted. Unfortunately, because of the ongoing investigation, we can't tell you any more for now.

With that, he stepped down and waved, walking through a door that took him to the hallway leading to his office. He never would have envisioned a scenario where he would have to take charge of Fitzgerald International alone. But beneath the gentle demeanor he was as determined as his brother ever was.

"Onward and forward," he said as he sat in his office, which had now become too small for his new responsibilities.

He was still too modest to consider himself owner, but undoubtedly he was now at the very least the largest shareholder in the company. He just shook his head at the thought and picked up the phone to call his wife.

"I was wondering," he started, "Would you like to work with me? I sure could use your support, not to mention your help. I'll have to spend a lot of time here, at least at the beginning, and I don't want to sacrifice all our time together."

"I can't say that the idea hadn't crossed my mind," Laura said. "But I wouldn't want to cost anybody their job."

"And you won't. You can work as a consultant, if you like. As things stand now, I'll need to hire a couple more people. In fact, we need to fill the positions left vacant by Jon and Max. I already have some head hunters looking into it just in case we can't find the right person within the company."

"I don't care about titles or things like that. If you need me, it's all that matters to me."

"I'm so glad you agreed, love."

"Me too," she said.

"We could work at the company together, just like William and Sophia!" he said nostalgically.

"That would be nice. I can't think of any couple worth emulating more."

"You don't know how happy it makes me to hear that," Vince said gently.

"Yes, I do," she said lovingly.

"You're right. Laura, you're too good to me," he said with delight.

"And you are to me, my love. How about lunch?" she asked.

"Love to," he said. "I'll pick you up."

"Okay, see you then. I love you," she said and hung up.

Vince looked around him and thought of 'Wills and Sophie'. Their presence was felt everywhere. He was sure they would approve since it was always their wish that the family would work in the company that William made so successful.

The obvious similarities didn't escape him, and he was humble and grateful to be the bearer of the torch passed on to him by his brother and sister-in-law. With Laura by his side running the company, he felt more confident.

***

Back in his room, Bradley got Jake's phone call around eleven o'clock in the morning.

"Great news!" he started. "There is a Maxwell Adams in the flight to Paris, with a final destination of Bern, Switzerland."

"Ah, man! Why didn't I think of that?" Bradley exclaimed regretfully.

"How were you supposed to know that?"

"No, I meant that I should have put my money in a Swiss bank. Why else would he go to Bern? They don't have any relatives there. It's got to be about money."

"But it gets better. He paid with a credit card and we can use the number to track him down wherever he uses it."

"Hey, that's great! When are you leaving?"

"Tonight. I've already booked our flights."

"I hope to be able to say the same for me soon. I can't wait to get out of here."

"You will. I saw the passport guy and apparently your name was familiar. You know, it's his business to know these things. Anyway, he suggested that you shouldn't leave through the airport since the FBI is looking for your face. He will contact you tomorrow to set up the drop off."

"Did you give him my cell number?"

"Are you kidding? The feds must be all over it by now. If I were you, I would get another one," Jake said.

"I should. So how is he going to get hold of me?" Bradley wanted to know.

"He'll call you there; I gave him your number. Don't leave your room until he calls, because he'll only do that once," Jake warned him.

"Did he give you my passport name?"

"Actually, my friend said that if you have credit cards or identification under another name, he could use that name; otherwise he'd chose one for you."

"Oh yeah. Great idea. That will make it easier for me. Tell him to use the name Fulton Tidwell," Brad said.

"Okay. Spell that for me."

"One more thing, Jake. Is there any way you can let me know about your progress with Max? Using my cell phone, as you pointed out, is out of the question until I get a new service. I have as much interest as you in making sure that he won't be a threat to us," Bradley reminded him.

"I can e-mail you, provided that your address is fairly secure."

"Yes, I have a number of those. Let me give you one I've never used. Ready?"

"Yeah."

"Brad at WorldNet.Com," Brad said.

"I got it," Jake said. "Remember that the message will be coded, but it shouldn't be hard for a college guy to figure it out."

"Got it. Good luck," Bradley said.

"Thanks, I'll be in touch," Jake said.

"Bye," Bradley said.

"So long," Jake said and hung up.

Bradley realized that he had, at the most, twenty-four hours to figure out the best and safest way to get out of the city and eventually the country.

The next day, more than eleven hours later, Jon finally got to walk out of the plane and into the terminal of the Charles De Gaulle airport in Paris as he waited for his connecting flight. He took a deep breath and his mind meandered through his prior visits to the city of lights. The Eiffel Tower had fascinated him ever since his parents took him up to the top as a little boy.

This time it felt different being there. Oddly, he had a premonition of something good, which he attributed to the warm childhood memories he had of the French city. He made a mental note to spend a couple of days visiting some favorite places before going back to the States. His thoughts were interrupted by the speaker announcing his flight boarding for his hour-long trip to Switzerland.

Three hours later in Bern, he was settling down for a good night's sleep in his hotel room. He couldn't wait to get a complete night of rest, without fear of someone coming after him.

Around the same time, Eve Anne was in Paris settling in her room at the Montparnasse Hotel after her flight back from her assignment in Bucharest. It had been an extremely fruitful trip and she couldn't wait to submit her article to the magazine and request to be considered for the follow-up assignments. She wanted to pursue leads she got from the Romanian Center for real life success cases to give more weight and balance to the story.

Still, after working long hours every day for more than a month, she was happy to be in Paris for a few days of relaxation and sightseeing before heading down to Honduras for her next assignment. She planned on spending the next day shopping, after getting in contact with her family to update them about her whereabouts. She tried to keep them current on all her trips because she knew how much they worried, especially about this trip, which was so soon after her accident. Thankfully she didn't have to lie when she told them she was feeling nearly one hundred percent recovered. Besides, any day now she would become an aunt, which she was looking forward to. She wanted to keep in touch to know as soon as the baby was born.

Back in New York, Jake and Leo's flight to Bern via Paris had taken off an hour earlier. Their plan was to call their boss upon their arrival and find out Jon's whereabouts based on his credit card use, which they were tracking all along.

Unsuspecting of the extent of the surveillance he was under, Jon was using his credit card for his trip and lodging charges, thus making himself an easy target to follow.

The day after his arrival, he went to the bank first thing in the morning to take care of the transfer of his funds. He requested to speak to the branch manager in regards to his account, and upon checking its status, the customer service manager led him to the office of the bank manager.

"Good morning," said the bank officer, extending his hand to shake Jon's. "I'm Wolfgang Neumann. How may I help you today?"

"Good morning," Jon said, shaking his hand. "I'm Maxwell Adams, the second signature on this account, and I need to transfer the funds into these two accounts," he said, handing Mr. Neumann the pertinent documents for his transaction.

"If you don't mind my asking, Mr. Adams, is Mr. Fitzgerald well?" Wolfgang Neumann asked.

"I'm afraid not, Mr. Neumann. Jon perished in an airplane crash last November."

"Oh my! I'm terribly sorry to hear that," he said sincerely.

"Thank you. It's been hard on all of us," Jon said.

"I'm sure of that," Mr. Neumann responded.

"Anyway," Jon said, "I could be persuaded to leave five hundred thousand dollars if you can offer me a good interest rate on my account. I do like to diversify."

"I'm sure we can offer you a very favorable rate, Mr. Adams."

"Then please transfer 3.5 million dollars to the investment account and one million to the corporate trading account. The numbers are in the paperwork I just gave you," Jon said.

"Very well, sir. What would you like to do with the balance in the account?"

Jon thought for a few seconds and then remembered.

"I completely forgot there was a balance prior to the five million dollar deposit! Please put three hundred thousand into my personal account and I'll leave the rest in your fine institution."

"Very well. That will leave you a balance of 1.2 million dollars. If you'll excuse me for just a minute, I will put in your request to be processed immediately and get your electronic card activated. It'll be just a moment," Mr. Neumann said, disappearing briefly.

A few minutes later he came back and handed Jon his card.

"The rest of your transaction is being processed as we speak. In the meantime, is there anything else I can help you with?"

"Of course, this account and everything relating to it is a confidential and secure matter," Jon said, seeking assurance.

"As always, Sir," Wolfgang Neumann said.

Half an hour later, Jon left the bank feeling relieved, with a spring in his step after arranging his finances, and looking forward to the next chapter in his life. Not only that, he felt like he had just found 1.5 million dollars, after forgetting that he'd used his bonus two years earlier to open the account. With his money matters in order, he was ready for a short vacation in Paris before going back to the States. After that, he needed to figure out a way to help his Uncle Vince. Jon knew more than anyone about the complexities of the job suddenly trusted upon him. Once that was achieved, he could get on with his new life.

He started to walk back to his hotel, feeling excited about his unknown and undefined future. He liked the small town of Bern, with its small population and traffic-free medieval streets. It made him feel as if he was living in another time. As he walked past the street fountains and cafés, he envied the couples sitting together and being affectionate to each other. As beautiful as the city was, he was sure it would seem more so if he had someone to share it with. How glad he was he'd never brought Madison along on any of his trips!

"And to think I was going to build her a little castle," he thought shaking his head.

As soon as he arrived at his hotel, he made his flight reservations to Paris for early the next day, using his newly issued card. Once there, he would decide once again where to hide when he went back home. He would have to build a new life and needed to figure out where that was going to be. In a cruel twist of fate, he'd come back just in time to see his whole world fall apart and be left behind by the ones he loved.

He reserved his hotel room through Sunday in St. George, a small town twenty-five miles outside of Paris, although he was beginning to question how much he could enjoy Paris and its attractions by himself. He shook his head as if clearing his thoughts. He would be Max all of his life. Nevertheless, he felt uneasy having used his friend's credit card. Now that he didn't need it, he decided to pay it off and cancel it as soon as he got back home.

That night, as Jon was falling asleep for the night, Jake and Leo had arrived to Bern and checked into a hotel room not far from him. The next morning, they called their boss to find out where to locate Jon. He gave them the name of the hotel and for good measure Bradley e-mailed him a photograph of Max.

At seven o'clock in the morning, Jon left the hotel and two hours later boarded his flight, arriving in Paris at ten o'clock in the morning. It gave him plenty of time to get to his hotel and go to the Louvre museum. It had been at least seven years since his last visit because he never had the time to do it on business trips. There was one thing he was sure of, he didn't need company to enjoy the museums.

An hour after he left, Jake and Leo showed up at Jon's hotel inquiring if he was there. After they were told that he had checked out earlier, they hurried back to their hotel and called their boss again.

"Boss, I think our information needs a little updating. We just missed him at the hotel by about one hour. Are there any other transactions after the hotel, like car rental, plane tickets, etc?" Jake asked. He listened for a little while.

"Okay," he said and hung up.

"What's up?" Leo asked.

"He said to call Marshall for the updates in the card charges. And that he wants to hear from us soon letting him know that we've taken care of business."

"Yikes!" Leo said.

"He warned me that the next time he hears from us we better have good news."

"Yeah, well. This guy is a slippery one," Leo said.

"Not slippery enough. His time is running out," Jake said, irritated.

"If Bradley was right and he came here to take care of financial matters, this Max guy is going back to Paris for a connecting flight to the States, and we can't let that happen."

"I'm calling Marshall," Jake said, dialing the number. "If he gives me the card number and access codes to the airlines, we can get it faster ourselves with our laptop."

After obtaining the information he wanted, Jake checked the credit card transaction records for himself, but the last time the card was used was at the hotel in Bern. The was no further activity after that. They booked a next-day flight to Paris, going with their gut feeling that Jon was obviously going back home. Jake spent his afternoon searching the Internet for international reservations under Max's name, without any luck.

In Paris, Jon was enjoying his afternoon spending most of it at the Louvre museum. Afterward he parked his rented blue Fiat down an alley near the Arc de Triomphe and went into the Napoleon Cafe for dinner. It was getting dark and the lights cast a glow over the city aptly named City of Lights. He sat by a window, enjoying the sight of people parading past him. After having his cappuccino, he went back to his car and drove to his hotel. As he walked into the lobby, the receptionist greeted him and he remembered that he needed to change his credit card charges, since he'd used Max's card without realizing it.

He walked up to the desk and requested the reversal of charges on the card he had given them when he first arrived and gave the clerk his newly issued one. After taking take care of that bit of business, he went up to his room.

Twenty five miles from there Eve Anne was sitting down to dinner with Matthew Morell, her cameraman/photographer and good friend. Together they had tackled challenging assignments, but their next one promised to be interesting, to say the least. Exhausted from a day of shopping, she opted for dinner at the hotel, which suited Matt just fine when she called him. He had had a long and tiring day too, after meeting with an old colleague of his who now lived in Paris.

"My feet are killing me," Eve Anne complained.

"Where did you go today?" he asked.

"You mean where didn't I go? I must have gone into dozens of stores. It's hard to come to Paris and go back empty handed to your family."

"What are you doing tomorrow?" Matt asked.

"I'm thinking of going to Les Invalides, but it doesn't have to be tomorrow necessarily. We still have one more day after that. Why?" she asked.

"Because," he said slowly and pulled out two event tickets, "I have a couple of passes for two tennis matches tomorrow at Roland Garros."

"How did you get them?" she asked, surprised.

"I have my sources," he smiled.

"I'd love to go. I tried to get some tickets before leaving the states, but they said they were all sold out. I don't know how you did it, but thank you," she said, kissing him on the cheek.

"The only drawback is that the first match is at eight o'clock in the morning and the second is at five."

"I'm sure there will be plenty of things to keep you busy in between matches," she said, amused, aware of Matt's appreciation for women.

He smiled with a guilty look as he read the expression on her face.

"What can I say?" he said, shrugging his shoulders, trying to fake innocence.

"Absolutely nothing. I've known you long enough," she said.

"My mother said, 'Shop around until you find the right woman,'" Matt said.

"Smart woman," Eve said.

"Yeah," he said with a proud smile. "That's my mom."

After they finished their dinner, each went to their room. Eve got on her laptop and e-mailed a brief message to her parents before going to bed and Matthew did the same. He always kept his loved ones informed of his whereabouts when working on assignments.

The next morning, at the same time Eve Anne was getting ready, Jon was getting up in his hotel room, feeling jet-lagged and tired.

"I guess flying in and going to the museum the same day took a lot out of me," he said to himself.

He turned the television on and came across the live broadcast of the French Open, which he watched for a while before getting up. He decided to stay in his room for the day, have room service, and search the Internet for a place to live back in the States. Now more than before he felt he needed to find somewhere to hide away and figure out how to deal with the thugs who killed his mother. He was determined to find out what the relationship was between the kidnappers and Bradley. Then he would bring them to justice, somehow.

He didn't want to think about it before, but the fact was he couldn't avoid facing reality now that he was going home. He tried not to think about it, but the mental image of Jake and Bradley together looking at him at the airport made him burn with anger. But sooner or later, he was sure Bradley would have to face it all. For now, he just wanted to enjoy his time in Paris, and at the top of his list was going to the museum Les Invalides before going back home. He settled in his room and decided to do some work on his laptop computer.

Between watching the French Open and searching for a place to live, the day went by quickly and before he realized it was six o'clock in the evening. He decided to go for a walk around town before having dinner and turning in for the night.

Eve Anne was also nearing the end of a day of tennis fun with Matt. With their flight to Latin America booked for Saturday, she planned to visit one of her favorite museums before leaving for her next assignment. She hoped that her trip to the small Central American country would go as planned, although the type of research for the article could carry risks. Still, the quicker she got it done, the sooner she would get back home.

Meanwhile Jake and Leo were settling in a hotel room, also in Paris, after their flight from Bern. The first thing they did after closing the door behind them was connect their laptop to the Internet access and once again spy on Max's credit card transactions. This time there was only one more entry, that of a room charge at Hotel Michel in St. George, but the charges were later reversed and the account closed. Leo looked for the address in the phone book and wrote it down for the next day. They were both tired and hungry, so they went downstairs to the hotel restaurant and had a late dinner before going to bed. The next day they planned to get up early to watch the last hotel where Max's card was used. At this point, their chances didn't look very good but they were running out of options and had to check every possibility.

CHAPTER 9

HELLO AGAIN, STRANGER

The next morning, Jon woke up feeling much better and ready to take on the day. He had decided the night before to drive to the Riviera on Saturday and spend the last day of his trip there, before flying home on Sunday. After taking the previous day to rest, he felt refreshed and ready to take on his unknown future, albeit cautiously. He got ready and went down to the restaurant to have breakfast before heading off to the museum.

Jake and Leo were also up early that morning to watch Hotel Michel, the only lead they had. Jake parked his rental car in a strategic location from which they could see the main entrance as well as the underground garage parking.

Around ten o'clock in the morning, to their jubilation, they spotted Jon leaving the hotel and followed him from a safe distance, being very careful not to be noticed. Jon took the highway towards Paris, got off at the Les Invalides turnaround exit. He then made his way to the museum with the same name. He found a parking spot a block away, which suited him just fine because it was a beautiful spring day—perfect for a walk in the side streets of Paris.

Unaware he was being followed, he blended in with the rest of the tourists going through the ornate gates into the building compound. He walked toward the main entrance, accentuated by its beautiful church that had masterful stained glass windows, topped by a golden dome with stunningly intricate gold designs that likened it to a jeweled crown.

He paid his entry fee and started his way around the rooms and chambers filled with the most impressive collection of arms, artillery, uniforms, emblems, photographs, etc. Everything imaginable relating to battle, going back beyond the Middle Ages, was there in display. Jon was glad to have the whole day free, because it had been many years since he had visited the museum. During his business trips, he didn't have the time to invest in seeing all of it. Something about being there made him feel like a little boy again.

"Maybe it was playing with my G.I. Joes," he thought, trying to explain his fascination.

As he made his way around one of the wings, he came into the dome, under which laid the crypt with the body of Napoleon Bonaparte, considered by his French countrymen as the greatest military genius. When he walked into the tomb chamber, there were a half dozen people standing around, some of them taking photographs of themselves standing next to the French emperor's tomb. Off to the side by herself, he noticed a young woman with her back turned to him, taking notes in her electronic organizer. Something familiar about her caught his eye. She was wearing a pale green blouse over a tan, loosely fitted skirt, with her auburn long hair gathered in a ponytail. When she turned around, he was stunned. He would recognize those deep green eyes in any part of the world.

At first he was speechless and didn't know what to do or say, in disbelief.

"Could this be that girl? No way!" he thought.

Over the weeks since he had come back to the physical world, Jon had thought of her often. He would find his mind wondering and fantasizing about her, never imagining that he would ever see her again. There was something about her that transcended this existence, that much he knew, but he didn't have a clue what it was.

After thinking about it, he finally worked up the courage to walk up to her.

"Excusez moi, parlez vous Anglais?" He asked.

She looked up at him.

"Yes," she said. "I speak English. I'm an American. What about you?"

Jon was awestruck upon seeing how beautiful she was up close. He instinctively checked her out, from her beautiful toes peeking out from her brown sandals to her full lips and striking green eyes, which seemed to match the color of her blouse.

She tilted her head and looked at him with an amused smile.

"Oh, I'm sorry," he said, coming out of his stupor. "Yes, I am an American. I'm Max," he said, extending his hand to her.

"Max, it's very nice to meet you. My name is Eve Anne," she said shaking his hand, which he took between his two hands and, while looking into her eyes, brought it to his lips and kissed it.

"You look familiar. I'm sorry to say I don't remember where I've seen you, but I'm sure it will come to me," she said.

"Let me give you a hint: Bryce Canyon," Jon said.

Her eyes and mouth got wide open.

"Oh yes!" she said. "You're the guy that hitched a ride with my friends Tim and Josh."

"That would be me. You remember me?" he asked, pleasantly surprised.

"I remember you from the hospital," she said.

"Me too," he said to her. "I remember you being wheeled down the hallway for some x-rays, and waving to your friends as you passed by. I think you said, 'Hi boys!' Or something like that," he finished, realizing he was giving away too much.

"Yes, for a minute the boys were pretty scared for me," she said.

"You have to admit that was a pretty unbelievable fall."

"Tell me about it," she said. "What about you? Whatever happened with the crazy woman who left you stranded in the middle of nowhere? My friends told me about it."

"I never saw her again," he said

"You don't need that."

"I figured that much."

"Good for you. So, what brings you to Paris?" she asked as they started meandering around the other sections of the museum.

"I had some business in Switzerland and decided to take a few days here before going back to the States. What about you?"

"I wish I was going home, like you. But this is just a stopover for me. I just came back from Bucharest, where I did an assignment, and tomorrow I am going to Latin America to do one about the poaching of mahogany forests."

"You are a reporter?" Jon asked.

"It's one of the things I do. Right now I am on assignments for Geographic International."

"Sounds like a worthwhile job."

"It is," she said. "It just gets lonely sometimes, after being away from home for long periods of time," she said.

"Yes, I can see that," he said.

"What about you? What do you do?" she asked him.

"Business administration," he said.

"Ah!" she said. "You must be here on business too."

"Sort of, but it's more for personal reasons." he said.

They fell silent for a few minutes while admiring the incredible display of objects of war before them. Eve Anne couldn't believe the coincidence of running into Jon again. She remembered him in the emergency waiting area, hanging around her friends. Many things from that day were hazy in her memory, but she remembered his presence from the time of her accident.

"Are you here alone?" he asked, interrupting her thoughts.

"No," she said, causing him disappointment. "I'm traveling with a staff photographer and there will be someone to join us in Honduras."

"So what's a beautiful woman doing looking at war stuff? Shouldn't you be shopping or something?"

"I did that the day before yesterday and this is relaxing in comparison. Besides, I just love this museum. The tourism institute should feature it more; there are a lot of things to be learned from this place."

"It's my favorite museum in all of Paris. Don't misunderstand. I love museums in general, but this is the first one I fell in love with as a little boy. It's what awoke my subsequent love for art and museums. I still remember the first time my mom and dad brought me here."

"Ah! How cute! How old were you?" she asked.

"I was six," he said musingly.

"I was ten years old the first time I came here," she said. "They had an exhibition of Seven Wonders of the World photographs and they were magnificent, especially the series of the Grand Canyon. I fell in love with the whole world right then."

"And now you want to save it."

"I'm no Joan of Arc; I just want to do my part," she said.

"And you do it so beautifully," he said under his breath.

"I'm sorry, I didn't hear that" she said.

"I said the world was created so beautifully," he said.

"I agree with that. If we would only take better care of it!" she lamented.

"Educating people is the key. We've come a long way since the environmental activists started to call attention to recklessness of businesses and people in general," he said.

"That's true, and it's that very fact that gives me the purpose to do what I do," Eve Anne said.

"And a very noble thing it is. I'm glad that there are people like you, whose work is dedicated to speak on behalf of our planet."

"You're not saying that just for my benefit, are you?"

Jon looked straight into her eyes.

"I mean all of it," he said.

She couldn't look into his blue eyes for very long. She was afraid he would be able to read her mind and realize how flustered she was, her heart beating fast in her chest.

"Well, thank you," she said.

"You are welcome," he said. "So, you said you're leaving tomorrow?"

"Yes. And you?" she asked.

"I was planning to go back to the States Sunday; which reminds me, I have to confirm my flight reservation," he said touching his watch.

"What are you doing tomorrow?" she asked.

"I was thinking of driving to the Riviera for a day."

"Ah yes!" she smiled at him teasingly. "An American's idea of paradise on the French coast."

He looked into her eyes, then at her sensuous full lips. He could almost taste them and realized that his stare was making her blush.

"My idea of paradise is true love," he said seriously.

"Then you think that paradise is a state of mind," she said.

"No. I think that a taste of paradise on earth happens when everything good in your life comes together in perfect unison, and for a brief moment, you almost can feel perfection in a physical state of being."

"You're pretty serious," she said.

He laughed when he realized how he might have sounded.

"You must think I am a real dork," he said.

"Not at all. A lot of people rarely think of what lies beyond our physical lives. I think that part of us makes us capable of the kind of love that never dies. Love never dies," she repeated confidently.

"You have no idea how right you are," he said.

"Of course I'm right. Besides, I am a bit of a romantic."

They spend most of the day talking and walking through the museum without realizing how much time had passed. It wasn't until the crowds around them began to thin out that they realized it was almost five thirty in the afternoon. Echoing in the background, they could hear the voice of the tour guides telling the public that in fifteen minutes the museum would be closing.

Jon and Eve Anne looked at each other. Neither wanted the day to come to an end. They silently walked out past the gardens and toward the gate, immersed in thoughts.

"Where are you staying?" Jon asked, breaking the silence.

"At the Montparnasse Hotel. And you?"

"I'm staying at Hotel Michel in St. George," he said.

"Charming town. Close to Paris Disneyland too," she said.

"I didn't realize that."

"What planet did you come from?" she teased. "You're less than five miles from it!"

He laughed. "Too bad you're leaving tomorrow. It's a fun place to go to, but not alone."

"Yes, that's true," she said.

"Will you have dinner with me?" he asked after working up the courage, afraid of wasting his opportunity.

"I'd like that," she said with a smile.

"My car is a block away," he said as they walked out the gates. "Did you drive here?"

"No. I walked from the hotel. I find doing that or taking the metro preferable to driving when getting around the city. You also get to see more of it that way."

"I know what you mean. Finding parking is always a challenge in Paris," he said as they walked toward his car.

They were so captivated with each other and immersed in conversation that neither of them noticed they were being followed. Jake and Leo had seen exactly where Jon parked his car earlier, and after he walked away they parked a short distance from him.

When Jon and Eve Anne got to the car and turned around to look at Les Invalides in the background, he noticed the two men who turned their backs immediately to them, in an apparent attempt to conceal their faces. Jon opened the passenger door and Eve Anne sat inside. Still looking back at the men, he went around the car and sat on the driver's seat, adjusting his rearview mirror to get a better look at them.

"Shoot!" he exclaimed, gripping the steering wheel when he recognized Jake's face.

"What's wrong?" she asked.

"I'm not sure you want to know."

"Sure I do. I'm a journalist, remember?"

He scratched his head as he observed Jake and Leo through the mirror. Clearly, they were waiting for him to drive away because they were just standing around pretending to be tourists.

"Well?" she asked.

His mind was racing. It was obvious he was going to have to deal with the situation now as opposed to when he got back home.

"How did they find me?" he said out loud. He looked at her apologetically. "I'm sorry," he said to her shaking his head.

"Why are you sorry? What's going on?"

"Okay. Here goes. I lost both my parents over a week ago," he started.

"I'm so sorry to hear that, Max, really sorry. I can't imagine losing one parent, let alone both of them " she said, putting her hand on his arm as a sympathetic gesture.

"They were the most loving couple I've ever known. But anyways, I'm sure those two men following me are the ones who tried to kidnap my mother. I was close by when it happened, and screamed at him to leave her alone, trying to make him stop. When he realized I'd seen him, he threw her against her car and she was pinned against it by their SUV as they made their hasty get away. She was pronounced dead when she arrived at the hospital. My father was so broken up over losing her in such a shocking way that he had a massive heart attack and died when he was told of her passing."

"That's a horrible thing to go through," she said.

"It's pretty devastating," he said.

He started the car and drove slowly toward the Champs-Elysees, keeping an eye on Jake and Leo as they got into their car and followed from a discreet distance, or so they thought.

"Actually, it's the way they would have wanted it," he said to her a few minutes later. "I couldn't imagine them living without each other. They always said they would go together and sure enough, they did."

"Wow!" she said. "I'd like to find a love like that."

"So would I," he said. "But anyway, apparently the kidnapers took enough of a good look at me because they tracked me down in Alexandria Bay, my parents' home town. They saw me as I was leaving my hotel, but I was able to lose them at the airport, or so I thought. Now they're here. How did they do that?" he said with frustration.

"Why haven't you called the authorities?" she asked.

"I was hoping to postpone doing that until I got back." He hated lying. "I've had enough to deal with the passing of both of my parents and the betrayal of my fiancé with someone I thought was a good friend. As if that wasn't enough, he was embezzling funds from the company."

"Who's company?"

"My family's," he said.

"How many siblings do you have?"

"I'm an only child."

"Double ouch!" she said.

"I had plenty of friends!" he protested.

"Yeah, but it's not the same. If you weren't an only child, you'd at least have someone to lean on now. I wouldn't trade my siblings for anything. So, are you going back to run your family business?"

"Not right away. My uncle Vince, my dad's only brother, is doing that now. I need to take time away for a little while."

"It's nice you can do that."

"I don't mean to change the subject, but do you see the silver Fiat three cars behind?" he asked her.

She looked back and spotted them right away.

"That's them, huh?" she said.

"Yes, and I've got to find a way to lose them."

"Take the Avenue Du Montparnasse," she urged him. "Then go around the building and into the underground parking lot. I'll keep an eye on them and when they lose sight of us for a minute, I'll let you know. Then you can go inside and hopefully lose them."

Following her suggestions, he navigated his way into the guest section of the underground parking of the hotel, accessing it with her electronic parking card.

They hurried and caught the elevator to the fifth floor. From one of the windows of her room, there was a clear view of the turnaround intersection. Eve Anne opened the curtains and they both looked out just in time to see the silver Fiat drive around on the outside lane of the one-way circular intersection. Jon and Eve were sure that Jake and Leo would make the turn into the hotel street looking for him, and sure enough, after standing by the window looking out for a few minutes, they watched them drive around the intersection one more time. Much to their relief, they seemed to give up and go away.

"Boy! You sure know how to make an impression," she said, walking away from the window.

"I'm so sorry about that," he said.

"Isn't it usually the girl who brings in the drama?" she asked teasingly.

"Well, now you are making fun of me."

"Just a little," Eve chuckled.

She walked over and sat on one of two high-backed French provincial chairs around a small coffee table and smiled mischievously at him.

"Okay," he said, breaking her amusing silence. "You have to admit, I seem to have gone a long way to make an impression on you," he said jokingly.

"Yes, I saw it with my own eyes, but you didn't have to go that far," she answered good-naturedly.

"I just wanted to make sure, you know?" he said, walking over from the window to sit next to her. "But seriously," he continued, "I've thought of you since the first time I saw you. And speaking of knowing how to make a lasting impression, yours takes the cake."

She smiled.

"Yes, I got to admit, that was dramatic, like a girl," she said, shrugging her shoulders and throwing her arms up in the air.

"Never in a thousand years did I expect to find you here. In fact, I didn't think I'd ever see you again," he said.

Eve Anne was taken back a little by his confession but was glad to hear him say it. However, she wasn't ready to tell him that she too had thought about him. Those hypnotizing blue eyes were etched in her mind, and in fact, she surprised herself at how well composed she was when she first saw him at the museum.

"I never expected to see you again either," she said.

"Maybe it's fate," he said.

"Do you believe in fate?" she asked him.

"Absolutely. Don't you?"

"Of course! But sometimes it's hard to tell the difference between true fate and a passing fancy."

"True," he said.

"So how do you know?" she asked.

"You just know," he said.

She leaned forward and Jon could smell her sweet perfume that aroused his senses. He was very tempted to reach out and touch her face but held back.

"Now the question is: what are you doing about your situation?" she asked, bringing him back to reality. He sat back and tried to look focused.

"I don't know how they've been able to track me down, but I guess they don't want me to go back to the States alive. There is no question as to my ability to identify them; if I wasn't able to do it before, I can certainly do it now, after running into them a few times already."

"You have to get them off your trail first," she said.

"Somehow I've got to get back and alert the authorities before they get to me, because it's obvious they want me out of the way."

"Yes, and in the worst way," she said. "Vehicle manslaughter committed after a botched kidnapping could give them a long time in prison. What I don't understand is why follow you all the way here, instead of just letting it go after you left the country?"

"I don't understand that either, especially because I couldn't identify them then. The only time I had seen one of them was during my mother's kidnapping struggle, and I was too concerned about her to really take a good look at him," he said.

"Do you have any suspicions as to who would have wanted your mother abducted and why?"

"My parents were the kind of people that didn't have enemies, so it's kind of hard to think of anyone." He stopped in mid-sentence as he remembered Bradley at the airport. "Except Bradley, apparently," he said, talking to himself.

"Who's Bradley?" she asked.

He ran his hand through his hair and sat back.

"Bradley was a childhood friend. He worked for my father's company because I gave him a job. Apparently he had been embezzling money by using his position as controller of the company."

"What a backstabber!" she exclaimed.

"It doesn't end there. I recently found out he had been carrying on an affair with my girlfriend for most of the time we were together."

"But how did you tie him into the scheme?"

"He was at the airport with the driver of the Fiat. They followed me there after I checked out of the hotel."

"That would do it," she said.

"I'd like to know why. It doesn't make any sense!"

"Sick minds have no logic. Maybe he just was a bad seed," she said.

"It's hard to believe that of someone who was supposed to be my friend," he lamented.

"I imagine it would be," she said. "Did you break up with your girlfriend because of him?"

"No. I didn't know about them until recently."

"Why did you break up with her?" she asked with curiosity.

"I was gone for over six months on a business trip, and during that time realized that she was not the one for me."

"That was a lucky trip. You could have been stuck with her," she said.

"Yes, I guess you could say it was lucky," he said pensively.

"How did you find out about them?"

"I overheard them one evening when I happened to be seated at the next table at a restaurant we used to frequent."

"Bummer! I'm sorry to hear that," she said.

"Don't be sorry, I am glad I was saved from that tramp."

"God works in mysterious ways," she said philosophically.

"You're not kidding! And how!" he said.

"Did you confront them then and there?" she asked.

"No! I wanted nothing to do with them and was just glad

to leave unnoticed which wasn't hard. They were so wrapped up making their wedding plans, they wouldn't have noticed me if I stood in front them."

"Is he wealthy or influential enough that it would warrant eliminating you? If he is already wanted for embezzlement, it doesn't make sense that he would be looking for more trouble."

"He's neither wealthy nor influential. He comes from an upper-middle-class family, but like you said, there's no logic to a criminal mind," he reminded her.

"It takes money to travel around the world chasing after someone like they're chasing you. I don't think those guys we saw today are in this alone. Even if your friend was in it, there is no telling what kind of people those men we saw today are associated with, especially since they are apparently willing to do anything."

"You can say it. They want to kill me."

"I don't know why else they would go through the trouble," she said.

"Which brings me to the fact that I have to get out of this city before they find me again," he said.

"May I suggest something? Since they seem to know where you are going, how about making reservations for two or more destinations; that way, if they have been following your trail, they would at best have to split. Better yet, make three or more reservations and that way your odds are better."

"I like that idea. I should make a reservation for going back home, of course, and two other destinations. Do you have any suggestions?" he asked.

"The world is your oyster. Whatever flights you choose should take them going the opposite direction of where you are heading, so I guess you have to figure that out first."

Jon got up from the chair and paced the room, wringing his hands while Eve Anne looked on. He stopped and looked at her.

"Where are you going?" he asked her.

"Latin America," she said.

"Specifically where?" he wanted to know.

"Specifically Honduras in Central America."

"Sounds like it would be a good place to hide," he said with a mischievous look, as if he'd just had a brainstorm.

"Yes it would be, but what are you saying? Never mind. It would be a good reservation to make whether you were going there or not," she said.

"Okay," he said. "Now I just need one more destination."

"How about somewhere fun. Greece maybe?" she asked. "They should easily believe that a young single guy would be heading there to enjoy the Mediterranean sights."

"Great idea! The island of Crete sounds good," he said enthusiastically.

"I'm glad you like it," she said. "You should have a wonderful time there," she said.

He stared at the floor for a few seconds and then sat next to her, putting his hands together as if making a plea.

"I know that you just met me and I am a stranger to you," he started apologetically.

"But I didn't just meet you, you know," she interrupted to remind him. He smiled, almost relieved.

"Yes, thank you for reminding me of that. Anyway, I know that it's too much to ask, but given the circumstances, I must. Would you consider letting me tag along with you to Honduras, at least until I shake these guys off?" he asked, holding his breath. She pondered for a few seconds. Something in her was glad he had asked.

"I don't know why not. I'll have to talk to Matt, but I'm sure he will be okay with it."

"Who's Matt?"

"Matthew Morell is my photographer/cameraman. We travel together."

"Of course."

"But don't worry. You and Matt will hit if off really well. He'll love to hear your story."

"My story?" he asked nervously.

"You know. The bad buys chasing you, the adventure. He lives for that kind of stuff," she assured him.

"Can I trust him?" he asked.

"Max, not everyone in the world is out to get you. Just relax. Some of us would gladly help you."

"That's true," he acknowledged. "And I thank you for that."

"You are welcome. Now, how are you making your reservations?" she asked him.

He leaned back on the chair and looked at the ceiling. He took a deep breath.

"I have to somehow get back to my hotel to check out and get my laptop and luggage."

"I can drive you there in my car, if you like; unless you feel more comfortable driving yourself."

"Are you kidding? It's a rental. I will take you up on your offer, thank you so much. Besides, they've already seen what I'm driving and are looking for that car. I can't afford to take any chances and be seen in it."

"Where are you going to return it?" she asked.

"At the airport," he answered.

"That works out good. We'll leave your car here and drive my car back to your hotel to get your things," she said.

"I really appreciate this," he said.

"It's okay. I'd hope you'd do the same for me, if the tables were turned," she said.

"I'm sure I would," he said emphatically. She smiled.

"When do you want to go?" she asked him.

"I'd like to wait until it is dark if its alright. In the meantime, if you have a laptop, could I perhaps use it to make my plane reservations?"

"Sure. I can also give you the information about our itinerary." She blushed realizing that he might think she was referring to the two of them. "I mean, Matt and me."

"Now it will be Matt, you and me. I guess we'll be the three amigos, huh?" he said. She thought about for a minute.

"Yes it will," she said, going into the adjacent room and coming back with her notebook computer. "By the way, I'm starved. If we have dinner in the hotel restaurant there's less of a chance to be seen. That is, after we are done here. I will call Matt and have him meet us there."

"Sounds good," Jon said. "When should I book my flight for?"

"Tomorrow at two o'clock on the Lufthansa flight to Honduras," she answered.

"What is the destination city?" he asked.

"That would be La Ceiba, but our final destination is further into the country."

"You'll have to tell me about the rest at dinner," he said.

"There will be plenty of time for that," she said.

"That's true," he agreed.

"I'll call Matt to let him know to meet us downstairs," she said walking to the phone on the small desk.

For the next half hour he navigated the Internet, making flight reservations and checking his e-mail while Eve Anne went to the bedroom and changed into a pair of slacks for dinner and waited for him.

On their way to dinner, Jon couldn't help stealing an appreciative glance at Eve, and just as he was about to pay her a compliment, the elevator doors opened and Matt came in.

"Matt! Hi." She turned to Jon. "Max, meet Matthew Morell, my friend and assignment partner. Max, I'm sorry, I don't even know your last name!" she said, laughing.

Jon smiled at her and extended his hand to Matt.

"Matt, it's a pleasure to meet you. Maxwell Adams, but my friends call me Max."

"Very nice to meet you, Max," Matt said with a firm handshake and friendly smile. The elevator door opened and the three of them walked toward the hotel restaurant.

"I can't wait to hear your story. Eve Anne said you were traveling with us," Matt said.

"Yeah. Hope you don't mind me tagging along," Jon said.

"No way! It'll be great having you with us. In fact, you just might have the adventure of your life while you're there," Matt said.

"I think I've had enough adventure to last me a while," Jon said.

"Then you are heading to the wrong place my friend. I've been to the Platano Biosphere twice before and it's always an adventure. But in a good way."

"That I can handle. It's the kind adventure I've been on lately that I can do without. Being chased around the world by thugs that probably want me dead because I am a witness to one of their crimes—that's not fun."

"I see your point."

Eve quietly observed the two men as they got engrossed in their conversation. She was glad to be the spectator for the moment, because before they met she was already sure that they would get along extremely well, and she was right.

The server came a few minutes later and took their order. They used their dinnertime to get to know each other, and after a while it seemed as if they'd been friends for a long time. They were enjoying their dessert when Matt volunteered to help Jon.

"I'll drive you in my car to pick up your things at your hotel, if you like."

"That would be great! I don't know how to thank you. Eve Anne had volunteered to help but I'd rather take you up on it. I'm sure you understand," he said, looking at Eve Anne.

"No problem. You don't want a girl around in case of trouble," she said sarcastically. "But seriously, if anyone is staking out your hotel, you don't want to take the chance of being seen going back," Matt said.

"No, I don't!" Jon said, stirring his cappuccino.

"You can hide in the back seat. It shouldn't be hard to pull it off at nighttime."

"Not at all," Jon agreed.

"Eve Anne, I was thinking, what do you think about Max posing as our Environmental Biologist? That way he can travel as a part of our group without arousing anyone's suspicion," Matt said to her.

"Good idea, Matt," she said.

"Max, my room has an extra bed and you're welcome to stay there for the night if you like, unless you want your own room, which wouldn't make much sense just for one night."

"Thank you, I'll take you up on your offer. The last thing I need right now is to leave a trail."

"That's what I thought," Matt said.

And so it was decided that the two men would retrieve Jon's belongings from his hotel. After that, their next business at hand was to pack up and get ready for the following day.

***

Jake and Leo were growing increasingly frustrated by Jon's ability to evade them so far, but it didn't deter them, in fact, it made them more determined to go after him. After losing him in downtown Paris, they went back to their hotel to regroup and plan their next steps. Calling their boss didn't make for any happy campers either, as he too was getting irritated about their inability to eliminate Jon once and for all.

"But boss, we're looking for a guy in a big city."

"Yeah! But who lost him after finding him, you idiots!" he screamed at Jake on the phone.

"We couldn't take the chance of getting the woman involved in this! We don't need any more complications than we already got. You can't shoot the guy in the middle of Paris with people all over the place. The last thing we need is to get someone else involved and make the circle bigger," Jake retorted.

"All right," the boss said, a little calmer. "Just keep it clean, and by that I mean no one else gets involved. But remember, we need this guy dead, and if he took a look at you two again, it's even more urgent for your sake that he's taken care of, and soon."

"Yes, boss. You know I'm good for it. I know it's taking longer than we thought, but we'll get him. I promise."

"You better," the boss warned him.

"I always get my man," Jake reminded him.

"So far you have. Be careful of that first time, don't let it happen to you."

"I'll let you know when we know what we're doing next," Jake said.

"Remember, now that he knows someone is after him he'll leave town, and he could do it not only by plane. He could use a car or even a train, so look at all the possibilities."

"Great! You had to throw that in," Jake said, annoyed at the thought of going in so many directions.

"Just pointing out possibilities, my boy. When you know something, e-mail me at the address that's on the mail I'll be sending you later with coded instructions, that is, if you can't get hold of me right away."

"Will do," Jake said and hung up the phone.

Leo brought the map they were given at the car rental office and they took a careful look at it and the roads leading away from Paris. Overwhelmed by the possibilities, they took a break from it and Jake signed onto his computer, hoping for leads about transactions on Max's credit card, only to come up empty. Then he proceeded to scan airlines passenger lists and after a few minutes he started to get the results he was looking for; but his fortune quickly soured when he spotted three reservations in Max's name each for different dates and all going in different directions.

"Ah shit! There are three flight reservations under his name, all of them for different days and different destinations!" Jake exclaimed.

"He's trying to throw us off his trail now that he knows we're on to him," Leo noted.

"At least we now have a lead as to how he's getting out," Jake said.

"Provided that it's not something he's using to throw us off his trail, like the multiple reservations," Leo said.

Jake looked at him, annoyed.

"What?" Leo asked defensively. "I'm just pointing it out. Don't listen to me. You're probably right. He could have all these reservations because he wants us going in opposite directions, away from him."

"That's exactly what I'm saying!" Jake said, feeling a little vindicated.

"Now we have to figure out which is the flight he would be taking."

"Let's see," Jake said as he sat back on his chair and pondered out loud. "If I was trying to get away, I wouldn't go back to the United States; it would be like going back to enemy territory. We already know that he had the chance to go to the cops, but instead he left the country. I think we can discard the reservation to San Francisco, which leaves us with Crete, Greece, and La Ceiba, Honduras? Where the hell is that?"

"Look it up in the web," Leo suggested because he didn't know exactly where the country was either. "But if I was him, I'd rather go to Crete and soak some Mediterranean sun."

"Who wouldn't?" Jake said.

He signed off the Web page he was on and looked up the map for Honduras. The last time he had seen that name might have been in middle school geography; it was such a small third world country of no consequence.

"Leo, my man, this looks interesting. Honduras is a small country in Central America; it just might be a good place to try to hide, or get lost. The question is: is it too obvious?"

"Hmm…Why Latin America?" Leo asked.

"Either he is going because it's the perfect place to hide, or it's a great way to throw us off his trail while he goes to Crete," Jake theorized.

They were both silent for a few minutes, each searching their brains, trying to guess the right answer. Both U. S. and Crete reservations would make sense. But the Honduras card thrown in was something totally out of the blue and that confused them both. The fact still remained: They had to make a choice and pick one. After a while, Jake broke the silence.

"We can make two reservations, one to Crete and one to Honduras. That way we'll have both of them covered. Either one of us can handle the Max surveillance until the one on the bogus target trip joins the other."

"I don't see a choice, as long as we can stay in touch. But of course, that depends entirely on where we finally end up going to get him," Leo said.

"I'll book one flight for tomorrow and the other for the day after, like he did. This way, if he's on tomorrow's flight to Honduras we will know, if not then we'll know he's going to Crete," Jake said.

"Now we just have to decide who is going where," Leo said.

"Yeah, but anyway you look at it it's a fifty-fifty chance, and I sure would like better odds than that," Jake said, pacing the room.

"What about Bradley? Doesn't he know Max? Maybe he could give us some insight," Leo suggested.

"Leo, that's brilliant! He supposedly has known Max since they were kids; maybe he can shed light on this for us. I'm going to e-mail him right now. Maybe we can get a reply soon enough to help us. In the meantime, we'll make the Crete reservation because it seems more logical for a single guy to go there. Honduras could very well be a decoy destination, it's too exotic. We'll wait a few hours to make the other reservation until after we've had a chance to hear from Bradley. I'll give him a few of hours to get back to me. If we're lucky, he can give us a good lead that would save us time and money," Jake said.

He went through his notes, found Bradley's e-mail address, and mailed him a message that read:

Having a disappointing time here. Paris has yielded
partial results. If I had to choose one place to get
away, and my choices were Crete, or La Ceiba,
Honduras, which would my friend choose?
It is of outmost importance to have your
opinion, as I value it when it comes
To being friends to the Max.

Sincerely,
J&L

"I hope he doesn't take long to get back to us," he said to Leo after sending the document.

"We can always go with our plan," Leo said.

"Yeah. It's just that taking off in different directions is not effective at all. One of us will be going on a wild goose chase and that will add more money and time to finish this job, which is taking too long already!" Jake said with obvious frustration.

"I know! And I agree with you, but we have to work with what we have," Leo told him, trying to reason with him.

"Hopefully Bradley has some ideas on this."

"Maybe," Leo said. "Are we going back to stake out Max's hotel?" he asked.

"Yes, we should do that even though I don't think we'll get much out of it because if he is trying to lose us, he most likely left already. He knows we're on to him now."

"That's true, but that's all we have to go on for now," Leo asserted.

"I think I saw some restaurants around the area. We'll case out the hotel for a few hours after we eat. If he leaves or comes into the hotel, he would likely do it at night."

"Sounds good. I'm hungry." Leo said.

"If Bradley doesn't answer by tomorrow morning, we'll reserve the flights and flip a coin to see who goes to Honduras because that flight leaves tomorrow afternoon and Crete is for the day after."

Leo nodded in agreement.

The two hit men seemed like a good pairing. They had worked together in many other jobs and their partnership worked well in part due to Leo's ability to keep Jake composed at times when he couldn't afford to lose control. Although Jake was apparently in charge, he knew the importance of Leo as his partner and considered him very capable.

After having dinner the men drove to Jon's hotel in St. George. They circled around a few times, and then parked in a spot where they could observe all the cars coming and going into the underground garage. After five hours of unsuccessful surveillance, they went back to their hotel to get ready for their anticipated trips the next day.

Unbeknownst to them, Jon and Matt had in fact come and gone, even as they watched, with Matt driving his car, which the thugs didn't recognize. After checking out, Jon and Matt went back to their hotel and made their plans for the next day, unaware that Jake and Leo were hiding in the darkness of the moonless night and at one time were just a few yards away from them.

The next morning Eve Anne, Jon, and Matt met at the hotel restaurant for breakfast, and afterwards went back to their rooms, gathered their luggage and gear they had packed the night before. At 11:30 in the morning, they left the hotel and headed to the Charles De Gaulle Airport, cautiously looking around and trying to keep Jon's car inconspicuous. By 12:30 they were at their respective auto rental counter returning their cars and at 1:00 in the afternoon they were checking in for their flight.

Jon decided to make use of his extra time before the flight and connected his notebook computer to one of the airport's terminal connections. He verified that his accounts were processed as he had instructed the bank, and after being satisfied by his inquiry, he mailed Marco a quick note.

I'm sorry to tell you, but there's been a change of plans.
For reasons that I can't get into right now, I'm at the
Charles De Gaulle airport waiting for a flight that leaves to
Latin America. I'm not sure how long it will be, but
I hope not very. I'll be in touch via e-mail
Whenever possible. I'll elaborate then.

Jon

Earlier on, several miles away in their Paris hotel, Jake and Leo were packed and ready for their flight. After making some coffee in his room, Jake signed on his computer and his gladness could not have been more evident. Bradley had answered his e-mail and it read:

Glad to hear from you. Sorry that Paris is not yielding.
As for me, after heeding the friendly
advice of our mutual friend,
I was pointed north, toward the land of pucks, which is where
I find myself right now.

In regards to our friend's choosing, there's a strong possibility
of a construction business link in
Honduras. If I were my friend,
I would choose Honduras. For the next
few days, you can also reach me
at 403-148-7400, ext. 2547 if you
need to. In the expected event of
forced relocation, I will try to keep in
touch on both mediums, as
I hope you will for the sake of our mutual benefit.

Hope to hear from you soon.
B.O.S.

The message was signed with "B.O.S.." the obvious initials of his full name.

"Leo!" he shouted happily. "Bradley says that Max has possible business ties to Honduras and if he was us, he would go there."

"Let's make our other reservation, then. What time is the flight leaving?"

"It departs at three o'clock, which gives us plenty of time. Although, it's going to cost us plenty to purchase last-minute tickets."

"Just make the reservations," Leo told him. "Considering what's at stake, I can't believe you'd complain about that now. It would cost us more if we had gone with the other plan, anyway."

"You're like a nagging wife."

"Screw you!" Leo said, sitting down.

"What language do they speak there, anyway?" Jake asked. Annoyed, Leo ignored his question as Jake continued searching for airline ticket reservations. To his consternation, the flight bound to Latin America was full and the earliest available seats would be the next day at the same time.

"Once again, we're trailing one day behind him!" Jake yelled, thoroughly disgusted and angry.

Leo didn't say anything. He didn't like the situation any more than Jake did, but he had better control of his emotions and didn't believe in making things more complicated. Keeping things simple was his motto, but there was nothing simple about the job they were on or his latest choice of profession.

At thirty-four years old, he found himself divorced, with gambling debts and a large child support payment when a friend introduced him to the Organization. At first he found making the money easy, just driving people around and running errands. Later on, his position moved up to delivering packages, and before he knew it, he started helping out on the jobs themselves, but he'd never killed anybody. He justified the lifestyle to himself by reasoning that he would only kill in self-defense, which was the reason he didn't work alone. But as he found himself immersed more in the underworld he also felt pulled away from his children, and that was wearing on him. However, he was a man of his word and was bound to help Jake finish the job they had started. But more than anything, he wanted for all of it to be over.

He turned the television set on and watched it while Jake continued to surf the Internet. They had nothing to do but wait until the next day to catch their flight.

After he was finished gathering information about their trip, Jake decided to call Bradley to get answers to some questions he still had. He looked at Brad's telephone number in his mail.

"Canada, ay?" he said, thinking out loud, as he dialed the

number, which after two rings was picked up.

"Hello?" Bradley's voice said apprehensively.

"It's Jake."

"How's it going man?"

"Ah, it's going. What about you?" Jake asked.

"I had to get out of town. My picture was all over the papers so I took your friend Marshall's advice to get out through Canada," Brad said.

"That's a good move; it's a much easier route to take."

"So you're going to Central America?"

"That's why I called. Have you ever been there?"

"No," Bradley said.

"What's this business connection you mentioned in your e-mail?"

"Fitzgerald International is in the business of building affordable homes in poor countries, mainly aimed at the U.S. retirees moving there on a fixed income. In places like that they can live like kings on little savings and social security payments."

"I see. Do they have businesses in Honduras now?"

"Not yet as far as I know, but it's just the kind of place they would be interested in building," Brad said.

"So you're not completely sure of where he is going, then. You're just guessing?" Jake asked.

"He has a lot more reasons for going to Honduras than to Greece."

"I guess so. What would be the chances of finding someone who speaks English there?"

"Probably good. I've been to South America, and although we had our interpreter, there seemed to be quite a few people that spoke English. The hotel where you stay can probably help you find someone," Brad suggested.

"Okay. Thanks for the info."

"Don't mention it. Hey! Keep me posted on what's happening. You know I have a lot riding on this."

"Yes, I know. I'll try to let you know what's happening,

provided I have the chance. I don't even think my cell phone will work there."

"If you could use my help anytime, let me know. I will be making my way down to South America soon," Bradley volunteered.

"Thanks. But Leo and I have it under control. The fewer of us to attract attention, the better," Jake said.

"My offer stands until Max is out of the way for good. I hope the next time we get in touch you will have the good news that he's dead."

"Me too. Talk to you later," Jake said as he hung up the phone.

"Did you hear that? There's an excellent chance that he is going to Latin America," he told Leo.

"Why don't we go to the airport now and check out the flights? We might be able to see the passengers before they go to their gates," Leo suggested.

"If they haven't gone through security, yes. Otherwise only ticketed passengers go beyond that point," Jake reminded him.

"I guess we owe that to nine-eleven too!"

"Yes, Leo my man. It's the way of the world now, but you're right. It wouldn't hurt to go by the airport and see what else we can find out. After all, we got all day."

"Yeah, but can we make it to the airport with enough time?" Leo asked.

Jake looked at his watch.

"Oh shit! It's twelve-fifteen," he said exasperated. "If we hurry now we might get there around the time the passengers start checking in. Let's hope he's not one of those guys who like to be at the airport five hours before his flight."

"Let's go then," Leo urged.

"We'll grab a bite to eat after," Jake said.

They left for the airport in their search but their trip would be useless, as they arrived more than an hour after Jon and the rest of the group had gone through the security check.

"Is there any way for you to check the list of passengers who got on the flight later on, or maybe tomorrow?" Leo asked Jake as they were walking to their car.

"OK, how far do we have to chase this guy?" Leo asked. "It seems useless to spend all this traveling, time and money when he obviously didn't report anything about the "accident," so he must have something to hide that's nothing to do with us."

"That's true. Which makes you wonder: What is he hiding?" Jake said.

"Who cares! Our job is done. I just want to go home," Leo said.

"The boss cares. He wants this man dead, and he paid us good money to do the job," Jake said.

"That may be, but I didn't sign up for all of this. Let's go home tomorrow. We're not doing anything here," Leo said.

"I'll talk to Bradley and give him the update."

They went back to their hotel room, made their online reservations and packed for the next day departure to go home. Jake made reservations to go home but didn't cancel their tickets to Honduras either, waiting until he got in touch with Bradley and let him know their plans to go back home, which turned out to be wishful thinking.

"Don't get in touch with me until the job I paid you for is done, there will be something extra for you when you give me the news I want to hear," said Bradley.

"Yes boss," Jake said and hung up, then turned to Leo. "You heard him. We got to finish the job."

"You mean you must, because I am going back home tomorrow. You can't change my mind on this Jake. Sorry, man."

Jake didn't want to argue. Somehow, he had to figure out a way to make Leo go with him to finish the 'job' they had been paid to do. But how? Leo was not going to change his mind and Jake was determined to take Leo with him.

www.ingramcontent.com/pod-product-compliance
Lightning Source LLC
Chambersburg PA
CBHW022128050726

47590CB00002B/451